ACE
III

Arresting,
Contemporary
stories by
Emerging writers

edited by
Julia Prendergast,
Eileen Herbert-Goodall
& Deb Wain

RECENT
WORK
PRESS

ACE Anthology III: Arresting, Contemporary stories by Emerging writers
Recent Work Press
Canberra, Australia

Copyright © the authors, 2022

ISBN: 9780645356373 (paperback)

 A catalogue record for this book is available from the National Library of Australia

Cover photograph: Christian Bass courtesy of unsplash
Cover design: Thomas Hamlyn-Harris
Set by Thomas Hamlyn-Harris

recentworkpress.com

Australasian Association of Writing Programs

RECENT
WORK
PRESS

Contents

Introduction

Julia Prendergast

The contributions to *ACE III* are diverse in form and theme. As a composite picture the collection represents an expansive vision for short-form writing. We include work by authors from diverse cultural and geographical locations, including – Australia: Gadigal Country, Dharawal Country, Wodi Wodi Country, Wurundjeri land, Naarm, Jinibara Country, Whadjuk Country, Turrbal & Yuggera land, Ngunnawal Country, as well as Dallas (USA), Mexico City, Greece, Norway, Tbilisi: Georgia, NYC, Chennai: India, Singapore, and Saudi Arabia.

Across the collection, there is a push and pull of 'felt presences': Gordon Weaver asks, 'in how small a space can [we] create the *felt presences* that animate successful stories' (in Shapard and Thomas 1983: 228, emphasis added). The concept of felt presences is at the heart of the contributions within this collection. The authors examine the conundrum and contradiction of human experience through carefully crafted detail. The brevity of short-form writing makes it an apt vessel for capturing the haunting incompleteness of human experience. Through flash and traditional length short stories, creative nonfiction, memoir, and hybrid forms, there is a compelling ebb and tow of ideas, as focalised through highly idiosyncratic 'register[s] of intelligence' (Wharton E 1997: 63). The authors cultivate narrative detail with intuitive hands and minds, fashioning abstracted realities that linger well beyond the final lines of the text.

At every turn, as we engage with the work of fellow authors, we consider how our writing and thinking is informed by the work of other practitioners – by wild acts of making. Editing is an act of attentive listening – it's deeply privileged work. As we listened, we wondered: What conundrum of lived experience is the author contemplating? The contributions pay homage to the crucial relationship between idiosyncratic voice and sharply rendered detail. The contributions leave us reeling, asking ourselves: How is it possible that story-work can enter our affect cycle as if it were lived experience?

We are indebted to the authors in this collection for the gift of engaging with their stories. This is the great joy of reading and editing, and the lure of writing – encountering the otherwise unsayable through the deft handling of sensory detail, bearing witness to the creative use of language as an act of homage to an otherwise irresolvable idea. It has been our great pleasure to listen to these authors – to have had our empathic compass expanded by their art.

The opportunity to provide publication pathways for emerging writers is made possible by the expansive vision – the profound and abiding generosity – of transcultural Arts' leaders. Thank you to Shane Strange, publisher at Recent Work Press, as well as Janet De Neefe: Ubud Writers and Readers Festival (UWRF);

The Executive Board: Australian Short Story Festival (ASSF); Kate Pickard: University of Western Australia Press (UWAP); Zowie Douglas-Kinghorn: Voiceworks/Express Media; Kate Noske: *WESTERLY* Magazine; Tim Tomlinson: New York Writers Workshop. It is (fully) glorious to be part of this Community of Practice.

We acknowledge the generous support of the Australasian Association of Writing Programs (AAWP), the peak academic body representing the discipline of Creative Writing in Australasia. AAWP offers a suite of national and international prizes and publication pathways, in support of emerging and established writers and translators, in partnership with many of the organisations listed above, including: Ubud Writers and Readers Festival (UWRF), Australian Short Story Festival (ASSF), University of Western Australia Press (UWAP), Voiceworks/Express Media, and *WESTERLY* Magazine. Many of the contributions within this collection were submitted to AAWP prizes.

The board of the Australian Short Story Festival is grateful for grant funding in support of this project: Restart Investment to Sustain and Expand (RISE) Fund. We utilised a portion of the grant funding in support of this collection, fulfilling the following grant imperatives: providing remunerated publication pathways and networking opportunities for emerging and under-represented writers from diverse cultural backgrounds; providing mentorship and income for two emerging editors. This represents a combined commitment, on behalf of AAWP and ASSF, to supporting emerging writers and editors.

Thank you to Thomas Hamlyn-Harris for the gorgeous cover design, for his patience and good humour, and his expertise in layout.

Finally, thank you to the hilarious and relentlessly delightful Eileen Herbert-Goodall and Deb Wain – for the editorial sisterhood and fine company, for their generosity and meticulous attention to detail.

Julia Prendergast on behalf of the editors: Julia Prendergast, Eileen Herbert Goodall, Deb Wain.

Wharton E 1997, *The Writing of Fiction,* Touchstone: Simon & Schuster.

Weaver G 1983, *Sudden Fiction: American Short Short Stories*, edited by Robert Shapard and James Thomas, Gibbs Smith, pp. 228-9.

This is Just to Say

Karen McKnight

I have hidden all the razors. This time inside a handbag hanging from the curtain rail in my bedroom. I put all the scissors in there and some small paring knives and write a note to myself reminding me of my hiding place. I hide the note too, but I probably won't remember where. A woman's handbag is a good place to hide sharp things, unless you forget and get picked up by cops and pull out a knife instead of a licence.

I clear the rubbish and clothes and other teenage crap from the doorway of my daughter's room to make a pathway for the paramedics. My date is up and standing to attention in his leather jacket, not knowing what to do. 'I have endless patience,' he said when we first met.

'Okay,' I said, 'we'll see.'

The bathroom floor is pools of blood, spurts of it are over the white tiles. She's taken pills too. I have Nurse-on-Call in my ear barking instructions. 'Is she awake! Is she alert! Keep her upright! Turn her on her side until help arrives!'

'Yes!' I say. 'Yes! Yes!' I don't tell them that I am simultaneously slapping on make-up – that I am still on a date and will need it – the make-up that is, to hold me together through the long hours ahead in Emergency, those fluorescent lights can be unforgiving.

'What is she doing now?' Nurse-on-Call screams.

The paramedics are big girls. They walk into the apartment with the authority of police. Trudging into the hall like Ghostbusters, armed and ready. Where's the poltergeist, I imagine them saying, where's the menacing entity that has been wreaking havoc and causing you so much trouble? It's in there, it's possessing my daughter, me as well from time to time – it can jump!

They head in and set down their equipment beside her bed and go to work.

While the minutes pass and the seconds count down, I say my prayers to Mary. I close my eyes and see my daughter in my mind's eye receiving a shower of light from the Virgin Mother. When I do this, my girl is usually smoking or putting on make-up or even cutting herself, so I say to Mary, 'Go harder on the beams,' which she does turning on the searchlights, scanning perimeters because my daughter will have flipped us the bird and walked away.

The back of an ambulance is like a tradie's van. Tools and cords and bits of equipment that do God-knows-what, occupy every surface. One of the big girls drives, the other sits in the back with us and makes small talk. 'Do you like school? Do you play any sport? What's your favourite TV show?'

My daughter shrugs, conscious now, strapped onto a bed and on her phone as we move through the night. Despite the fact she's cut herself severely and overdosed on pills, she's on Snapchat. Which probably means half the population of Melbourne's fifteen-year-old's will have seen this on her 'story'.

The lights inside this thing are excruciatingly bright. I wince at my bag sitting on my lap, stuffed with provisions, things I grabbed at the last minute, anything I thought we might need. Socks, an overripe banana, an Uncle Toby's Muesli Bar – one that's sat years at the back of the cupboard. You'll eat anything at 5:00 a.m. in a hospital emergency room cubicle. You'll eat shit if you think it'll keep you awake.

It wasn't always like this. We were once normal people, with normal sized problems. But then she started scratching herself, making neat lines across the top of her foot with a pin, concealing them with a sock. 'Look at you, one socked girl,' I'd joke. A year later, I am living every parent's nightmare, breaking bad, doing the once unthinkable, whatever it takes to keep my girl alive.

The new normal has become dialling triple zero and waiting for the quiet flashing lights of an ambulance in the early hours of the morning. It is sitting sleepless on a hard, plastic chair beside the gurney where she lies, waiting hours for a doctor to assess her and get another version of the events – the dosage or the cutting instrument, the time of the act, the motivation, 'Did you intend to kill yourself?' they ask.

The new normal is having a date follow the ambulance to the hospital, having him hold my hand in the emergency room, while I hold my daughter's as the wounds are sutured and glued. She squeezes my hand while they do it. 'It hurts so much Mum.'
This guy will see more than a new lover should, more than a parent even. He tells me he will cry about this at his counselling session.

'I just want to say to your daughter, *why?*'

Then it is getting home with her all chirpy, as though nothing out of the ordinary ever happened. Me putting the kettle on, telling my date, 'I'll just be a moment,' then going to the bathroom to mop up all the blood and spew with towels, stuffing them into the laundry basket. Coming back in smiling, saying, 'Cup of tea?'

Him looking at me incredulous. 'How about a vodka?'

As soon as she gets in the car, she's shedding clothes like she's on fire. She strips down to tiny, skin-tight black shorts and a loose-weave crocheted halter-neck. As we walk down the street to the Abbotsford Convent, she is removing her bra and stuffing it into her backpack. Her fifteen-year-old arms are exposed, covered in deep criss-cross cuts in various stages of healing. She wears those cuts like a fashion accessory, flouncing them around like they are better than normal arms. They're her arms, she says, it's her body and she's fine with them.

'What are you looking at?' she says to me.

'Nothing,' I say, but my heart is breaking, knowing that people will stare and judge, and I pray she'll always be this confident.

Ancient trees of the convent grounds sigh in the breeze. Those old gums would no doubt have seen girls like her, poor wayward waifs sent here in times past to be reformed by the nuns, cleansed of their 'madness' and their 'sins' in twelve-hour laundry shifts. Made to wear brown sacks and pudding bowl haircuts. I wonder if it worked, my angry self thinks, whether it worked better than Parentline with their string of 'trained professionals' waiting for your call, waiting to empathise and say things like, 'Gee, that must be really hard.' Maybe try saying, 'When you tell me to go fuck myself, it's upsetting.'

She is deliberately walking ahead of me. We have not come to the convent seeking redemption though. I've already resigned myself to the fact that, at least I, will now burn in hell. We are here on a drug deal. One that will be tacked on to the end of a mother-daughter date, Goddamnit – my attempt to normalise things before I do the fortnightly drop off to her dad's. And, if I am totally honest, my attempt to alleviate some of the guilt I am feeling about the rest of my parenting: of loving her but not liking her sometimes, of having no strategies to deal with her, no boundaries, no consistency, no ideas that work – not fucking one, about being a good mother – apart from those that involve me drinking, getting a bottle out of the cupboard and pouring a lot of it into a glass and then down my throat. Now that's a strategy that works! Then I become Good Mummy. Fun Mummy.

'You're such a stress head,' she says. 'You need to smoke weed.'

We find a table inside the Convent Café. I order a coffee while she looks at the menu. When the waiter comes up, she orders the Big Breakfast Eggs and I see another thirty dollars rolling out of my wallet and it's not even 10:00 a.m. The cannabis drop will be another hundred and fifty, giving the reality of a second job at the local Chick'n Shoppe another nod. I sip my coffee and give her a smile, then look out to the convent gardens wondering if the little bastard doing the deal will show. Checkpoint Charlie is behind some tree apparently.

'Are you sure he's coming?' I say.

'Yes,' she says annoyed. 'I've told you, it's all been arranged on Snapchat.'

I take a breath and hold it. 'Okay,' I say, upbeat.

Dope was meant to be a temporary answer. A quick fix until we found a medication that actually worked, or a strategy better than the psychiatrist-suggested 'snapping a rubber band against one's wrist', to control cutting. 'You just need to keep them alive until maturity kicks in,' her GP said to me on the quiet. No. Better the passive, giggly, zoned-out teenager in the beanbag blowing smoke rings, than the darkly depressed, self-harming girl listening to suicide songs – *Fe fo fi, I want to fucking die.*

I look around.

'Has he responded yet?'

She scoops baked beans onto toast and chews. 'Mum. Please. Just chill.'

I purse my lips and picture the afternoon – her a mess, me frantic. Dropping her off at her dad's then speeding off to the far reaches of the western suburbs, places way past Altona I've never even heard of, where garden sculptures are burned out cars, and scrawny dogs and kids are hard to tell apart, to end up at a bikie's front door in my Laura Ashley frock, shooting the breeze about grow lights and hydroponic plants before he hands over his specialty strain – Gorilla Glue – but not until he's sure I've tried some.

When my date turns up at the apartment, I greet him with breasts heaving, though more from worry than from sexual desire. I shove a drink in his hand.

'She's turned off *location services*,' I say, 'cheers.'

'Cheers,' he says.

We swig our drinks.

He takes his bag off his shoulder. He looks nice. He's had a shave. I go to kiss him.

'When?' he says.

'Like hours ago.'

We plonk ourselves in opposite chairs and spend the evening talking about her.

'This is sexy,' I say at ten o'clock.

'Ha, I know,' he says.

We go brush our teeth then get into bed in our underwear and hold hands. As we lay there in the dark, she texts me.

'Phew,' I say.

He moves towards me.

I can feel my eyes closing, being pulled under, to somewhere far away. I turn away from him. 'We need to talk,' I say to the wall.

I'm breathing in, I'm breathing out. I'm breathing in, I'm breathing out. It's the 4:00 a.m. wake-up again. I open my eyes suddenly because I can hear her, hear her moving about in hallways in her white hoodie, fingers hooked into the sleeves so you can't see her arms. Moving through rooms with bare legs. I lift my head up and listen out but it's all quiet, too quiet, and I realise I'm in an empty bed.

I'm on the M1, off to work, when I get the call from her father. She's gone missing. I take the exit ramp and pull over, listening to him going over all the details.

'She's smoking in the bungalow. I told her not to smoke in the bungalow and she goes yeah, yeah, and I come back and she's smoking in the bungalow. So I say, don't smoke in the bungalow and she goes yeah, yeah and I come back and she's smoking in the bungalow. And when I venture in there, the heater is tipped over and there's cups of drinks spilt over on the floor near it, and she's taking sleeping tablets and I'm not allowed in, like fucking hell!'

'I know,' I say to him, 'I know. I'll see if I can find her.'

I hang up and sit in the car for a while, watching people in other cars racing past on their way to where they are meant to be. I call her but she won't pick up. I imagine what will happen if I take another day off work. My boss has stopped saying hello and goodbye to me. Compassion fatigue. I've missed so many days now that, when I do go in, I'm in a daze, staring at my in-tray and it all looks meaningless, picking things up from last week and I can't remember a thing about them. It's like someone else's desk, someone else's work, someone who walked away from the job one day, picked up their bag and left.

I dial her number again. This time she picks up.

'Dad's a fucking dick.'

'Oh darling, he's just trying to—'

'Don't talk to me about him, you never believe anything I say.'

'That's not true,' I tell her, but it kind of is true. Part of me is convinced that she has us over a barrel. The panic attacks timed, the depression when it suits, the cutting a big *I'll show you*.

'Of course I believe you. Where are you?'

'Where's Dad?' she says.

'He's driving round the streets, looking for you. You ran off from the car.'

'Tell him to go home.'

'Okay, but where are you?'

I contemplate the inevitable – having to turn the car around and pick her up from the side of the road somewhere – the look on her face, the weight of her falling into the passenger seat, the car heavy with load, the drive home in silence, the call to my boss ... then the sense of desolation around the hours ahead.

'I'm going to school,' she says.

I drop the phone in my lap, look up out the windscreen to the sky where I expect to see a band of angels descending with trumpets.

I put the phone back to my ear.

'You're amazing!' I say, but she's hung up.

'I'm leaving the situation,' her father tells me. 'She needs one abode, one set of rules. Don't fuck it up,' he says.

'What do you mean?' I feel like laughing and crying at the same time. I press the phone closer to my ear.

'She needs to be contained. I'm happy to have her here but I'll be locking the door at night while she's out in the bungalow.

'What do you mean, locking the door at night? She's a child. What if she needs you?'

'She's stealing stuff. What's she going to take next?'

'You told me you put everything of value in your filing cabinet. What else do you think she might steal? Furniture?'

'Who knows.'

I take a breath.

'Well, I'm clearly the best person for her to live with,' I say, swallowing. I can hear her crying in the other room. 'What do you mean, don't fuck it up?'

I hang up the phone and go into her room. She is on the floor hugging her knees, her face a mess of mascara tears. I stand there, knowing that I am clunky, that I don't know how to love her, that she will probably push me away. But I get down onto my knees and hold her, pull her in close. Her head lolls against mine as I kiss her bleached hair.

'It's all going to be okay,' I tell her, and we sit there together amidst the make-up and the dirty clothes and all the nameless crap, most likely stolen, strewn across her floor. 'It's all going to be okay.'

Auburn Road

Deniz Agraz

Mum and I alight the train at Auburn. We are out on our own for the first time since we arrived in Sydney a week ago. We've been cooped up at Uncle Kemal's house in Turramurra and too scared to go outside alone after he told us that this country was full of venomous spiders, swooping magpies and drunk men begging for money outside the train stations.

'Stay close to me,' Mum hisses in Turkish through her clenched teeth as we step outside the station. She grabs my left arm with one hand and clutches onto her handbag with the other. We shuffle along the bustling footpath like that for a while. 'If you get lost, we won't be able to find each other. Neither of us knows enough English.'

I look at the buildings lining the street ahead of us flaunting shop signs written in letters I have never seen before. Inside, imported goods huddle together on the shelves. We pass a grocery store. An elderly Asian couple is standing at the door with a trolley. The woman points at the hairy, red fruits on the display and calls to her husband. He replies in a language that sounds melodic but incomprehensible.

'Nobody speaks English here anyway,' I scoff.

We stop to admire the bags of star-shaped wooden spices displayed in the shopfront. I bend forward to take a whiff and cover my nose.

'It smells strange, Mum.'

The small hairs on my arms stiffen when I remember that only a week ago, we were still in Isparta where I was surrounded by familiar scents.

I catch our reflection in a restaurant window. Even though Mum is wearing her high heeled boots, she is shorter than me. We stop and stare at the rows of fried meat hanging behind the steamy window as if we are in an art gallery.

'*Anne*, is that chicken?'

'Must be a duck,' she replies, pointing at its feet.

I have never had duck before, but my mouth is watering at the thought of biting into its glossy skin and savouring the juices. A girl around my age in school uniform is sitting inside by the window. With her eyes glued to the magazine spreading over the table, she dips her chopsticks into a steaming bowl of soup and catches clumps of noodles. As she crams them into her mouth, she looks up and our eyes meet. She smiles. I smile in return and burn the image of my first Australian exchange of smiles into my brain. My stomach growls. I think duck will taste just like chicken. But, obviously, you eat it with chopsticks.

'Your uncle told me there is a Turkish supermarket in Auburn,' Mum says, her eyes scanning the buildings. She pronounces Auburn as 'O-burun' which means 'that nose' in Turkish.

I giggle at the Nose suburb.

Mum does not hear me. 'Remind me when we get there to buy *biber salçasi* and bulgur, I will make *kısır*.'

'*Anne*, can we eat duck instead of *kısır*?'

When we arrived in Australia, Uncle Kemal was late to pick us up from the airport. While we waited for him, I watched from behind the glass window while a grey-headed woman hailed a taxi. 'Look at that old woman in mini shorts!' I exclaimed pointing at her. 'She is dressed like a young person.'

'Don't stare at people,' Mum scolded. 'Westerners don't like that.'

I wasn't sure if Mum really was angry at me or for being stranded at an airport in a foreign country where she didn't even know how to use a public phone.

'I want you to be on your best behaviour at your uncle's house. We'll have to stay with him until I get a job and rent us an apartment.'

I stayed quiet and kept my observations to myself until Uncle appeared in his white Mitsubishi van.

'Not every immigrant gets to see this view on their first day,' he said as we drove across the Harbour Bridge to his house. I pressed my nose against the car window and studied the white building sitting in the middle of the sea. Its curvy triangle roofs looked like the jester's cap. Mum had shown me a picture of the building in the magazine we looked at in the plane.

Across the road, two men are sitting on plastic stools in front of a shop. They both have dark hair and chunky moustaches like Grandad and one of them is smoking a *nargile*. 'There's the Turkish supermarket!' I exclaim and tug at Mum's hand.

'Where?' she asks with excitement. Her fingers around my hand tense up as I point at the shop.

'Where do we cross the road?'

Earlier today, Uncle warned us about crossing the road only when the light is green. 'Don't do the Turkish thing and cross the road anywhere. Use the pedestrian crossing,' he said while giving us a lift to the station.

We stand at the pedestrian crossing and wait for the road to clear. The first passing car slows down and then stops. We keep standing there. The driver gets impatient. She sticks her head out the window and beckons us to cross. Mum's shoulders sink. She squeezes my hand, and her long nails dig into my palm. I take a step forward and pull her with me towards the road.

As we approach the supermarket, the handwritten signs in Arabic letters become clear on the front window. The man who has been smoking *nargile* puts the pipe down and smiles. He starts talking to us but neither Mum nor I understand him. Mum holds her hands up with the palms facing the sky and shakes her head.

'They are Lebanese not Turkish. Look at the flag on the door,' she says.

'How come they smoke *nargile* then?' I defend myself and learn that *nargile* isn't only smoked in Turkey.

We continue walking. A few doors down, rolls of fabric in many colours are leaning against a shop window. They flutter in the wind like flags on poles. Mum slows down her steps and the fingers enveloping my hand relax.

Mum loves sewing. In Isparta, she would spend hours looking at the sewing materials at the street markets while I followed her around and carried the plastic bags. In return, at every *bayram*, she made me a new dress that would provoke jealous stares from the neighbours' kids. I could never tell her that I would rather wear blue jeans and the pink turtlenecks from Benetton. The existence of this shop is a sign that my new life in the southern hemisphere will be just like the one I had in Isparta.

'Let's look at this shop,' Mum says.

'But I don't want a new dress.'

'I want to make pillowcases for your uncle,' she replies.

I sigh with relief and we walk in. Inside the shop is dimly lit and I squint as we enter. It takes me a few moments to notice the Asian woman with salt and pepper hair sitting behind the counter. She is wearing a cream linen dress and holding a butter knife in one hand. The sweet scent of the apple she has been peeling permeates the shop. Upon seeing us, she stands up and smiles, showing the gaps between her teeth. Mum looks at her and yells out, 'Hello' stressing each letter of the only word she knows in English. It sounds as if she is forcing the air out of her throat. This is the first time I witness Mum trying to communicate in another language. She sounds like a stranger. The shopkeeper says, 'Hi' as she wipes her hands with a tissue.

Mum straightens her back and starts striding around the shop and I tail her, a step behind. With her hands on her waist, she makes her way around the rolls of satin, crushed velvet and embroidered lace.

Suddenly, she stops in front of a roll of blue fabric and rubs it with her palms. Her eyebrows lift. She gathers a section of it in her fist and pulls it. The fabric runs between her fingers. Mum's face lightens up. 'This is good quality cotton,' she turns around and tells me. 'See how smooth it is. It has no gaps.'

The shopkeeper, who has been watching her from behind the counter, walks towards us. The plastic slippers she is wearing makes that familiar 'shi-pidik, shi-pidik' noise every time they hit against the tiled floor. It is the same noise that Grandma's slippers used to make at dawn when she walked to the bathroom to wash herself before the morning prayer.

The shopkeeper points at the rolls at the entrance and says something to Mum who lets go of the fabric in her fist.

'Do you think she is angry at me for touching it?' Mum asks.

She rubs her hands onto her skirt uneasily and asks if I understand what the shopkeeper has been saying.

I had just started studying English early this year when the only English teacher at school quit after having a heart attack in class. I spent the rest of the year playing *yakartop* in the schoolyard during the English hour. Mum knows this but she must be secretly hoping that the years of watching American videoclips on MTV may have taught me a word or two. I shake my head.

'How do you ask the price in English?' she asks.

'I don't know, *Anne*. I think *para* is "money". Say "money".'

Instead, Mum opens her handbag and takes out her wallet. I figure that she is going to show the woman some coins to hint that she wants to know the price. But the woman says, '*Kaç para*' meaning 'How much is it?' in Turkish. Mum, her eyes widened with astonishment, blurts out a laugh and repeats, '*Evet, kaç para?*' – Yes, how much is it? She sounds happy for the first time since we arrived in Auburn.

The shopkeeper lifts her left hand up in the air and stretches out all her fingers." *Beş dolar metre*,' she says, pronouncing the 'ş' like a 'h'. She gently pats Mum's shoulder with one hand and points at the entrance with the other. '*Kırmızı*,' she says meaning 'red' and makes six with her fingers. '*Altı*.'

'Ohh, she has it in other colours too,' Mum mutters and walks to the doorway to inspect them.

I walk to the counter to look at the fashion magazines and notice the glass bowl next to the cash register. It is filled with confectionaries wrapped in shiny paper. I take a glance at them and my stomach rumbles.

The shopkeeper bends down on the floor and pulls a plastic stool from underneath the counter. She beckons me to sit down. I am overflowing with curiosity and it is impossible to simmer it down. 'You country what?' I say, trying to remember the phrase Ömer *hoca* taught me early this year.

'Vietnam,' she replies. '*Türk* Auburn *çok*.' – Turkish Auburn many. She throws her hands in the air and draws an invisible gigantic bubble.

I nod to show that I agree even though we haven't seen a single Turkish person since leaving the train station.

She grabs the glass bowl and holds it out to me. The candies inside resemble a chest of hidden treasure. Gold. Ruby. Diamond. I take a red one and say, 'Thank you' in English with my voice cracking.

I put it on my lap and look at the writing on the wrapper. The letters look just like the ones in Turkish but they have more hats and tails. When I try to read it out loud, the shopkeeper laughs. I join her with a giggle.

I unwrap it with the expectation that a piece of chocolate will reveal itself. But it isn't chocolate. It's yellow. It's soft. It's unfamiliar but not pretty like the star-shaped wooden spices in the window.

Not knowing what I am about to put inside my mouth, my heart starts thudding in my chest. Still holding it in my hand, I run to Mum who has been busy rummaging through the basket filled with cut pieces of silk. '*Anne*, she gave me this, but I don't know what it is.'

Mum turns arounds to have a look at what I am holding. She scrunches her eyebrows. 'Must be a candy. Eat it. It's impolite to throw away what people offer you,' she whispers.

I return to my seat and hold the candy in front of my nose to inhale it. It smells like nuts. I rub it on my mouth and lick my lips.

I can hear the shopkeeper speaking to me from behind the counter, trying to encourage me to eat it. I gather all my strength and take a small bite. The candy crumbles away between my fingers. What melts inside my mouth is bursting with a familiar flavour. 'It's peanut candy,' I yell to Mum from my seat. She turns around to give me an approving look and returns to her exploration. In one go, I cram the rest of the candy into my mouth and lick my fingers one by one to taste the very last of it.

As the shopkeeper cuts three metres of the red cotton fabric for Mum, I remember the phrase Ömer *hoca* had taught us in one of our rare English hours. 'What is your name?' I ask.

'Thuy,' she replies and hands me a business card. T-h-u-y. She points at her name and shows the letters one by one. With a serious face, she spells them out.

'Maybe she was a teacher in her country,' Mum says as Thuy folds up the fabric. She puts it in a plastic bag and hands it to me.

As I am readying to leave, I hear Mum saying the words 'Turkish, super, market' one by one. She points at the street, hoping that Thuy might understand that she is asking for directions.

Thuy walks us to the doorway and stands there, facing the street. First, she holds her right arm straight then bends her wrist towards the right. 'Turkish supermarket,' she says.

'Okay, it's around the corner,' Mum translates but I already know.

'Bye, *arkadaş*,' Thuy says as we leave calling us her 'friends', I repeat and wave at her.

Outside, Auburn Road is filled with colours, shapes, and sounds that we didn't even know existed until a week ago. The inside of my mouth is still coated with the sweet stickiness of the peanut candy. Mum takes the plastic bag from me and holds my hand. She strokes my palm with her fingertips as we watch a gaggle of chattering schoolgirls in uniform crossing the road where there isn't a pedestrian crossing.

The Immaterial Quality of Creating Matter

Andiopi Athanasiadou

We all gathered to watch him work. They kept knocking on the door.

His hands were not beautiful; the joints were crooked, the fingers were enormous, the fingernails black, destroyed by paints and varnishes.

From the container to the canvas, colours gathered light and moisture. He went to the canvas and spread them without a design, in thick brushstrokes, baldly, without correcting things. Red primer and strokes of white – for the fat – brown for the seared meat's crust, some bloody juice dripping on the metallic plate, next to it a glass of wine, and the room was bursting with delicious scents.

The miracle took place there, in that very arm, with nerves and muscles floating in the air: the photosynthesis. His aura, his special quality, was inside that arm, bound to him by the shoulder. It was there that the wine fermented and the meat was roasted. One could see the arm flow and spill, the wine matured in his blood, the meat he just painted cooked slowly in the heat of his body, every bit of it created in his mind. The man knew how to make meat.

He threw a white, stained cloth on the table. The floor glowed with the glimmer of the fireplace. I could see the flames dancing.

'Bread,' someone whispered, but he was almost out of colours. He abandoned the brush and used his fingers to scrape some colour from the bottom of the box; then he placed on the tablecloth, stealing its whiteness and the yellow from the flames, a fresh wheat loaf.

With the same hand, he broke the bread and passed it around.

Outside, the creatures knocked hard on the door.

Sometimes he came back spent, bruised, exhausted, dragging with him blossoming branches, flowers and seashells, in shapes we had never seen before. Sometimes he brought a dying two-headed bird or other creatures that lasted for a little while and then turned to dust, but not before he had the time to draw them again.

We knew, then, that he wandered through a landscape he himself had created and that he walked deep inside the forest, near purple waters.

One time, we found a creature, half-fish and half-goat, in the water tank; it disintegrated at dawn. The creatures he found never lasted. In the evenings he cursed himself, 'impostor', 'conjurer', he rambled, 'not a creator'. He wanted to make them last and create a universe – origins. He made matter, but not life, not immortality.

I was returning from the fields one day when, behind a pile of chopped wood, I heard a meowing sound. It was a woman, stark naked and bright white, her marble face unbroken, her long, red tail swishing. She had caught some rodent and was tearing at it with her teeth, as if it were fruit, and she sucked the blood. She looked at me with blind eyes and fled, lightly as if she could fly.

I knew he had created it. He had finally made a creature that could last. Otherwise, there would be no point in feeding.

Later, he took us to the forest where they lived. It was a place he had painted, of course. They needed to stay close to where they were 'born'. The tall, purple trees and the reddish cypresses with their star-shaped leaves trembled; the sky was a lake reflecting sunlight, but dark and greenish like a swamp. The landscape led to a beach where the sea was like any other sea.

'It is very hard to bewitch the sea,' he said, but the creatures' desire for water was so expansive that the sea quickly filled with beings – amphibians and others resembling fish. The creatures played near the sea and rolled on the beach, biting each other and laughing with peculiar cat smiles, showing glimpses of teeth.

It was paradise.

He loved it most of all. He began working on grand and wild projects to make the place more beautiful. Dramatic sunsets, frozen thunderstorms, frayed clouds, grey and blue mists, colours he discovered in his eye's iris; he even weaved stars with golden yarn, swarms of stars we had never seen before.

The creatures, beautiful and proud, were very cruel to the other living beings that shared their forest. Finally, what they carried inside them – what he didn't know he had given them when he added the satin white of their skin on the canvas and the fox red in their hair – revolted.

Red – it is all the fault of red. Fire, blood, meat.

The creatures multiplied in such a monstrous way that they all united into one body and tied their tongues together and created nooks for protrusions never designed for their bodies. We saw the beastliness and thought it was cannibalism.

Seven days later, we heard the first heart beating like a distant, hollow thunder, inside the belly of this finger-born Aphrodite. We fell silent.

The creatures were now autonomous and separate from us.

Blood had spilled during labour.

They multiplied. They took over our land and kept eating, they sucked everything, locusts revelling in destruction. They drove us away from the forest, the sea and the sky, forbidding us to go outside of the few remaining houses. We shut ourselves in the granary he used as a studio. It was empty. He was running out of colours and we were hungry.

Then, he painted the Great Rain. The water level rose every day in the forest and the creatures drowned or died from starvation. We remained in the granary and ate what he could paint. The granary was made of wood and floated like a big boat on the water.

When we got out again, eight days later, the water had started receding and we couldn't see any of the creatures.

Loneliness crept inside our hearts. What was once 'they' became just 'us'.

Swipe Right

Angharad Lodwick

I knew straightaway I was dead.

For starters, nothing hurt anymore, and I can tell you right now it was a bloody relief.

The second giveaway was that it had been a long time since I had been anywhere this schmick. It looked a bit like a hospital waiting room or a Centrelink office with white tiles that went on forever. Black ropes directed me to the only counter in the place.

I moved towards it with the funny feeling that walking was just for show here. The guy behind the counter seemed reasonable, I guess. Looked like something between a banker and a bikie.

'G'day,' I said, lifting my chin.

'You know where you are?' he asked without ceremony.

'Yeah, I reckon so.'

'Righto. Well, here's your key. Lift's over there,' he said, indicating behind me with his eyes.

'Cheers.' I grabbed the Labrador-shaped keyring and put it in my pocket.

'Anything else?' I asked, keeping a measure of confidence in my voice.

'Yep. Here.' He handed me a phone.

'Nice one. Know any good numbers?' I joked.

His response was a raised eyebrow and a question of his own: 'You ever used a dating app?'

I laughed aloud. Had *I* ever used a dating app?

'You bet,' I said with a wink. Then I thought about this for a second. 'Are there women here?'

He didn't bite. 'See for yourself.'

I held up the phone and looked at the screen. Relieved I didn't have to squint anymore, I saw it was my grandmother. That crazy old bat.

'You want to meet with someone here, you swipe right. Don't want to see 'em, swipe left. You want to see her?'

I shrugged. Why not? I guess she was the one who bought me my puppy for my eighteenth birthday. I'm not even religious but the pup was so clean and white and perfect, there was only one thing to call her.

I swiped to the right, and Nan's face disappeared.

'I think this one's broken. Any chance of an upgrade?' I joked as I handed it back to him for a look.

'Huh,' he said, frowning at the screen. 'Grandparents are usually a safe first bet.'

'What?'

'Well ... I guess she doesn't want to see you.'

'What do you mean? Why wouldn't she want to see me?'

'If someone wants to see you too, you'll match with them and then you can send them a message and meet up. But if they don't, well, look.' He held up the phone so I could read the message that had popped up. I skimmed through the long, wordy message about something to do with me nicking her pain meds. Jesus, Nan, that was ages ago. Get over it.

I watched him press the back button, the message vanished and the words *No Matches* appeared on a black screen.

He handed the phone back to me and I locked the screen and put it in my pocket like it was no big deal.

'Thanks mate,' I said with my biggest grin. 'I'm not really much of a tech guy anyway. So, are there any good parties on? Any bars? Maybe something a bit more stylish to wear? I'd be happy to make it worth your while.'

I had no idea what opportunities there were here, but that had never stopped me before. It was always good to suss out your options early.

He gave me a stony look. 'Check into your room first; you'll figure it out.'

Figuring he wasn't good for much else, I turned away. The lift was right across the white tiles and before I knew it, I was standing in front of the doors. I pressed the only button inside, then looked back at the counter. The man was still there, but he looked a little different from a distance. Softer, or something. As the doors closed, he watched me with something like pity. Well stuff him, I didn't need anyone's pity.

After what felt like an eternity, the lift finally arrived at my floor. The doors opened into a hallway that stretched on and on either side with colourful patterned carpet just like down the pokies.

I pulled the keyring from my pocket to read my room number, but there was none. I checked the door directly in front of me and sure enough there was my name on it in clear black letters. The key fit, no problem, and I stepped inside.

It was a bit like one of those old 70s motel rooms, all oranges and browns. I'd stayed in plenty like it over the years while I was still on the move. I kicked off the terrible no-brand runners I was wearing and fell backwards onto the bed. It was a bit hard, but at least it didn't take me forever to get comfortable anymore. I put my phone and key on the bedside table and picked up the remote I found sitting there.

I wasn't really into TV, but there wasn't much else to do so I turned it on. You'd think they'd at least splash out for higher definition. The first show looked like a soap opera or something. I changed the channel, but it was the same show. A priest and some guy dressed in black. I flicked and flicked but the stupid thing only seemed to get the one program. I settled back and decided to give it a go.

Looked like a pretty miserable story to me. The priest was giving a sermon and there was a plain cardboard coffin to the side. No photos or anything. Just some undertaker or something sitting in the front row. Poor dead bastard didn't have any f—

Oh, hell.

I shifted to the end of the bed, leaning forward to take a closer look. The priest started saying some rubbish about Jesus and forgiveness, and the mortician or whatever they called them sat there nodding. Paid to be there; that'd be right.

I switched the depressing thing off and put the remote down. To my surprise, when I looked back up the TV was gone. Great.

I decided to go exploring but when I stood up, I realised the door was gone too. Nothing but ugly brown wallpaper where I had walked in. I checked my bedside table; the key and remote had disappeared as well. What was I even supposed to do here? I opened the wardrobe, but it was completely bare. There wasn't even a Goddamn minibar.

Being dead seemed just as shit as being alive.

Just as I was contemplating how to put a hole in the wall for something to do, the phone buzzed. I picked it up and checked the screen to see a new contact notification. I tapped the thumbnail. My old mate Johnno!

I swiped right and what the hell? His picture disappeared. A message popped up with some bullshit about how I invited his younger sister around to meet my dog and *took advantage*. Come on, Johnno. She was over sixteen and as if she wasn't keen for it. And I didn't return her calls, but I didn't need that kind of grief. It was supposed to be a bit of fun; not my problem she took it too seriously.

I went to reply and tell him exactly that, but there was no reply button. There wasn't even a delete button. Just his name, the message and *Return to Main Menu*.

I clicked back and there they were: Nan's message and Johnno's. I still couldn't believe Nan didn't want to see me. I read through her message again. Blah, blah, *I was in so much pain at the end*. Come on, everyone knew she was just carrying on.

There weren't any more new contacts, so I put the phone down.

This was going to be a long bloody afterlife.

It seemed like eons between notifications, and time stretched longer than I could ever have imagined, broken up only by the buzz of a new contact. Even though I always swiped right, over and over they all said no.

Swipe. My first housemate? I just *borrowed* that rent money, and I would have paid it back eventually if she hadn't been so angry about it. Why should I have bothered to talk to her about it if she was just going to yell at me about *broken trust* and *we relied on you*. It took me ages to find another place to live that would let me keep my dog.

Swipe. My old boss? I was *going* to bring the ute back, I told him that, and the accident wasn't even my fault. Yeah, OK, maybe it wasn't the best time to roll a cigarette, but the other car came out of nowhere. I couldn't possibly have been expected to pay him back after he fired me. I had a really hard time getting jobs for a while after that and poor Halo went hungry a lot. I don't know why these people couldn't be a bit more forgiving.

Swipe. My business partner? I mean, yeah, I borrowed his investment to pay off some debts first, but after I collected the deposits from the customers, I was totally going to do the work. OK, yes, maybe I shouldn't have spent it *all* on speed and a new sound system, but it was my thirtieth birthday party; people were expecting a good time. Why is it so hard to be understanding? Then the bastard dogged me by calling the cops. I had to leave Halo behind for a while when I was on the run, and she had to fend for herself.

Swipe. My ex? Well, yes, I guess we didn't end on the best terms, but I wouldn't have shoved her if she hadn't been so unreasonable about sorting out the assets and giving me what I deserved. Sure, the car was in her name, but I was the one who drove it the most, and she only covered my rent a few times. Besides, she should have been asking me for forgiveness. She was the one who called the RSPCA on poor old Halo when I was arrested.

Swipe. Jesus, even my mum? It wasn't like she needed the money; she had dementia for chrissakes. By that time, I'd been in jail for years, and when I came out, I had nothing. No one.

Swipe. Swipe. Swipe.

I would have stopped checking the phone each time it buzzed, but I had literally nothing else to do. No movies, no music, no Xbox. I didn't seem to need to eat or sleep or go to the toilet or anything. Most of the time I just lay on the bed staring at the chipped paint on the ceiling or reread through the messages.

It was worse than jail.

There was only one message that I ever swiped left on. My old man. That lying, selfish bastard. His dumb face disappeared, and a message box opened up. I was tempted to just write *go fuck yourself* and leave it at that, but then I really thought about it. I had no intention of ever meeting him here (and I wasn't even sure whether you could change your mind once you said no anyway) so it seemed like my only chance to tell him what I thought without him interrupting me with his own special brand of charming spin.

I took my time to tell him exactly how much of a manipulative prick he was to me and Mum, how entitled he was and how I hadn't been able to wait until I got my P-plates, took my pup, and drove the hell away from that house.

I pressed send, and his face and the message disappeared. I was relieved. I didn't want to see his ugly mug or the angry words I had written.

I don't know how long I had been there when I got the notification. I was expecting it to be another old girlfriend, another so-called mate, so I nearly dropped the phone when I saw that beautiful, blonde smiling face in the photo.

My hands shook as I swiped right, and my heart was in my mouth as I waited for the inevitable message.

It didn't come. The screen went black, and the word *MATCH* filled the screen in white letters.

A sob came out of my mouth, but it was cut short by the sound of my phone ringing. All it said was *Incoming Call* and I fumbled with the buttons to answer.

'It's a match. Are you ready to meet now?' the familiar voice said.

'Y ... yes,' I stuttered, my voice cracking. It was so long since I had spoken to anyone.

'Through the door. Take as long as you like.'

'Thank you.' I breathed, turning to where the door had been when I first arrived. It had reappeared; I ran towards it and wrenched it open.

On the other side I found myself in the kitchen of my last place, before the cops came. It was grimier than I remembered, with empty cans and unwashed dishes everywhere. The dog bowls on the floor were empty.

I heard panting, and I slowly turned around. There she was.

I dropped to my knees, and she ran into my arms.

'I'm sorry. I'm so, so sorry.'

Genealogy Questions for the Aunties

Ashley Somwaru

5. What do you know about your family surname?

बंसी :

        filled with punctured holes

                crossed legs

pruned fingertips

        some say it's hidden in Radha Rani's skirts

सोमवार :

        or under the rue

blotting Aja

                in his cupped hands

syllables – eroded

11. What stories have come down to you about your parents? Grandparents? More distant ancestors?

Remin' meh, yuh was bawn before or afta daddi pass away? He been ah give dem pickney dem caramel an' call dem beast. An' cross he foot so when he sit an' knack ah drum an' sing. He use to ketch a pandit by he tongue if he say somethin' wrang. Me think dah boy ya so is daddi rebawn. When he come out, he cross he foot just so. Yuh been ah come right afta? Yuh fadda tell meh yuh svara like a swan flyin' out yuh throat. An' meh does hear yuh does do a ting with yuh fadda dholak. Yuh mussi tink yuh ah man.

9. Did you have family chores? What were they?

In Johanna, abbidese couldn't go school if we nah pick de rice or bora or mind de cows. If yuh cyan do wah yuh suppose to, yuh cyan leave. When we ol' nuff, meh fadda pull we out. Somebody haffi tend de farm an' we haffi eat. One time, de cow stomach knot up an' swell an' e' turn ova an' dead next day. Nobody ah watch am. How meh feel bad.

1. Are there any physical characteristics that run in your family?

When meh been small small, meh family call meh blackie.

17. How did your family come to live here?

Only nine ah we go an' some leff back. Meh big buddy gaan away an' bring we come afta he go school an' marry. Alla we in 2nd street, Kensington stay till we gi' kick out. Meh been ah come wid middle school education buh we nah get money so meh fin' wuk. Only pickney go school wid lice floatin' top deh hair. Waan by waan dey marry we off. Meh daddi an' mudda nah tek worry no mo'. We become next side problem.

13. Of all the things you learned from your parents, what do you feel was the most valuable?

क्रोध

          the kind that makes women become rocks

                    and banana trees and

राक्षसी

        murmuring

                you'll never know

     you'll never know

3. What is the funniest practical joke you ever played on someone?

We use to hol' a dragonfly by de wings an' snap off de tail. Dada tell meh sista she go end up like dat if she dey by sheself. She jus' pick sheself up an' go London. How ol' she dey now an' she going all ova de place, nah listenin' to nobody askin' yuh nah go marry fuh real? Imagine, who go do she dead wuk and send she away if she get no chile?

6. Who was the oldest relative you remember as a child? What do you remember about them?

One time meh brudda get licks bad an' de man teff all he ting. Since den, he tell he daughta doh marry no dougla, no man from Laventille. She 'ent listen. She own fadda didn't walk she down de aisle. Nobody hear from she afta dat.

10. Describe a typical family meal. Who did the cooking? What were your favourite foods?

We does have de gyul dem lay out banana leaf for when de man dem come afta dey done finish prayin'. Alla we ah spoon pun'kin an' bodi an' aloo an' archar along de veins. Den we does pile buss up shot fuh scoop all de sauce. Ant running along yuh food when yuh eat. Da'is how yuh know yuh eatin' good. De children go in the bush and eat mango 'til 'is dey turn to eat. We does tek wha leff back.

22. As a parent were you strict or lenient?
I sey watch story heh. Apna Bazaar get plenty plantain, 5 fuh one dollah. So meh pickin' pickin' and 'cross street is Didi's gyul wit one man. How she skin ah show. Bubby pokin' all through she shirt. I sey if dat was my chil', she wudda neva leave de house like dat.

4. What was your religion growing up? What church, if any, did you attend?

यदा यदा हि धर्मस्य ग्लानिर्भवति भारत |
अभ्युत्थानमधर्मस्य तदात्मानं सृजाम्यहम् ||

    ghanta and buzzard feet
        sanjeevani and cremation ground

    bottom-house wuk

    lingam dug up from the field

    dakshina exchanged for prayer

    havan kund inking
        the whites of your eyes

परित्राणाय साधूनां विनाशाय च दुष्कृताम् |
धर्मसंस्थापनार्थाय सम्भवामि युगे युगे ||

think of the word 'cross' as a woman
                unmarried and prancing down the street or
drum beat on a broken inhale
bush after bush after bush
slip of tongue—kshama
        one who hasn't bowed down to her husband—
                Vishnu with a grip tight on his gada

18. Do you have any health problems that are considered hereditary?

When meh daddi was sick, he tell alla we is because we does raise he pressah. Whatever he sey, we gah fi do it. Yuh cyan ask questions. He want he foot rub, alla we fight to go massage he 'til he fall asleep. Is blessings, yuh know. Deez days, yuh tell ah gyal fuh do something, she schups and gaan she way. Dem young gyal nah even waan give yuh a glass of wata. Dey say, yuh nah get hand? If meh daddi been hear dat, e' wudda been buss mouth. He say yuh gah fuh go pick banana, yuh cyan ask why. If a bacoo unda da tree, walk next side. Dis gyal sey she too scared fuh do it, buh she get send back anyway. Dis gyal go an' ask pandit why she cyan sit down an' do prayers fuh sheself an' dey tell she, e' just dey so. Me feel meh pressah raise when meh see deez pickney dem. How dey chul chul. Doh even waan sing lil bit. Dey steady sneak away.

29. What is the one thing you most want people to remember about you?

Hear. Me nah talk nobody bad. Me does only talk wah meh see.

7. Were there any fads during your youth that you remember vividly?

Yuh see Sona gyal? Like she cut from de same marble as Gauri Ma. Everybody does follow she 'round. She smile big big an' say hello auntie, how yuh do? Alla we dey behin' she, wah she waan eat an' so. But watch, Dabit daughta real nasty. Da gyal cudda chase away all dem roach. How dem small pickney laugh when she come 'round an' poke she big belly. Dey does point a flashlight at she fuh see she face. Buh is just joke. Me nah no wah buh next ting happen, an' she make Sona gyal cry. No one go by Dabit house no mo' afta dah. She go big school an' come back buh nobody waan talk to she. She enta ah room an' everybody dey quiet. We does call she big mouth cuz now she does fight people wen dey sey anyting. Meh tell she wha man go want yuh if yuh look so. She say, auntie, nah watch me so. Buh is for truth. Ah man waan sleep next to dah? Meh see she an' me so happy she not meh chile. Meh daughta skin clear clear and she do up she face good. Big mouth gyal does twist up sheself. Me does haffi squint an' look at she. Me tell Dabit, yuh shudda had sons. Dey cudda do mo' fuh you. Cut yuh grass an' shovel snow. An' bring home one nice gyul fuh mind pickney. Dis big mouth gyal... yuh guh haffi mind she yuh whole life 'til yuh dead. Meh sey, if she was fairer, she wudda been real pretty. If she was fair, everybody wudda like she.

A Boy Called Luke

Patrick Eades

My mother called me with the news. She was halfway through a sentence by the time I placed the phone to my ear. She talked like she cleaned the house, a hundred miles an hour and with enough vigour to erase the hardiest stains and a good portion of your residual hearing.

'— visit Uncle Kadin in the hospital this afternoon. Pray for him, thanks be to God he make a recovery, we pick you up at three-thirty, make sure to be ready.'

'Mum, what's happened to Uncle Kadin?'

'What? I tell you already, Abdul. You do not listen. He have cancer of the prostate.'

Cancer.

I stopped listening to my mother. I thought of Uncle Kadin, an old man by now, eighty at least. I had always imagined he would die of a heart attack. Fat as a cow and happy as a child, he would be missed by many.

Tears wet my cheeks, but they were not tears for my dear Uncle Kadin, they were tears for a boy I used to know. A boy called Luke.

*

I was nine years old when I first met Luke. I arrived at my new school feeling more scared than when the man with the upside-down smile helped us on the boat headed to Australia. My backpack hung off my shoulders like an anchor. I watched kids run and yell and scream in the playground. I had never seen so much joy. Or white skin. The looks I received from kids running past let me know they would not share their joy with me.

'Hey there, Buster.'

A small boy stood in front of me with gelled hair and lingering baby fat. I stared at the harelip sprouting from the middle of his face, cutting his smile in half.

'I'm Luke.'

'Abdul,' I said, not sure if I should offer my hand in greeting.

'Uddle, that's a funny name.' He paused for a minute. 'Want to come look for stink bugs in the bushes on the back oval with me?'

And, like that, we were friends.

Luke was the only boy in our year five class not to call me 'sand monkey'. In fact, every time someone called me that he would throw a pencil at them, which he paid for later in hurtzme donuts and sack-whacks. But Luke wasn't afraid of dishing out punishment himself. After one of the boys called Luke an endangered Australian elephant, Luke spent lunchtime undoing the screws on the boy's chair. When the bully returned from lunch and slumped into his chair, it collapsed like a Baghdad apartment tower and a rusty screw gouged the boy's calf. A shocked silence descended upon the classroom, only to be broken by Luke's maniacal laughter from the corner. I asked Luke later if he felt bad about the boy's leg and he said the only thing he felt bad about was that modern medicine had learned how to prevent gangrene.

Luke invited me over to his house one November weekend to catch tadpoles. His mother beamed as she opened the door.

'It is so nice to meet a friend of Luke's,' she said. 'He talks about you all the time!'

Luke shared his mother's smile without a hint of embarrassment.

'Yeah, Mum. This is my friend Abull.' (He was getting closer). 'He came from eye-rack.'

We caught twenty-seven tadpoles that afternoon, and Luke detailed our adventures during show-and-tell the following Monday. Luke spoke so fast Mrs. Hardy had to remind him to breathe between sentences. My brown cheeks turned crimson and I slouched beneath my desk.

'Hey, sand monkey. Did you catch the freak disease in the pond too?' Brendan asked, and the classroom erupted in laughter.

Lunchtimes we spent searching for new insects to add to Luke's bug collection, or building tree houses out of paddlepop sticks and discarded lunch bags for the possum who lived in the bottlebrush. Luke never wanted to play with the other boys.

The other boys played football – they called it 'soccer' – and sometimes Luke would catch me staring at their game as he held out a Christmas beetle in his hand for me to look at. I feigned enthusiasm, but I cared more for that ball than for his stupid bugs.

Every now and then Luke would be absent from school, and on one of those days I shuffled over to the boys organising the teams and asked if I could play. Brendan (our class captain) told me they had a no freaks allowed policy, and any friend of Luke's was a friend of a freak, which also fit their exclusion criteria.

Back home in Iraq, I had been the best football player in my village. My feet danced like a jackal, the power in my skinny legs enough to frighten any who dared to goal keep. Football was my escape. Escape from the gnawing pains in my stomach, escape from the roar of the bombs which shook our house and from the stench of burned animal flesh at dawn. Now I had really escaped, but I had lost football.

When I told my father, he said football was a silly thing to miss. You could miss Cousin Ali, or the hill our village was built on, or Masgouf after the river had been running clear. But to miss a game? That was foolish.

I was a fool.

One lunchtime Luke and I were collecting lady beetles from the piles of freshly mown grass on the back oval. Something struck Luke in the jaw and dropped him. The missile turned out to be Brendan's football.

'Hey, Freak. It's your lucky day,' Brendan said, as he loomed over Luke and the pile of grass clippings. 'The gardener cut your lunch up for you.'

Brendan's friends made mooing noises and laughed.

A tightness clutched my chest. I urged myself to stand up for Luke the same way he stood up for me. I willed my arm to throw my fist into the side of Brendan's smug little head. I wanted to lower my head and charge at Brendan like a bull.

But my legs wouldn't move.

Frozen to the grass like a stick-figure snowman, I watched.

Brendan flashed a smile at his friends before grabbing Luke's hair in his meaty hand. 'Eat your lunch, Freak.'

'I have already eaten my lunch. I had a cheese and pickle sandwich, a roll up, and—'

The rest of Luke's menu was cut off as Brendan thrust Luke's face down into the grass clippings and ground him into them.

Luke never cried, never called for help. Two steps and I could have shoved Brendan off him, but fear anchored me in place. A sour heat burned the back of my throat.

When Brendan grew tired of his torture, he wrenched Luke's head back up with enough force to snap his neck.

'Had enough to eat, Freak?'

Luke nodded his head, a strand of grass caught in the cleft of his upper lip.

'Good,' said Brendan. 'Bit more grass in your diet, bit less Maccas, maybe you won't be such a fat shit.'

The others laughed. Brendan released Luke's head and stepped away. He stooped to pick up the soccer ball, and I took that to mean it was over.

My legs became my legs again, and I moved to Luke. I extended a useless arm towards him, still on all fours, his belly hanging almost to the ground.

'Hey!' Brendan yelled at me.

It wasn't over.

'What are you doing?'

I said nothing, my arm hanging in the breeze like the wilted branch of an olive tree. I looked at Luke, but he was staring at my extended hand, avoiding my eye.

'I heard you like soccer, Abdul,' Brendan continued, while he rolled the ball up and down his forearm.

Football, I wanted to say. 'Yes,' I said.

'Want to play with us?'

I looked at Brendan, my future spinning in his hands. I knew there would be a catch. A choice.

Later, I would realise our lives are built on the choices we make each day. They are the bricks laid down to give us shelter from the winds of change, the roof to protect us from dark clouds above, and the doors to welcome in lonely travellers. Or the barbed-wire fence to keep them out.

I let my arm flop back to my side, shot one last glance at Luke, and trotted over to the others. His face looked like a wounded calf when its mother abandons it knee-deep in the mud of a drying waterhole it will never climb out of.

I kicked the ball with such fury that lunchtime. Brendan and the others thought I was trying to impress. They didn't understand. I kicked the ball as if it were a tiny replica of my coward-self.

There was no going back. Luke refused to talk to me. Every now and then I would find a spider or a millipede crawling in my pencil case, and I would turn to see Luke's face challenging me. I turned away.

I remained friends with Brendan and the others for the next few years, but as high school approached, I asked my parents if I could apply for one of the selective schools in the city. They were thrilled, and spent their meagre savings on a tutor to help me with the entrance exam. I studied hard so I could go to a school where there was no boy called Luke sitting alone beneath the branches of a flame tree each lunchtime. Like other immigrants, I studied to escape.

I was fifteen when I ran into Brendan on the bus, and he asked me if I'd heard about Luke.

'Leukemia. Fuckin' rough, eh?'

I thought he was joking at first. Don't want to catch *Luke*-emia – turns you into a freak!

'Went to his funeral last week,' Brendan said. 'A few of the teachers came too. Mrs. Hardy cried like a fountain.'

That afternoon I went home and packed all my football uniforms, boots and balls into garbage bags and carried them down the road to the charity clothing bin. I walked home barefoot, my soles now soft enough for the pebbles to sting.

*

My mother wouldn't shut up the whole way to the hospital. My father concentrated on the driving, saying little. And I sat scrunched into the back seat, saying even less.

'If only you studied harder, Abdul. You could have been the doctor looking after Kadin. No – the surgeon – saving his life with delicate touch and such skill ...'

We made our way to the oncology ward, and I saw the unmistakable bulge of Uncle Kadin, resting on a hospital bed with two gowns tied together like cling wrap across his stomach. His room was packed with family and friends. Photos adorned the walls, flowers tumbled off the windowsill. My mother rushed forwards and wrapped her skinny arms around him as best she could.

Uncle Kadin chuckled, pushing her away. 'Rafiqa! I'm not dying, I'm fine. The operation was a huge success. God plans for me to live to one hundred at least. Although I do worry they may have left a few implements inside – look at the size of my gut now!'

We all laughed along with Uncle Kadin. I said my greetings and left the room, telling my father I needed the bathroom. I should have felt relieved, joyous at the good news but I didn't.

I wandered the corridors of the ward. I peeked into the rooms as I passed, some full of visitors, life overflowing. Others barren as a desert, blank eyes staring at the ceiling, waiting for what lay beyond. I continued out into the sunshine, beyond the bright yellow walls of the cancer centre to a bench facing out towards Botany Bay. An engraving on one of the wooden slats caught my eye.

In loving memory of Luke Price. Always in his mother's thoughts.

I wondered how often, in those final months and years, as her son's blood cells multiplied and the time they had left flew by at hyper speed, did she ask: what sort of God would come up with a plan like this?

It wasn't hard to find Mrs. Price. I found Luke's house from memory, tucked in the bosom of the valley, protected by red gums and bottle brushes. It had aged. The yellow paint had begun to flake, the

Greensleeves doorbell had lost its voice, and afternoon shadows cast a chill as I waited at the door.

'Abdul.'

Mrs. Price had become smaller. The years had stripped her flesh and bowed her spine, while I had risen and fattened, on the cusp of my own descent. She pulled me in for a hug and I felt her bones creak with the effort.

'I wasn't sure you would recognise me, Mrs. Price.'

'Please, dear. It's Mary. We aren't who we were thirty years ago.'

No, we aren't.

'You look well,' I lied.

She laughed. 'Still as polite, but even more handsome. The years have been kind. Come on in.'

She made tea while I sunk into the floral lounge. The side table next to me displayed a picture of Luke in a silver frame. He was older than when I had known him. His eyes had sunken, and his puppy fat had fallen off, or been eaten away. His parents stood either side, their arms clutching at him, trying desperately hard to smile but not quite pulling it off.

'That was six months before he left us,' Mary said, returning with the tea and a plate of shortbread biscuits.

'I'm sorry,' I said.

Mary took her cup of tea and blew on it. 'A friend of mine once told me three kids was the perfect number, in case one of them is a screw-up and ends up in jail or turns out to be an arsehole. We could only have Luke, but I knew he wouldn't be a screw-up. I just didn't plan on him dying.'

I began to say *I'm sorry* again but held it back. I had missed my chance to apologise.

She turned her eyes to me and smiled. 'Luke talked about you constantly. Said you were the greatest soccer player he ever saw – you scored thirteen goals in one lunch period. He went on about that for months. Do you still play?'

He never told her.

'No,' I said, shaking my head. 'I became an engineer.'

'An engineer? That's nice. Luke wanted to be a scientist.'

'How is Mr. Price?' I asked.

She turned back to the photo. 'Bill and I split up a few years after. We couldn't go back to being the two of us again.'

I nodded like I understood.

'What about you, Abdul?' she asked. 'Are you married? Children?'

'No,' I answered too quickly. It was a sore point my own mother kept jabbing.

'Why not? You won't be young forever.'

My mother said the same thing after each of my failed relationships. She said after what we had been through, I should be grateful for what I have – a home free from war, a career and a blonde-haired woman who would have been happy to marry me. All these things were true and yet they were not enough. Some instinct inside me whispered that the grass beneath my feet was not as green as it could be, and to settle for pine green grass when the world is such a vibrant palate of emerald, lime and parakeet would leave me empty.

Mary tapped the side of her head with a bony finger. 'Ah ... before I forget.'

She placed her cup back on the table and positioned her hands carefully on the armrests of the chair. She rose slowly and, still bowed, hobbled across to a chest of wooden drawers next to the sole window in the room. Another photo frame sat on top – Luke and I standing on their back verandah, Luke holding a Tupperware container full of tadpoles and murky water up like a trophy while I posed like a warrior with the net.

Mary tugged on the brass handle of the drawer second from the bottom, but it refused to budge. The back of her withered arm trembled with the effort, and I rose to help.

I forced the drawer open with a squeak, and pulled my hand away. Dust coated my fingertips.

'The bastard never opens,' she said, smiling wryly. 'Must be moisture in the air.' Mary extracted a faded yellow envelope from the drawer and placed it in my hand. *Abdul* was written in loose cursive on the front.

'You're the last one,' she said. 'Go on; open it.'

My fingers trembled as I eased open the envelope. I pulled out a single sheet of lined paper and read by the pale light of the window.

Dear Abdul (see, I got your name right – finally!),

I hope this letter finds you well. I know it will find you when you are ready.

Maybe you are an old man now, you have a family and a job and can drive a car – get a Beetle! Maybe you are still at school, still dancing across the grass with a ball magnetised to your foot, a cloud of dust and boys who think they can play soccer trailing behind you. I am glad I got to see you play. I wish I could have played like you, but I wish a lot of things.

I want to thank you for being my friend, my best friend. I don't blame you for following Brendan onto the soccer field, if I had a leg like yours, I would have done the same! I'm sorry I treated you badly afterwards, I've never been good at letting go. Now I don't have a choice. I don't want you to feel guilty, or sad for me. I'm dying, but I'm not sad.

Maybe it's the chemo sending me loopy, but I've been having real strange dreams. I'm standing in the rainforest (Daintree, Amazon, Monteverde? I can't tell) and there are millions of beetles flying by. You are standing there too, and so is Mum, Mrs. Hardy, even Brendan. Then everyone starts to break apart, and I'm crying – I reach out to grab hold of my mum to stop her crumbling. My hands come away with beetles, the brightest colours I've ever seen. And then I look down and I'm made of beetles too. All of us – now beetles – start flying through the forest. But I'm not one of the beetles, I'm all of them and none of them at the same time. It feels strange, but peaceful. Soon it starts raining in the forest, huge fat raindrops bigger than butter-king Billy, and they knock us out of the sky. We become the rain drops, and fall to the ground, soak through the fungi and the rot and detritus into the earth. I know I am gone, dead, whatever you like to call it. But I am still there, same as everyone, just different.

The dream feels real. More real than anything else right now. This makes me very happy. Now I know I will see you again amongst the forest. Maybe the beetles play soccer, and this time I can play too!

I hope you have a happy life, Abdul. You were a kind boy, so I think you must be a kind man. Thank you for our friendship and thank you for thinking of me again. All things come to an end, but now I think the ending might be a return to the beginning.

See you soon, Buster.

Luke.

A single tear dripped off my cheek and onto the paper, the weight of its impact rattling the page in my hand. I felt arms around my chest and her chin pressed against my back. She squeezed with an intensity that took my breath away, and I stood helpless in her grasp.

'My poor, poor boy,' she whispered, over and over.

I said nothing, but waited until the strength left the wiry muscles of her forearms, listened to the creak of her bones as she extracted herself, and bowed my head as she rubbed my hair, if only to look away from Luke's smiling face in the photo.

I folded the letter, placing it back into the envelope.

'May I keep this?' I asked Mary.

'Of course.'

Mary walked me out front after the tea, and I remarked upon her retaining wall leaning precariously over the driveway. The wooden boards were rotten and gap-toothed, weeds breaching the joins.

'A few weeks of rain and it might collapse.'

She nodded without looking. 'You're probably right.'

I wanted to leave. I wanted never to return to this empty house where I had spilled tears unworthy of the woman who roamed its vacant rooms, where I had dipped into a sadness she couldn't leave behind. It is natural to flee pain. It is why we jump on leaky boats, why we numb ourselves with pills and alcohol and reality television. But when an opportunity presents itself to share this pain, to spread its burden and lighten the load of others so their legs may carry them a little further, how can we turn our backs and still live with ourselves?

'I could help, you know, with the wall,' I said.

'I think it might be too far gone, dear,' she said.

I felt a flick against my shin and glanced down. The bush around here was known for redbacks. Relief washed through me as I knelt down and saw a Christmas beetle on its back, legs scrambling in the air. I used my finger to gently flick it over, and it took off with a hum of its wings.

I looked back up at the retaining wall. I could see which areas would need to be dug out, visualised the angles for the support posts I would place, calculated how many of the horizontal slats would need renewing.

'No,' I said. 'I don't think it is.'

Ode to Uśas: This Time Let's get the Dawn Right

A Narrative for Cinematic Virtual Reality

Soudhamini

Part One
Maya

It was as if she had eyes at the back of her head, he wrote.

Maybe it came from being around children so much
in the kindergarten that she worked in.

Or maybe there had been some betrayal in the
past that had taught her to cover her back.

But one day Rafael swivelled around in his
study and found Maya by the fireplace, so

contained he thought she might have
always been there.

Getting up from his desk, wedged between the
window and two groaning bookshelves, Rafael
went for a walk.

Reaching a deserted pier, he stood for a long moment
staring out to sea, savouring the wind on his face,
the discreet murmur of waves, the shriek of a
receding gull ...

And turned around, to see Maya recording,
holding the microphone like an extended
antenna in front of herself

Stepping on silent cat feet so she
wouldn't disturb the fish

Or the weekend fishermen standing
with inscrutable patience beside their
fine fishing lines.

He knew he had not written this and
wondered where the impulse came from.

She continued to record all kinds of things.

The grass at dawn under the towering redwood trees,
sunlight in the church's stained-glass window

the breath of canvas in the museum
through oil, acrylic, watercolour ...
encased in wood, metal, glass ...

as if to distinguish how each material
and combination thereof
mediated its rhythm.

Dozing off at his desk one afternoon
Rafael woke up startled to find the
recorder pressed against his chest.

I'm recording growth, she said,
not ascertaining your feelings.

Still he regulated his breathing
hoping to win her trust.

Systole, pause.
Diastole, pause.

That's the heart not the breath, she chided.
Don't confuse the two.

Then, which do you think is closer to thought,
she asked, leaning back on her haunches.

He realised he did not know either.

In the kindergarten the next day,
Maya placed a small camera in the
centre of the room along with the recorder.

Image and sound, she explained to the curious
children. Do you mind?

Their faces stared back at her, eyes
wide and curious on the spherical screen.

We will need to get permission from the parents,
warned the Principal. And if anyone objects, we
wouldn't be able to continue.

Maya nodded in acceptance
and shifted to the plant nursery.

On her computer that night

the audio waveform was a phosphorescent green
shimmering against her cheek like a muted flame.

The plant images looked quite bland next to it,
until she zoomed in to reach just colour and light.

Chlorophyll, she breathed in awe.

Seated in one of the octopus arms of the
panopticon in the State Library's Reading
Room, reference texts strewn
around his table

Māya, Rafael read   1
is both real and virtual.

As manifest world, it is real.

But to be truly real it must remain
unmanifest, and is hence virtual.

Immanent.

Part Two
Kshetra
Field

The body
is the field of the mind.

Ensconced in warm sheets Maya is sleeping
and dreaming of the forest.
The sound of agitated birds rents the air.

Rafael had left early in the morning
to the Asian market in search of
fresh produce.

A quiet, blue and grey figure
in the midst of its riotous colours.
Purple, yellow, green, orange, red
and a dazzling white.

Talking in tongues, Rafael thinks.
Singing in seconds as they
circle each other endlessly in their
curvilinear spectrum.

In her dream too Maya is sleeping
but this time on the forest floor,
her cheek pressed into the moist earth.

And in that dream
all she can hear is water.

Lush backwaters
lapping gently against the horizon of her mind
as sleep, dream, and a reluctant wakefulness
mingle in a soft radiance so lambent and
soothing she is loath to stir.

On the return journey,
Rafael sits with one hand resting
protectively on the bag on his lap
bursting with produce, the tram
undulating around him like a
rattlesnake.

From somewhere behind him, two
young boys are speaking excitedly
in Chinese.

Across the aisle a woman is
watching a show on her mobile
without headphones

but as everyone else is wearing them
no one seems to mind.

Reaching home
Rafael begins to slice it all into fine shards
while a glass of red glistens
approvingly nearby.

Bell peppers, onion, tofu, shrimp
and the finest, freshest coriander (not parsley)
subtle and heady in its contained fragrance.

A woman's voice levitates in the air
from the direction of the study

Long drawn out *drupad* notes   2
gouged out from inexhaustible depths
of body, mind, tradition and unfailing
riyaz   3

Rafael raises his head to listen
and hears Maya moan

Soft but unmistakeable
in the pause between notes

Maya is dreaming

of a hunter drawing his bow
notch by careful notch
as if it were a musical instrument
so the arrow would sing
clear and true as it flew.

She is dreaming

of the fleeting arrow
now proceeding on its own momentum,
the bowstring left shuddering bereft
in the hunter's limp hands.

She is dreaming

the taste of venom
in the tip of the arrowhead
speeding unreflectively to its target,
on her tongue.

And she hears as her own

the agitated heartbeat of the nesting bird
as the arrow hits its eye

The dull plop of the
stillborn egg,

The Brahmaanda   *4*
Cosmic egg

Dhukkam ... Dhukkam
Sorrow ... Sorrow

Rafael hears the words clearly
though Maya does not speak them
in her bird voice,
only moans.

Treading softly, he enters the study
and dons the virtual head gear

to see Maya lying with her eyes wide open
staring straight into the lens/him/the audience.

What is this world that you inhabit and
want me to be a part of?

Why do this to yourselves?

The words echo eerily amidst the still
rustling wings that he too now hears.

Is it not yourselves you hurt?

Rafael nods,
her image bobbing
within the headgear.

Perhaps you did not realise it in the past
or the hitherto anticipated henceforth.

Maya's gaze is still pinned
relentlessly at him/them.

But certainly in this caesura
now here/nowhere

you cannot but know.
Surely ... surely.

Rafael removes the headset and sits staring down ... at the table
first ...
then out the window ... then scanning the room, his refuge and
sanctuary,
that he is not sure he even recognises anymore ...

Rising fluidly from the forest floor
in her dream within the dream,

Maya leaves behind an indent
fertile as a vegetable patch.

Sleep-stalking the still wailing birds
she comes to a gurgling stream

and following its winding trail
she arrives at a hut.

In the dappled light and shade of
thatch within, she finds the young
old woman *AdI Shakti*,

agile warrior guardian of the
forest.

Turning,
in another corner Maya sees
a young man smearing moist paste
around the eye of the bird
held gently and secure in his
leaflike palms,

a scarlet-hued paste
shot through with green, brown,
red and a golden yellow.

Its other eye closed in affinity
the bird lies motionless

only its chest feathers heaving
lightly with each breath.

A moan beginning once again in her throat
Maya begins to walk forward

Even as a voice rings out behind her

Come now. I have been waiting for you.
What took you so long?

And so they begin,

young-old and old-young
women, belts wrapped tight
around their waists

Raise, cut, bend, look,
turn, hit, chop, raise,
turn, chop, raise, bend, raise,
turn, hit, chop, raise,
change ...

Until all four directions
beginning with the southwest
are duly propitiated.   5

We hurt perhaps to hold,
Rafael offers tentatively,
and to conquer direction.
Dhik Vijay   6

Improvising as he holds on
by the screeching tips of his
fingernails, to the dizzying
turns of Maya's centrifugal
tale.

Circle within a circle
story within a story
dream within a dream

and him at the very edge
precipitous
flailing ...

Not conquest, says Maya
voice alone within the headset,

Salutation

To the earth and its diagonals.
Vandana chuvadu.   7

Rafael nods in acquiescence
even as another voice booms out

Those that hurt must also heal.
That is KalarI dharma.   8

Heal whom, Rafael wonders,
themselves or the Other?

The question dangles tantalisingly
across the ever-deepening depths

and now it is Shakti's turn to look up
through and across intersecting worlds
to speak directly to him/them.

It is always yourself you hurt, Aadhaam　　　　　　　9
imagining an Other where there is only
another.

Distended a false pause,
an illegitimate capitalisation
between free-flowing syllables.

A pause you must now bridge
with reflection

for Prakriti to resume.

Bending over a bowl of frankincense,
her long hair shielding it from dispersing

Maya draws deep of its heat

Fanning its fragrant essence towards
the bird clasped to her chest.

The seed in the mind
is inception not conception.

Shakti stands in wide angle
close-up, the forest fanning out
flaring out behind her like
dreadlocks

her patience stretched thin
across the aeons, with no
borders or limits.

Burnt seed
offered on bird shaped altars
in anticipated reparation
of ancestral thought crimes.

Patriarchal stratagems
for a never-ending future

That has nevertheless
drawn to an end
now.

10

Rotten seed
Spat out from the earth's navel
In umbilical repudiation.

Rafael closes his eyes.
And his world turns dark
in every direction.

Only Shakti's voice
remains, deep
and urgent.

But the seed on the tongue
is Initiation.

Dharma Kshetre Puru Kshetre   11

In this field of earth-mind-body,

A righteous war has been fought
between past and future

For this immeasurable
instant to be born.

Kshana Kshane

A moment within a moment
In a time within Time

When new seeds must be planted
and preserved.

Once again Maya is dreaming
water, one stor(e)y and one
world up

Underground wellsprings
surfacing to nourish
the newborn seed.

Bijaakshara
Indestructible word-seed

Whispered in a pregnant darkness
and beginning already its lone journey
down the uterine tract of the universe,

Racing steadily to overtake another recent
more internecine passage.

12

This time Rafael decides to work at the National Library
to access a wider set of translations
both authoritative and intuitive.

The *Sudarshana Chakra*
he comes to understand

conjugated from
Su – auspicious
Darshana – mode of seeing
and *Chakra* –
the serrated wheel of time,

Moves orthogonally
always at right angles to
the Self.

The shortest distance between any two points
on the shifting trajectory of the everchanging self

Must always refer back
to this centre.

It is always therefore a radius
that is also a hypotenuse.

Heedless of the other researchers,
the exacting tick of the grandfather clock,
and the dull rattle of the long-stemmed fan
directly above his seat, Rafael
flings back his head.

And to keep the cutting edge of Time
in continuous, auspicious vision

One must
see with one's feet.

Dulce Madre de Dios!   13

This Rafael well understood

Having chewed the city underfoot,
masticating it day after day
until it became a part of him,

unclear where he ended and
the city began.

But always, always
siempre siempre
his eyes turned elsewhere,

Hearkening to
Country,

That distant unknown
that yawned like a sea
beneath his feet

Gurgling
its ritual incantation
of custodianship

in an unfamiliar tongue
that his feet nevertheless
acknowledged with every step.

Is Māya measure or measureless,
Rafael wonders suddenly,

The thought stopping him in his
tracks, as he strides through the
deserted city, accompanied only
by the plaintive ring of his
own footfall.

Delusion or emergent reality?

The question stares him back in
the face from the shining wet
cobblestones

as he swivels on his heels,
a full 360-degree turn

before tapping back on
stone to take the next
ten-ta-tive
step for-word.

Somewhere in the distant
beyond, music begins,

Percussion that flows like
melody, compact yet
fluid,

and to the sound of tinkling
cymbals, Tamil syllables set to a
Spanish beat, *nattuvangam*   14
for flamenco.

Rafael/Aadhaam/*Vaastu Purusha*   15
begins to dance

body undulating,
ululating,

with the urgency of a
waterfall.

Plunging
rising
swirling like a
dervish,

fluent as air

and hypnotic as a
flame.

Gathering every known
element and those yet
to be discovered
unto himself

to cleanse cure scour
and scourge
the planet.

The planet in himself
and he
mercurial yin yang spirit
in the planet.

Part Three
Ananda
Joy

And so it came to be

That as the first glimmerings of
Dawn, subtler far yet
More dazzling than any
before it, breaks through
the horizon

Under an ancient tree
In a timeless forest

Prakriti
begins to dance
once more.

Toes moving
like the long arm of a compass
de-scribing its infinite circle,

The long arm of a clock
marking its incessant rosary
of seconds to de-still the hours.

Re-membering
warrior ancestry
animal ancestry
spirit ancestry
divine ancestry.

The courage to fight
courage to protect
courage to create
and recreate.

Stance, reflection.
Posture, reflection.
Movement, reflection.
Form, reflection.

Self
Reflection.

And the world
inclines
to move again.

The first tendrils beginning to surface
pushing their way through the moist earth
still fertile from the lingering trace

of Maya's presence
and Shakti's gaze.

Chords, arcs
quadrants, semi circles
darting radii
and dazzle-edged diagonals

Opening, converging
expanding, conserving.

A whole new order
of abstraction
suggestion
evocation

Bud petal
Bud leaf
Bud fruit vegetable

Buds complete
and self-sufficient
unto themselves

Terminal.
Axillary.
Adventitious.

Trees rising high
Reaching out with strong arms
rippling with knotted musculature
towards sun and sky,

Grasping with eager hands
at light and air
the sap rising swift as mercury
in their veins
as they gnaw for space
to grow and expand.

Fruits ripen
wreathed in colourful grins, their
cheeks filling out with fragrant juice

promising to burst at the seams
and spill their nectar
into the earth's parched throat

So Nature could once again
be replete.

Part Four
Uśas
The Dawn

Time am I

Not person
or number

Singular, dual, plural
First, second, third.

Self-fulfilling
promise

The day must
dawn.

An *Agon*

tearing open
tear-ing open

the unending night.

Un enfolding

A space to know
of *knowing.*

An *Immanence*

already Before.

Pit Stop: A Memoir

Nina J. Winter

I met Carla in a bar. A singer, raised in Spain, of French and African-American parents, she was living in Japan, performing her songs in fluent French, Spanish, Japanese and English at an intimate Tokyo bar. She was slim and striking with large brown eyes and short dark curls. When I heard her sing, tears filled my eyes. I wanted to *be* her. She was the most intoxicating person I had ever met. She was also, astonishingly, one of the unhappiest.

'I don't know who I am,' she told me. 'I'm not really American or French. I'm not Spanish. I'm not African. I don't belong anywhere.'

Carla didn't have a home. She was adrift, inventing her own history as she coasted like jetsam, catching hold in one place, then letting go and ending up in another ultimately unfulfilling one.

I know where I'm from. South Hedland. It's not an exotic place. Just a spatter of houses between the desert and the sea in the Pilbara region of WA. In 1975, my New Zealand-born parents and I crossed the Nullarbor Desert in a large white ute pulling a small white caravan over the red-dirt highway from Melbourne, Victoria, where I was born.

My memories of the place we landed in are yellowed by heat, like my photos of that time. The town was not much older than I was, built by an iron ore boom after a massive iron ore deposit was found at Mt Whaleback in 1957. Captain Peter Hedland sailed into the harbour in 1868 from Perth on his boat the *Mystery*, which he built on the banks of the Swan River.

Hedland marked the harbour for a port and his modest vision is, nowadays, the highest tonnage port in Australia and one of the busiest in the world. What might at first glance seem to be remarkable vision is somewhat tempered by the fact that he failed to mention the colossal sandbar that sealed the entrance, making it accessible only at high tide, in good weather. In the eighties they dredged the channel and it now allows ships that weigh up to a quarter of a million tonnes each.

In my childhood the port was still forming. We pulled up at the very outer edge of the even newer hodgepodge of asbestos housing called South Hedland, eighteen kilometres inland from Port Hedland, built on higher land to avoid storm surges that inundated the port area. It was as if my parents (or the car) gave up at the first hint of a town after all that spinifex and dirt.

We lived in our caravan at the Wesnova Caravan Park for three years, one foot in the scrub, one in the town. Mention South (or Port) Hedland to anyone who's passed through it (for few choose to stay) and people are predictably unoriginal in their descriptions (*shithole* being the most common).

It hardly ever rained and our rain, when it did come, came all at once, in furious purple cyclones that forced water into our house, through every tiny hole imaginable, stripping the leaves off the poinciana tree and the paint from cars. Us kids would run out of the classroom and dance in a whooping celebration of something so magical and rare. The hard red earth, baked into resilient rock, was slow to yield to the shock of so much cool water, which slid over the cracked-clay surface into the deep ditches that were cut to channel the runoff. We would splash around in them, running barefoot through the altered landscape, cartwheeling and screaming. When our muddy swimming holes receded to red-clay puddles, I caught the tadpoles that magically appeared and housed them in Peters ice-cream tubs to watch them transform. One leg, two legs, three legs, gone!

The insects, too, came all at once, in packs, swarms, plagues. Giant angry biting ants swarmed our driveway. Stinging caterpillars marched top-to-toe like tiny links of furry sausages, tiny poison-spitting sausages as it turned out. My father bought a Mr Whippy ice-cream van, then later traded in *Greensleeves* for the hissing of the deep fryers and grill of the Ampol Restaurant, one-half of the Ampol Roadhouse, which stayed open late into the night every night. The bright lights of the service station, a welcome beacon to trucks and travellers arriving out of the darkness, also attracted all the insects for miles. Gun-metal-grey Christmas beetles crept their way toward the light on thin rickety legs, like old-timers on walking frames. Plagues of locusts moved much quicker, devouring what spindly grass we did have, and each other. Swarms of flying ants arrived and dropped their wings suddenly in shimmering brown piles and became earth-bound. Cicadas left their entire exoskeletons gripping to the trunk of our mulberry tree and filled our nights (and heads) with their pulsating chorus.

Geckos called out kak-kak-kak in the night as they colonised our houses, keeping watch over us from the walls. Little brown frogs persisted in our bathroom. They peeped at me from inside the spout, from under the toilet rim and from the corners of the shower.

Quiet and shy, plain-Jane beige with little round black eyes like plastic pinheads, they came and went as they pleased. One night I stepped outside and saw the front of our shop rippling in the moonlight. Hundreds of frogs were huddled together on the crushed-quartz surface – making the building come alive, alien-like – as they bobbed up and down in croaking song. I gently stroked one of the little frogs, not plain anymore but transformed into something special, something I never saw again.

I would have thought it a dream, or a child's reinvention of a much more mundane event, like the time I was eight and the shower water ran orange. At first I thought there was something in the pipes causing it, but then I put out my tongue and tasted the water. It was true … Fanta. It *was* Fanta. I ran and told my mother, who agreed with me it was a miracle until years later when she told me it was rust you idiot.

But I had *tasted* it …

Anyway, the frogs my mother agrees were real.

Everything in the town was tainted the purple-red of a deep bruise – from the iron oxide in the soil that backbones the state's economy and stains the houses and more: legs, lungs, hearts, souls.

And the heat, always the heat. But at least I also had the sea. My father loved to fish far out to sea and my mother paced the boat, keeping us kids onboard and making sandwiches. We pulled up one fish after the other, sometimes two or three fish on the same line: coral trout, bluebone, red emperor, giant trevally, Spanish flag, cod, snapper, mackerel, the occasional twisting sea snake or sandpaper-skinned shark, all eager to take our smelly bait, like the huge tiger shark Dad once chased Mum around the boat with (no one lost an eye).

We slept overnight on the boat or on sandy atolls off the coast. My favourite island had a little wooden sign painted 'Echo Beach'.

Here we cooked our fish in tinfoil and roasted spuds in the coals and toasted marshmallows.

I explored these islands like I was the first person to set foot on them, and it always felt like I was. The water was always warm and the sand crushed-shell white and filled with treasure. I collected baler and cowrie shells, sand dollars, Chinese fingernails and, with care, cone shells. I carved pictures into cuttlefish bones, shook dried white anemones like mini cheerleader pom-poms and, once, startled a blue-ringed octopus resting in a discarded snorkel into flashing his indigo rings at me. I splashed through the shallows, causing stingrays to shoot in every direction and scrabbled after crabs on the rocks. I swam until I was burned a deep freckled pink and my skin peeled like a thin layer from a paperbark tree.

I once camped with a friend and her father and brothers near Cowrie Creek Gorge where we spent hours with our hands in the mud-clay, shaping mini tea sets to bake in the fire. We slept side-by-side, all five of us, like a packet of snags, plus the dog, sheltered by a giant tarpaulin that allowed us to stare out at the close stars. Later in the night we were woken by her father and driven to the shore where, in the dim moonlight, we could see the soft sand undulating above the high-tide mark. Hatchlings of the sea, baby turtles just a few seconds old, were impatiently flicking their way out of their sand nests. They sprinted as fast as their tiny flippers allowed to the lapping water, like mini-Olympians off the blocks. The light from our torches confused some of them and they turned and dashed for us instead, mistaking our lights for the moon, Mr B said. I gathered up these disoriented flapping babies, marvelling at the striking blue and silver markings that glowed in my torchlight, and ran them into the shallows, waving them goodbye as they splashed into the unknown. So small, so new to the world, yet so driven in purpose. It was more magical than Christmas. In the morning it was as if it were another dream.

For family holidays we drove the interminably long road to Broome to stay with our cousins in an old wooden bungalow with wide, shuttered verandahs on which we chased each other around and later took long sweaty naps when the day became too hot. Their pindan yard had even less grass than ours and was dominated by a bloated boab tree with felted nuts that we scratched pictures into, then cracked open and ate the sour white flesh until our stomachs churned. Down at the jetty where we would scoff our fish and chips my uncle would spear fish between the pylons. He shared the water with large sharks that were also searching for something to scoff, lured by the flow of blood from the meatworks on the bay, where he worked.

Cable Beach had the biggest waves of my world and was once littered with massive sinister-looking jellyfish. I was terrified of diving through a wave and having one splat on my face, like a cruel cream pie. My cousin and I covered one with a sandcastle. From the water we saw a woman kick through our creation. Surprised by its jelly base, she wobbled on one foot before falling on her back in the sand, legs splayed in the air.

At thirteen, my family turned up at my boarding school in Perth at the end of the year towing another caravan. 'Surprise,' they said. 'We've sold up in Hedland: the shop, the house. The dog's gone, we've given away the cat. You're not going back.'

And a couple of months later we set off on a holiday to New Zealand.

My family never returned to Australia. Instead, we ended up in the east-coast town of Whitianga, a tiny tranquil town usually described as quaint or beautiful (and hardly ever as a *shithole*).

Instead of the giant red and black eyes of Sturt's desert pea and the soft lavender spikes of the mulla mulla, I now had roses, camellias and daphne. Hydrangeas and jasmine. Lush lawns that needed constant mowing. Instead of the shrieks of galahs and sulphur-crested cockatoos there were the songs of tuis and bellbirds. It was cold ...

At twenty-one I left New Zealand for Japan, where I met Carla. I then wandered through Asia and Europe for a few years, floating like flotsam, looking for a place to land. Until one day I asked myself, where? My answer came in a dream: Broome. So at twenty-six, my suitcase and I hit the now-sealed highway on a Greyhound bus from Perth, headed to Broome.

I was told the bus would stop in Port Hedland. But it didn't, it pulled up in South Hedland, at the Ampol Roadhouse. The Wesnova Caravan Park was still standing next door. The familiar smell of the petrol bowsers hit me when I stepped off the bus. I picked some rocks off the ground of the same ore that had lured the thousands of immigrants and misfits to this region, moving towards the promise of money or away from their past. The world can't get enough of the steel that is made from this dusty ore and once again my hands were stained the familiar purple-red.

In the distance, I could see the top of the 'Silver Spider', still the tallest landmark in town. Terrifying in its height and strangeness, to me it had resembled a Martian tripod from Orson Welles' *War of the Worlds* and I had always cycled as quickly as I could past it, scared to peer up at its giddy height.

Now exposed as an unremarkable and not even particularly tall water tower painted a dull grey, I turned my back on it and approached the redback-spider-lined tin fence of the roadhouse – my old back yard. The poinciana tree still stood sprinkling the yard with its Lilliputian leaves and flowers of fire. The brass tap in the middle of the patch of determined grass, under which we used to sit in an old Red Band cooking oil tin, was also still there.

Across the other side of the yard ran the chain-link fence, once tightly strung, now bowed in resignation to its fate, through which I could see the netball court where I had played my first game of netball. At age six, I'd run after the other girls two years older than me, confused and shaking my head in tears if anyone tried to throw the orange leather ball at me. Next to the courts I could see the football oval where I played T-ball and, later, softball, on Sunday mornings. This was the site of the yearly carnival, which excited the pants off us kids with its one ride – The Tumbler. For a dollar you could bash at an old car with a sledgehammer or belt each other with pillows on a slippery pole. My favourite was the coconut shy, where a dollar bought you three shots at knocking over and winning a coconut. Clowns with round open mouths. Dodgems. Fairy Floss. Ticket stubs littering the ground like giant's confetti next to the chocolate wheel where I never won anything but my nanna – the queen of raffles – won me a gimcrack tea set which I treasured as fine china.

My hands shook and I bit my bottom lip but could not stop the tears from falling. I felt elated to return to a place so special to me as well as a strange nostalgic sadness for this insignificant, dilapidated building on the verge of being knocked down and replaced by a modern Caltex. I felt a deep love for this place – the land in its vast flatness seemed to stretch my soul to the horizon, like skin over a giant drum.

The other passengers stared as I stood crying in the carpark, clutching my camera. I entered the shop. Everything was changed yet the same. I ordered some chips. My dad used to work the fryers and the bain-maries were always full of the truck-stop staples: chips, battered fish, chico rolls, crumbed chicken, crab sticks, dim sims, none of which I cared for except for the chips. Hot, golden salty chips I helped myself to whenever I wished. The shop was now packed with shelves of groceries that customers could reach themselves, instead of the high wooden shelves behind the counter. I'd have to haul myself up to stand on the counter to reach the items when I was serving customers. At six I had started helping Mum, carefully filling the office desk with level piles of coins for the banking. To bank our heavy swags of coins we had to drive to Port Hedland, past another local landmark, the sparkling salt pyramids of the Leslie Salt Company.

The mixed-lolly counter was now gone, replaced with a bait freezer. In my childhood the counter was lined with boxes of half-cent, one- and two-cent lollies, which kids spent forever choosing what to spend their five, ten or twenty cents on. I was usually allowed to help myself and if Mum said no, I snuck behind the counter and sneaked handfuls anyway. Spearmint leaves, milk bottles, witchetty grubs, freckles, raspberries, milkshakes, strawberries and cream, black cats, bananas, chicos, fake teeth, snakes alive, and candy shapes with inspirational words: love, peace, hope. In the jars above the refrigerated chocolate counter were stacked red spinning-tops and whistle pops, packets of 'fags', kool fruits, redskins and wiz fizz sherbet, lolly gobble bliss bombs, tattoo bubble gum, and lolly necklaces. Ice-cream for rolled cones came in tall twelve-litre tins which my brothers and I finished with spoons, my youngest brother in nappies in danger of falling in, headfirst.

I bought a punnet of chips and ate a few. They were lukewarm and soggy, nothing like my dad's chips. I ditched them and half-heartedly bought a packet of red frogs.

My parents had passed through the Pilbara on a mission to make some money and return to where they belonged. This place, a pitstop.

I returned to the bus.

'I'm from here,' I told the girl sitting next to me as we pulled out onto the highway, my fingers smudging the window. 'I'm from here.'

The Stuff of Salvation

Joanna Morrison

You can see the ocean from up here on the stage. The sun, sinking into the water, makes everything look soft, and when the pub is quiet, you can hear the water. Breathe with it. It's not quiet tonight though; there are six or seven clusters of diners and drinkers all gathered around the heavy oak tables, waiting for us to start. I watch the candlelight on their faces, flickering, erratic. It catches their hands too, resting around their drinks, tracing grooves in the oak.

Aaron is beside me in his corduroy shirt, his hair tied back but still escaping to fall across his face. He plays the opening chords of our first song. I can feel the vibrations beneath my feet, and I close my eyes, preparing myself for the feeling that comes when I sing. It's like dreaming, or sailing with the wind behind you. The way birds must feel when they fly. If I couldn't do it – if I wasn't allowed to reach inside people with my voice and touch them where it hurts – I'd just be a drifter: unmoored, unnavigable.

I know when it's working, too, because they can't take their eyes off me. Neither can Aaron. When he harmonises with me, it feels as though he's singing through me. Or at least, that's how it used to feel, back when we were an item. When I was part of the furniture at his place – as much a fixture as his bed, close to the floor; and his hats, on the hatstand that looks like a twisted hand.

He always had something new to listen to on his playlist, always turned it on as we walked in. We were listening to The Gorillaz when it happened – that brittle moment that formed around us like salt crystals on a string. My fault, really. I said something I couldn't take back: *What if I lived here, with you?*

Aaron looked away then, picked at something that wasn't there on the knee of his trousers.

I couldn't speak at all. Felt like I was dissolving, burning up in a blinding light.

'Moving in together is the death of any passion,' he said, finally looking at me. He'd been there before; he didn't want that for us.

He doesn't love me, that's the thing he wouldn't say, but which I've since come to understand. He thinks I'm sweet, but he has no safe, permanent place in his heart for me. Not the way I do for him, will always have for him. *Always*, I think now, into the ache that is the distance between us on stage. I still want his hands on the nape of my neck. I want him wanting me, breathing on me. I want the smell of his hair, right here with me. But he's filled up on me, had enough; wants something else for dessert.

I play a random chord – F# minor – and smile at him, an unimpeachable grin. If he wants to pretend he never looked into my eyes and talked about how we and everyone else on the planet were made of stardust, and how the cosmos and all of time and space had colluded to bring us into being – into that moment between his sheets, that moment in which he ran his fingers along my clavicle in a prelude for doing the same with his tongue – if he wants to act as if that never happened, I can too.

He smiles back at me, wariness in the tilt of his head. This is our new routine: I deny him the satisfaction of a scene; he looks at me like a parcel he's found on his porch, something he didn't order. The hurt of it shows though; I know it does, despite my efforts to hide it. It leaks out in the form of scathing remarks, disguised as banter on stage, or shaped like sabotage. Like now, when I cut off the striding Spanish-style guitar solo he's been working on as an intro to our next song – cut it off with a firm series of strums on my own guitar and a *thank you* into the microphone. He looks at me, and I know he knows I'm not cool about things.

I start up a different song instead, the loudest song on our list, wanting to scare off the feeling in my throat, the choking feeling that nothing will ever be fine again and everything will always be dark. It doesn't work though, because our voices slip around each other now; they don't hold one another and thrum together the way they once did, like the start of a miracle, or the end of misery.

Later, when Aaron's gone home and I've given up hoping he'll come back, and the waiters are wiping down tables and most of the customers have left, I allow myself another tequila, because maybe that will stop the gnawing behind my eyes and the constant return of the memories I don't want to repress but can't afford not to – of Aaron in the dark, of his being in the world. There is a man next to me. I don't know how long he's been there, but I'm suddenly aware of him, so it's possible he's just arrived. He smells of aftershave and garlic bread instead of sandalwood and guitar strings, and this distinction is both repugnant and the stuff of salvation.

I look up at him and see something in his face that diminishes my wretchedness just a little. He wears a look of admiration, of respect. There's desire too as his eyes move over my face. It's a relief, like breathing again after the heaving ocean has held you under.

'Can I buy you a drink?' he asks, because I blew him away up there and he just wants to be near me. He doesn't say the last bit, but I can tell.

I'm half-tanked already, which makes his attention that much more dangerous; he's beginning to look like an antidote.

'Vodka and lime,' I say. 'If you insist.'

'Too easy,' he says, and while we're waiting he says, 'You're very talented, you know?'

'Not really,' I say, though I know it to be true, because Aaron told me once, and I still haven't quite shaken the habit of believing everything he says. I take a large gulp of my drink; it tastes like poison. That's how you know it's good.

'You have this presence up there,' the man is saying. 'You know?'

'Well, thank you.'

'I'm Ray, by the way.'

'Well, thank you, *Ray*.'

His leather jacket creaks as he reaches across and brushes my hair off my neck with a hand that trembles, just slightly. I smile at him and it's all the invitation he needs. His hand comes to rest on my leg, and he buys me another drink. Listens closely as I overshare, about who-knows-what: trivial stuff. He sits closer with every drink, and before long, he's so close it's absurd. I laugh out loud, which is when he leans closer still, and kisses me. It's not unpleasant. Quite nice, really. Enough to begin pulling me up and out of grief, though there's a faint scent of zucchini around Ray's neck. Just a trace, beneath the cologne.

We go out to his car and it's sordid, but I'm drunk and why not? Though I begin to wonder why he hasn't taken me home, to a house with a bedroom in it, and a bed in that. And I notice a cream jumper in the back seat, beside a copy of *The First Stone*. I don't ask him whose things they are, though I should. Instead, I let him drive me home, sticking my hand out the window to slide it over and under the air we're pushing through.

The next time we're together, Ray drives us both to my place and I take him to my bed. When I start to cry, he brushes my tears away and tries to bring me close against him. He thinks he's moved me; doesn't realise I've been dragged under by a tide of emptiness, a lack of feeling for him so absolute it's frightening, because what if Aaron felt this same lack as he lay with me? Even just a fraction of it?

Lying heavy and still in his arms, I tell him about Aaron and what he made of my adoration.

'It's fine though,' I say. 'It's not like he promised me anything.'

'Being with someone like this *is* a kind of promise though, don't you think?'

'Not really,' I say, wondering what kind of promise he's reading or writing with his fingertips running up and down my arm.

A fortnight later, Aaron arrives at the pub with a bruise under his right eye; he looks as wounded as I feel.

'Ouch, there,' I say. 'What happened?' I'm smiling, but not cruelly. There's something sweet about his face, all swollen and sore.

'Some dickhead attacked me this morning,' he says, putting his amp on the stage, 'as I was taking my bins out. I turned around and he just went for me, punched me and ran off.'

'Did you get a good look at him?' I ask, imagining someone in a hoodie making off with his phone and wallet, though he probably didn't have those on him at the time; he usually takes the bins out in his boxer shorts ... which I can't afford to think too much about.

Later, the bar is quiet; our glasses are empty. Ray winces as he reaches cross-body into his jacket for his wallet. He tries the other hand instead and it's awkward for him, having to double-back with his right arm. His left hand on the bar is red and bruised.

'Was it you?' I ask. 'Did you hit Aaron?'

'Yes,' he says, a smile creeping over his sheepishness. I say nothing, so he goes on, 'Followed him from the gig last week to see where he lives. Went back a few days later.' His smile fades at the look on my face; he looks away.

'You left-handed?' I say, for something to say. Something other than, 'You shouldn't have,' which is what I'm thinking but don't want to voice, in case he thinks I see his gesture as a gift of some kind.

I take hold of his hand to study the bruising. He pulls it away, slips it into his pocket, but it's too late; I've seen it – the white band of skin I've somehow managed to miss until now, around his ring finger.

'I know what you're thinking,' he says, turning and turning his wallet on the bar, the leathery whack and swish of it becoming a rhythm I can't stand.

'No, you don't,' I say.

And neither do I, but he stops fidgeting, which is something.

The Way He Walks

Christina Eastman

There is something about the way he walks. The spring in his step, the jolt from the crack of his knees, his blunt pace. In between those short movements – within those small moments – is an exchange. An exchange of life for time, and love for pain. His stride is firm, confident, the only thing that remains constant. His walk is sure. As sure as the Earth moves around the sun, ceaseless. Its manoeuvre is timelessness and time itself, an orbit creating linearity.

Time is but a shadow.

Time is the dark.

There is something about the way he walks. He walks at night. His walk is loud. Patience in each step, a rhythm he carries into a warm melody that soon falls out of tempo and into dissonance, a sound that perishes, enveloped by the silent dark. He soaks and bathes in the music of his quietude – his power and his magic. What he throws into the dark never comes back.

I watch him walk every day. His steps like a metronome, persisting in the motion of mystery. In a wink, his walk is noiseless. Muted, bleak and bland. The skin, stretched and bound around his decaying marrow, slowly disintegrates and unravels like a secret. With each step, he wrinkles and flakes, alone, piece by piece, under the stars. Sometimes he is in a hurry and begins to run. His flesh shrivels as if consuming itself, until it becomes paper thin and translucent, until his figure is but an opaque window in the moonlight, his pain a mere whisper in the wind. He is truly alone. In the dark, his senescence is fluorescent, and his walk invisible.

In between those short movements – within those small moments – is an exchange. An exchange of life for time, and love for pain. Sometimes he looks back. I can see him glancing over his shoulder.

He looks for me.

He longs for me, but never sees me.

I have only ever been in front of him.

The Chop

Emma Darragh

I am five and my hair is long and brown like hers, but it is not very beautiful. The way she brushes my hair tells me this. She drags the sharp bristles across my scalp, down through the knotted lengths, to the knotted ends.

'Vivian, you've been sucking your hair again,' she says, her grip on my head tightening.

I squeeze my eyes shut. She pulls my hair so hard I can feel my forehead being dragged back across my skull. I could end up half-bald like Mr Dawson at school, like—

'I said, you've been sucking your hair again.'

'I'm sorry.'

'It's disgusting.'

She plaits it, tugging each skein of hair so tight it might rip right out.

'If you don't stop sucking your hair like a baby, I'm going to cut it off. I'll give it the chop. Understand?'

I picture the scissors, creeping up close to my head. I picture myself looking like a bald man. 'Yes, Mum.'

She twists the elastic band around and around that little coil of hair, the bit that's always wet, that always smells sweet, the hair that hangs down like a soft rope.

Our mother's hair is as long as Rapunzel's except it's brown. Her name is Mary Anne and she's not a princess in a tower but her hair floats behind her like a bride's veil. It makes her look like a beautiful horse, soft and shiny.

Sometimes she makes long plaits from it and wraps the plaits around her head, and she looks like a girl, not a mother. Sometimes she wears it in a high ponytail like *I Dream of Jeannie*. But mostly she wears it out like a brown-haired Barbie doll. It reaches so far down her back that she can almost sit on it.

Sometimes, just before lunch on a Monday, she drags us down the street to our neighbour Glennys' house. Glennys used to be a hairdresser before she had her kids. She has two boys the same age as Susan and me and she's a bit sad that she doesn't have any little girls' hair to do.

Glennys carries a chair into the kitchen and our mother sits in it. Glennys lets Susan and me have a turn at using her spray bottle and we both wet the hair for Glennys.

'You want to have a go?' Glennys says, opening and closing her skinny silver scissors.

'Yes, please!' I say.

'Don't even think about it,' our mother says, turning around and looking at us with squinting, grey-blue eyes.

Glennys just laughs and takes our mother's head in her hands. 'Straight ahead, Mary Anne,' she says.

Glennys combs the wet hair and starts making little snips. The hair falls down on the tiles. When Glennys is finished cutting, she combs our mother's hair, very gently, and sweeps the cuttings into a pile. Our mother takes the dustpan and tips them into an envelope she pulls from her handbag.

Now that I'm at big school, it's just Susan that goes with her on those Mondays.

When Susan was a baby, her sticky little fists would get caught in our mother's hair and our mother would cry out in pain and swat Susan's hand away or put her down on the carpet in the middle of drinking her bottle. 'Naughty!' she'd say. Susan would throw herself down on the floor and kick her pudgy little baby legs. Milk would spurt out on the carpet in fat white puddles.

Some days our mother cracks six eggs into a bowl and rubs them into her head and down the lengths of her hair. Other days she washes her hair and walks around smelling like beer.

On Saturdays she always pulls and twists my hair into a ballerina bun for ballet over in the church hall. She stabs my head with bobby pins and the hairspray gets in my eyes and nose and makes my hair crunchy. But on Sundays she sleeps in, and my hair gets to be free. The top is still crunchy with hairspray but the rest of it unfurls like a thick brown ribbon. On Sunday nights she washes my hair in the bathtub, using a plastic measuring cup to wet my hair with sudsy bathwater. She rinses it off with cold water from the tap, making me shake and shiver. The cold water is supposed to make it shiny.

'Stay still,' she says, brushing.

I *am* standing still. But she's pulling my hair so hard I keep losing my balance.

'Vivian! Look at this.' She flicks the end of my hair towards me. 'It's all ratty.' She drops my hair. 'Stay here,' she says.

She disappears down the hallway.

Is she getting the scissors? If she gives me the chop, she'll make me look like a boy and everyone will laugh at me. And it'll hurt.

I wipe my sweaty hands on my school dress and pray quietly to God.

She doesn't bring back the scissors though, just a new hair elastic.

'You're going to end up with a big hair ball in your stomach and you'll have to go to hospital to have it cut out of you.'

Like a bird's nest.

'Get your thumb out of your mouth.'

As she drags the brush through my hair, I imagine her carving out my scalp.

Susan is lucky. Because she's only three, Susan's hair is too short and wispy for a big hairbrush. Our mother combs Susan's hair with a pink baby comb and sometimes puts little headbands or clips in it, even though they always fall out.

She pulls my hair into a tight, tight ponytail and then plaits the ponytail. She ties a blue ribbon around each elastic. It hurts to turn my head.

I have the longest hair in my whole kindergarten class. I already know that today Ryan Redmond will come up to me at recess or lunch – or maybe even in the classroom when Mrs Lawrence isn't looking – and he'll yank on my pony-plait like it's a chain or a cord and he'll say: *Whoosh, flushing the toilet!* Or *Click, turning on the light!* Or *Toot tooooooooooooot!* Like he's a train driver.

When I walk through the school gate I can't help it, I hold on to my hair and then slip it into my mouth, just for a little while, while nobody is looking.

We wait for Dad to come home from work. Sometimes it takes a long time and our dinner isn't hot anymore.

Tonight, he walks through the back door and lets the cold wind inside. Susan runs up to him. He has leaves stuck to his shoes.

'What time do you call this?' our mother asks.

I look at the oven clock. 'Six-fifteen,' I say. We've been learning the time at school.

'I got held up,' Dad says.

'Where's the milk?' Mum asks, 'and the bread?'

'Bugger,' Dad says. 'I'll go after tea.'

But our mother takes her car keys off the hook near the phone and says, 'Don't bother, I'll do it myself.'

'I'll go after,' Dad says.

But our mother just takes the keys and marches down the hallway and slams the front door.

Six-thirty. She hasn't come back. Dad says, 'Well, girls. You must be starving.'

'Where's Mum?' Susan asks.

'She's at the shop,' Dad says. 'Go sit at the table.'

Dad spoons out a pile of apricot chicken onto the plates. And a pile of peas from a bowl in the microwave. He brings over a saucepan from the stove and opens the lid and looks in. 'Oh,' he says. Then he looks up at us and smiles. 'Whoops. No rice tonight. That's okay. We don't need rice,' he says. 'Especially when we have ice cream for dessert.'

'Yes!' Susan and I say.

'Maybe,' Dad says, pointing his finger at our plates.

Seven-fifteen. Our mother still isn't home. Dad starts washing the dishes.

'Where's Mum?' Susan asks.

'Well, she must be at the dairy, milking the cow herself,' Dad says. He dries his hands on a tea towel. 'Now it must be bath time.'

Eight-fifteen. We are in our winter pyjamas and she still isn't home. The ends of my hair are wet from the bath.

'What's Mum doing now?' I ask.

'What's Mum doing now?' Susan copies me.

'She must be at the bakery, baking the bread,' Dad says. 'And it's time you girls got to bed.'

'But it's not eight-thirty yet,' I say.

But Dad scoots us through the kitchen to our bedroom and tucks us into bed.

In the morning, Dad makes us toast. For a treat, he lets us have a cold Milo with a spoon in the mug and lots of dry Milo on top.

'Where's Mum?' Susan asks with Milo all over mouth.

'In bed, asleep,' Dad says. 'Finish that and get ready for school, Viv. You too, Suzy Q.'

I go to my room and put on my uniform and unplait my hair. It flows out of my head like a waterfall. When I come back out to the kitchen with my hairbrush, Dad is wrapping a sandwich in foil and squeezing it into my lunchbox.

'Does Suze take lunch to pre-school?' he asks me.

'Yep,' I tell him.

Dad butters more bread and opens the Vegemite again.

The best thing is that Dad doesn't even brush my hair at all. I wear it out to school and it flies behind me like a kite when I run around the playground at recess.

We eat dinner at five-thirty. Beef and potato casserole and a glass of milk. Our mother's plait is loose, like the hair could escape at any minute.

'We need to brush your hair after your bath, Vivian,' she says. She takes a bird-bite of her casserole. 'Or it'll be impossible in the morning.'

My hair is knotty and puffy and there are probably leaves and twigs sticking in it.

She washes my hair and the shampoo gets in my eyes.

'Soon you'll be old enough to do this yourself,' she says.

After my bath, once I'm in my pyjamas, she makes me sit on the floor in front of the lounge. She wraps the towel around my head and rubs it, hard. Then she takes her brush and starts down the bottom, at the ends.

Rip rip rip.

'Ow,' I say. I can't help it. I try to hold it in. The *ow* won't stay in my mouth, though, and it comes out again, softly.

'Shhh,' she says. She's watching *A Country Practice*. I try to keep my eyes open because I want to see Fatso, the wombat.

I put my hands on my head, to keep the hair from being ripped out. *Rip rip rip.*

'For God's sake, Vivian,' she says, halfway up my hair. 'I'll chop this goddamn hair off myself if it ever gets like this again.'

A tear squeezes out of my eye but I don't really cry or make another sound.

'Hopeless,' she says in an angry whisper.

I imagine scissors so close to my head, big sharp blades could cut your ears off.

At school we learn about the letter *S. Soft snakes sliding s ... s ... s ...* We're singing the last *s ... s ... s ...* and that's when Ryan Redmond grabs my pony-plait and waves it around in time with the music, hissing with his stupid little mouth. Mrs Lawrence sees him and puts him in the sin bin for five minutes.

But soon he's back at our table, poking his tongue through the gap in his top teeth.

Mrs Lawrence gives us all a spirally snake to colour in. She puts out old ice cream tubs full of pencils and crayons, little dishes of sequins and tissue paper. And glue. And scissors.

'Snakes aren't pink, silly,' Ryan says to me.

I keep colouring and ignore him.

'I *said*, snakes aren't pink, *silly*,' he says again.

I stop colouring and look up at him, at his stupid tongue and his stupid gappy teeth and I pick up my scissors and snip them at him. 'I'll give you the chop if you don't shut up,' I tell him.

He widens his eyes at me and, to show him I'm serious, I snip my scissors closer to his face.

He sits back in his chair and starts peeling the paper off a green crayon.

When I've finished colouring my snake, I cut around the spiral shape, concentrating on the curves. When I'm finished, the paper coils around itself. Mrs Lawrence comes over and ties a piece of wool to it so we can hang it from the ceiling.

In the afternoon Miss Holly from the office comes to our classroom with a note that tells our parents to check our hair for nits. I hide it at the bottom of my bag.

At bath time, Dad stands shaving in the vanity mirror. I can see him from my spot in the tub. His face is all white with cream and he's keeping an eye on Susan and me and shaving off his face hair at the same time.

Susan and I have just made bubble-beards when our mother comes barging in with a soggy piece of paper in her hands.

'What's this, Vivian?'

The nits note.

She turns and looks at Dad. 'Donna Wilson just rang and told me there's nits going 'round.'

Dad stops shaving, even though his face is still foamy. 'Okay?' he says, lifting up his eyebrows.

'Head lice. Yesterday – you didn't do her hair yesterday,' she says. Then she turns to look at me. 'Has anyone been away from your class? Anyone sick?'

I hold the wet face washer against my chest and shrug.

'What about that Sarah Chilcott?'

'I don't remember.'

She steps into the bathroom and leans over the top of me and takes hold of my head. I squeeze my eyes shut, and my teeth together, and she starts splitting my scalp with one of her pointy fingernails. I hunch up my shoulders and wait for her to stop.

She finally releases my head. 'I'll check you after your bath,' she says.

When I get up on Sunday, Dad makes me a bowl of Coco Pops and he gives Susan a piece of peanut butter toast with sultanas on top of it. That's her favourite.

'I'll be out in the shed, Viv. Just yell if you need me, sweetheart.' He pats me on my crunchy head and then goes outside, leaving the back door open. I can hear him using the saw and I like the sound of the wood being cut, it's like a song.

Tonight is hair-washing night. And nit-checking night – again. My head feels itchy just thinking about it. About that small comb and that foam that smells like a hospital, and my neck feels tired thinking of how long I'll have to *sit still*. Because even though I don't have nits she's going to do it again, the comb and the foam, just to make sure.

Dad is sawing. Susan is watching *Cartoon Connection*. Our mother is sleeping.

I go to her sewing table and find her scissors with the red handles.

They are heavy and silver in my hand. Like from a fairy tale.

I carry them to the vanity near the bathroom where we brush our teeth. Then I get a chair from under the bench. I drag it back to the vanity and sit down in the chair but I can't see in the mirror very well. So, I climb up onto the vanity and sit with my feet in the sink.

When I look straight ahead into the mirror, I can see myself in the mirror behind me and the mirror at the side of me. I can see me, hundreds of me, getting smaller and smaller.

I turn away from that mirror. In the main mirror there is only one Vivian.

I don't have a spray bottle like Glennys but I turn on the tap and splash some water onto my hair with my hands. Then I pick up the scissors and put the fingers of my right hand into the handles and practise a few cuts in the air. The scissors are heavy but they sound smooth and they sparkle in the light.

I wrap my left hand around all the hair I can grab and, watching myself in the mirror, try to cut it.

But the mirror makes things confusing and I can't get the blades around my hair so I look down at my hair and the scissors. The clump I'm holding is thick so only a few strands cut and they slip through my fingers and slither down to tickle my leg. I let go of some of the hair and try again.

This time it works. I pull my hand away. I look up into the mirror. It looks like I'm holding an animal's tail.

I hold my hair up. Hold it up above my head. Straight up. This time the mirror isn't confusing. I cut again.

Seduction: Imagining Leonard Cohen

Sudeshna Baksi-Lahiri

Glancing at her watch, she quickens her stride to reach the imposing Victorian building at the edge of High Park. Walking briskly up the wide, stone steps, she hopes the reading hasn't started: she wants to be hypnotised by the poet's magnificent voice and words. Entering the gloom of the vast empty foyer, she pauses for just a moment, taking in the elegant rosewood table and its flamboyant centrepiece. 'Odd,' she thinks in passing. 'It doesn't really fit with the classical ambience of the place.'

The drone of voices, broken by sudden shouts of laughter and the delicate clinking of glass, draws her to the far end of the hallway and the slightly ajar double doors. She takes a deep breath, runs her fingers through her hair, and enters the room.

Taking stock, she looks around. Scanning the motley gathering in this well-appointed space with its glittering chandeliers and elaborate sconces, she searches for that one distinctive face. And then she sees him standing there in his impeccable black suit, surrounded by a coterie of admirers, maybe just friends – a bit aloof, yet leaning in with a listening expression marked by the hint of a sardonic smile. A cigarette droops from his fingers, the ash long and curved – will it drop, she wonders, before he takes a drag? She'd like to see him inhale – his cheeks sucked in, lips pursed, the glowing tip of the cigarette as the nicotine courses through his veins – and then, the release …

> *I stumbled out of bed*
> *I got ready for the struggle*
> *I smoked a cigarette*
> *And I tightened up my gut …*[1]

She's been listening to him recently, in case she has the guts to go up and meet him face-to-face. She'd love to meet him, no two ways about that. Preparing, rehearsing, steadying herself to say … what? She still doesn't know … but at least to say it with confidence and calm, even though her knees might be knocking themselves silly under her flowing Egyptian dress.

His words disturb, yet captivate in their simplicity – *Your letters, they all say you're beside me now, then why do I feel alone?*[2] And his exquisitely resonant voice, drenched in sensuality – *The hyacinth wild on my shoulder, my mouth on the dew of your thighs*[3] – has continued to be an indelible part of her rather prosaic, yet remarkably unpredictable life. While his songs and poems do not consciously influence her choices or the trajectory of how she moves forward, they clearly colour the connections she makes with those around her.

She wonders what he's thinking at this precise moment. Is he bored with the event and would like to escape to his usual haunt to meet up with friends? Or is he steeling himself to do his bit to market his book and not let his agent down? From what she's read about him, she knows he's gracious and humble, but he's also vain enough to want his work to be critically recognised *and* have popular appeal (like any other artist). But given his dark and tortured writing style, these two desires have often been at odds.

She knows she's been staring at him, with thoughtful intensity, like an artist on the very edge of committing her subject to canvas. In another world, in another era, she might very well have been his groupie. She hasn't moved from near the doors. He must've felt the touch of her gaze – because a second later, he lifts his head and looks directly at her from halfway across the room. He does not change his smile, but takes the drag she'd imagined him taking – and through the smoky haze of the exhalation, he inclines his head, bowing ever so slightly – and beckons with his eyes.

'You can do this,' she whispers soundlessly to herself, as she gathers her dress and thoughts, and walks across the gleaming marble floor towards the man she's admired from afar and for so long.

A (Familial) History of Magic

Rafael E. Fajer Camus

Lola, Abel, and I are standing on the terrace of the clinic, over-looking the beach. We're watching the beachgoers, wondering why they're there since it's prohibited to set foot on the beach. Patrol cars come and go and the people on the beach disperse, only to come back once the patrols are gone.

The day is overcast. The ocean matches the sky: a bluish grey with shifting intensities. It's enchanting, magical.

A woman wearing a white t-shirt and a long white skirt walks towards the ocean. We can't make out her face, but we can see she's carrying a couple of bags. Her shoulders slouch with the weight. Her feet drag in the sand. She's looking around, her eyes darting in every direction. She seems not to want company ... no witnesses maybe. She doesn't look up at our terrace. She doesn't see us watching her.

She puts down her bags and commences a ritual, lifting up her arms, holding something in her hands. She sways from side to side. I think I hear some chanting. She throws the item into the ocean. She repeats the process with a few more things she takes out of the bags. The three of us are curious. Abel goes back to the office and fetches his binoculars. Lola and I look at each other. He catches our puzzlement and says he had brought them in case there were bikini-clad girls he could spy on. Lola and I chuckle.

We take turns looking through the binoculars. The items have been washed onshore. The woman leaves before we can glimpse her face through the lenses.

Lola: What are those? That whitish thing looks like a fish head, don't it? But that feathery thing ... part of a bird?

Me: Nah. I don't know what those are but I'm sure they're not that. That would be sick. It's probably just some garbage she's been hauling around.

Abel: Look at them man. They're dead animals. I'm fucking sure.

Lola: They really do look like quartered animals.

I take the binoculars and look more attentively.

Me: Actually, I think they might be. But that's just weird. I mean, we're probably just ... I don't know. Listen I have to go. I have a session to lead, and I still haven't prepared the music for it. I'll catch you after. Let me know if she morphs into a gorgon while I'm gone.

Abel: Music? What for?

Me: Guided imagery through music. That's what I do mister. You'd love it.

Abel: I think I'll stick to spying on beach witches, thank you very much.

Me: Aight, catch you in a bit.

I lead the session. I come back. Lola and Abel are staring at Lola's phone. They show me the photos they took of what the woman had thrown into the ocean: the body and head of a cock ripped from one another, a dead fish with a sliced lemon next to it, a closed bag with a dead animal (specifics unknown) and a dead pigeon, all laying on the beach, the surf hitting them.

We research online about black magic rituals entering the details to get specifics: frenetic witch dancing while throwing animal parts into the sea, meaning of cock decapitation in magic rituals, the effects of sliced lemon on dead fish (the unexpected results of this last search were particularly interesting to Lola – she's a great cook). We learn that the woman is trying to separate a family, to have the wife (of what we assume is her lover) killed and the children severed from their father. Lola is freaking out. She can't stand still. She's trying to say things but the speed of her speech is unintelligible. From the little we can make out we realise that she believes in magic. Abel is also uncomfortable. His body is still, a bit too still. He's biting his lip. His eyes are focused yet absent. After a brief negotiation (very brief, both had the same idea), they delete the images on their phones just in case the bad juju can be transmitted through them. I'm intrigued. I think about magic.

Magic is everywhere. In Mexico people use magic to find love, to win elections, to become rich, to hurt enemies, to exorcise demons, to predict the future, to talk to the dead, to change destiny, etc. It's a powerful thing, magic. My family is no stranger to the phenomenon. We have a history of magic.

My dad was very ill for many years. He had cancer and Guillain-Barré syndrome. He suffered for a good amount of time. The illness changed him – from being a homophobic controlling prick, he turned into my best friend, a sensitive, understanding man. He became a dream father for our family and an admirable human being. But not without a great deal of pain. My mom suffered immensely with his illness too. They were each other's first and only love and remained married until eight years ago, when my father died of a massive brain haemorrhage while visiting me in Paris.

When my dad was at his worst, my mom and dad were at Mexico City Airport waiting for a flight to San Diego, where my father was being treated. A strange woman came over to talk to my mom. The woman told my mom that she was a psychic and witch and that she could help. She convinced my mom by explaining how my dad was in danger of dying and he needed a cleanse. My mom was amazed by this woman's knowledge of my dad's proximity to death. She thought the woman was psychic when it was evident my dad had one foot in the afterlife (or lack thereof).

My dad was bald and weak from chemotherapy. Still, my mom needed something to hold on to. She started seeing this woman every time she came back to Mexico City, hiding these consultations from the rest of the family.

The witch became my mom's counsellor and provider of all things magical: candles, mirrors, flowers, cups, etc. They started doing cleanses to rid the house of curses that she insisted jealous people had performed on the family.

My sister had a painting of a cartoon vampire hanging on her bedroom wall. The woman looked at it and found that it too was cursed and needed to be disposed of. My mom did as she was instructed and disposed of the painting.

Then the woman had a vision. On a specific night she could perform a spell and cleanse all the bad magic surrounding the family. She would need 500,000 MXP in cash, just to purify them, and she would need all the family jewels to do the same with them. She told my mom that jewels, being crystals, can hold curses with intensity. The woman disappeared with all the family jewels and the cash.

My whole family was outraged. But with time we all came to understand my mom's desperation to save my dad. She was trying to take a shortcut. Magic in a way is exactly that, a shortcut to a desired outcome. We want something and we perform a ritual to get it without doing the hard work of understanding the causes and conditions that might lead up to what we want. The result for my mom was the loss of all her jewels and the continuation of my dad's illness and recovery through medicine.

Magic changes the world. It changed my family. But when it works, it works. People give it power by adding meaning to magic. They engage in rituals full of signifiers that influence the mind. And that influence may in fact change the outcome of a situation we desire to influence. If I'm a religious believer and feel that I'm possessed, then I give power to the rituals that my religion deems necessary for the condition. This belief may be the thing that allows me to break free from a condition that I consider to be a possession. In fact, the process is psychological and neurological, through the influence of symbols that carry strength through meaning. I won't go deeply into this. It's a huge topic and I'm no expert. It's just a basic appreciation that helps me understand how people use rituals to effect changes in themselves, in their conditions or in the world.

I'm thinking about this while Lola is lighting incense to clear the space of bad energy. My older sister Eugenia calls. She tells me how her therapist, who is also a psychic, just revealed to them that Eugenia's youngest daughter is also a witch. What happens when they tell my niece she's a witch? She starts having nightmares about visions of violence and horror that keep her up all night. She hadn't had them before the revelation.

A few weeks ago, my other sister Sabina told me about a tarot card reader she wanted me to consult. At that time, I wasn't sure but now, as I watch Lola trying hard to clear our room of bad magic, I think it's a great idea, amazing even. I call immediately.

The video call is a catastrophe. He was trying to get information out of me through adulation and questions. I gave him nothing. He kept getting everything wrong and then saying how I was just so pure of energy and fantasticalness. So, I go fish. I tell him about my addiction. Magic happens.

Psychic: You experienced addiction as a bug on your shoulder. For other people addictions are horrifying and difficult, for you it was just another step while walking your path of light. It was so easy for you that you want to make it easy on other people.

I'm *fuming*! My head wants to explode. I want to reach into the screen and squish the man's head with my fists. Pulp it!

Me: Yeah. That's good.

He goes on and on: You are special. You have the ability to bring peace to those in need, those fighting addiction. You are an example of how to make the path easier, how it is possible. I see you will succeed in your recovery. You have qualities that will enable you to ...

I just agree and nod and listen trying to dissociate my actual state of outrage erupting in my interior from my exterior, all Zen and equanimity.

Idiot (I mean Psychic): By the way, all the proceeds from my calls go to addiction centres around the country.

When I hear that I immediately hang up roughly, shaking, considering breaking the computer. How fucking dare he! Cheeses! What I thought was going to be a fun investigative call that I could write about turned into a rage inside me that is about to turn violent, that I'm writing about. This man knows nothing of the war, the pain, the fear of addiction. To have experienced the most intense pleasure ever known to humans and have it destroy your life, to know the pain and desire to feel it again and to know that if you do so you might stay crazy or may even kill someone; it's a daily fucking war. *Fuck him!*

I'm angry at magic, angry at people wanting to take shortcuts to destinations. I'm angry at my family for falling into these traps again. I want to call them and scream again. But I know this is not the right moment to do so. I sit with my rage and let it subside. Then I ask myself the question: are you not trying to use shortcuts to happiness? *Yes, I am.*

My unhappiness and desire for happiness drove me to seek drugs. I confused pleasure with contentment. At the time I thought drugs would bring me happiness. They brought destruction but, with it, the knowledge that drugs are not the cause of my happiness. They served that purpose.

I call my sister to talk to her about her psychic. She listens, she says she'll never talk to him again.

Sabina: By the way, do you remember we had to do an inventory of all your belongings that burned with your apartment? That painting of the woman reading, it turns out that the artist (Santiago Corral) did a series of paintings while he was in a mental institution. Yours is one of them. He was hospitalised because he burned down his apartment.

La Poupée Cubaine

E.R. Pulgar

She danced before she met him. Before Miami, before Manuel Rivas, before her daughter Emmanuela took up space in her belly, Milena Ronveaux had no dash adding another last name to the one she inherited from the French colonial part of her ancestry.

In place of the life she had become accustomed to on the island, in place of the guayaberas and the coral necklaces and the sound of son playing on the malecón, she had lavender perfume, swanned feather boas, packs of Virginia Slims, clear six-inch heels, and skimpy sequin gowns designed with Josephine Baker in mind.

They didn't call her by her name. When she had paid her dues at the club run by Madame Minerva Luciernaga, a Venezuelan immigrant from the island of Margarita who had been in Paris for 30 or so at that point, she was christened with a new identity: '*la poupée cubaine.*' Milena, la muñeca cubana, the Cuban Doll of Menilmontant, the jewel of Club Mannequin.

On the streets, they called her Honey. Some said the nickname came from the colour her eyes shone in bright sunlight. Others say it was the taste of the nothings she whispered in the ears of her lovers. Still, some maintain that it was the way the streetlamps on the Boulevard Voltaire made her bouncing strawberry blonde curls and brown skin radiate as she strutted the streets, searching for a trick to turn.

She was an ungoverned twenty-five-year-old Cuban woman in Paris, trying to figure out what that meant and survive it.

She lived alone in the no-man's-land between the 20th and the 11th, between the vintage chandelier store and the Cimetière du Père-Lachaise. It was a nice pocket of an otherwise rough part of the arrondissement, where it opens to the Quartier des Amandiers. The studio was close enough to the club for her to walk there. Not too big, not too small, the place was unique in the fact that her rent was being paid by none other than the landlord himself. It was an oasis in an area that was still sketchy enough for her to walk with a coat that hid her body from anyone that couldn't pay for it.

Her first hours in Paris were marked by motion. She had just landed from Havana and spent the last of her money on the taxi from Charles de Gaulle airport to Bastille. She knew no one, but was beckoned by the name of the neighbourhood. No place to stay, no family, no masters, no rules, no job. By the time she had stumbled into Club Mannequin, she was desperate. Drawn to the lights, memories of old jobs, and a framed photo of Eartha Kitt near the entrance, Milena Ronveaux entered the establishment.

The Madame noticed her delicate yet muscular frame right away. From the way she walked into the club in heels she suspected this was not the case of a novice dancer. They locked eyes, and The Madame curled her purple acrylic nails, beckoning Milena approach her. A few cigarettes and martinis later, the women got to talking business.

'Mira, mi vida,' she would say between puffs in the raspy tone of a lifetime smoker, 'a trick is a trick – it's our duty to turn them. When I was still working the intersection, before my hair got grey and this cuerpazo was still a cuerpazo, I lived in this man's apartment rent-free. It was a great start. His name is Saturno, and he's an idiot like all men are idiots. He liked me. He fed me and I needed to save my money. I used it to open this club you sit in now. He found me working the same corner where you might end up if you stick around this part of town. He's pretty hard to miss, if you're looking for him: old white guy in a nice suit and a monocle. If he likes you, he may even pay your rent. There's just one thing you have to give.'

'What do I have to give?' she asked the patrona after lighting up a smoke.

Minerva leaned into her face until they were nearly kissing, putting her hand under Milena's chin as a wisp of smoke curled its way out of her teeth. The Madame grew grave, hushed, thoroughly tinging her words with the ancient wisdom wielded by anarchist whores since the days of Grisélidis Réal.

'What women have given to survive from time immemorial,' she whispered, grabbing Milena's cheek with sorrowful concern. 'It may hurt at first, but you'll get used to it.'

According to Minerva, Saturno Pagliaccini was an Italian expat who acted like the clown his last name implied he was. Old and pale as a dying tilapia, he was a well-known john amongst the workers of the Boulevard Voltaire for helping younger girls get a footing in the city for the price of their company. He had pockets deep as the Mediterranean Sea and, despite his old age and weak-willed air, was known for having a cock as thick as a Coke can that he knew how to use.

That night, Milena Ronveaux walked the streets searching for a trick, Cuban accent dusting rusty French pronunciation. Sure enough, an hour or so into her shift, a john came out of the shadows hobbling on a cane. He was wearing a dusty opera jacket, pale, a vein popping out from his forehead into a constellation of liver spots. He was grabbing at his crotch and licking his lips like an anteater.

She was not ready for his dentures to fall out. It took everything in her not to laugh.

'Monsieur, you ... dropped these.'

Lace glove in hand, holding back a gag, she picked them up between her index and thumb and shoved them back in his mouth. He licked his lips, veiny cobalt blue eyes wide open, a still-breathing corpse.

'A little one with such a strong hand ... I like that in a bambina,' he said. 'One of Minerva's girls?'

'Yes sir. My name is Honey, the sweetest new thing at Club Mannequin.'

He smiled at her, holding onto her arms as he leaned on his cane.

'Mi chiamo Saturno. Come back to mine for a drink?'

They went home, and for someone so clumsy he was indeed quite skilled and even elegant in his way. Milena hated that her first time having sex in this new city was with a client, but a girl's gotta do what a girl's gotta do.

The next day, Saturno asked her to stay in the studio apartment below his penthouse and gave her a weekly allowance. Soon after, Minerva offered her a slot dancing regularly on Wednesdays. The Eiffel Tower shone out of her window, a faint and distant constant.

Free rent and free money was convincing until it wasn't. Milena felt a darkness in the pit of her stomach every time Saturno and her slept together. After a few months, she began to feel herself more kept woman than a worker in control of her trick.

She often overstayed her shifts at the club, dancing until the tips of her heels were ground to dust. She found freedom in the club, in the music, in the exalted divine feminine energy that pulsed through the space.

As Saturno made her lose pleasure in dick, she began to focus on the women who came in. She became known at the club as a diva who catered to men and women, who came with a fresh pair of six-inch clear heels every week after destroying the last pair on the pole. Sometimes she let them whisper 'mi muñeca' between her legs. Sometimes she wouldn't even charge. In her dark little world, tenderness was worth more than tender.

Every Wednesday a beautiful woman with a large afro came in, ordered a whiskey tonic, and sat right in front of Milena's pole. She never made any moves as Milena swung around, but she tipped well. Milena didn't know why a woman as beautiful as her was smoking her Wednesdays away, watching her. She reminded her of her Tía Mercedes if she had become an older lesbian. Minerva told Milena the woman was from the south, but that was all she knew.

She was seemingly a bit older than Milena, face marked by light wrinkles from smoking, nails made long by the technician that same day, eyebrows freshly waxed. She was always in a full face of makeup, dark foundation propelling her melanated and moisturised face. Her afro was wide as a crown giving her an air that would have dwarfed the opulent shine of the Sun King himself.

One night, she dared to approach Milena, who was entranced by the way her hair moved in time to her hips. The woman walked up to her and put a 50 euro note between her breasts. She grabbed Milena's face, holding it with one hand between her index and her thumb. She stared directly into her eyes. Milena slid off the pole and guided her by hand to the back room where the girls took care of one-on-one clients.

'Ma poupée, ma poupée, ma poupée,' the woman whispered, pressing her forehead on Milena's. At that moment, they were the only two people in the packed club, the noise and music swallowed by two women whispering at each other under neon lights.

'What's your name?' Milena asked, coy and deeply interested.

'Call me Francine,' said the older woman, smiling with a chic gap in her front teeth. 'Et vous, poupée?'

'Call me Milena,' she said. 'I live nearby with an absolutely terrible keeper. I wish every day I could leave this all behind. Let me not bore you with the details.'

Francine pressed her lips to Milena's. They kissed for what seemed like hours, free of charge. That night, Milena quietly took her home, and Francine taught her about sex she hadn't thought possible.

As dawn streamed into the room, the faint toll of a nearby church bell ringing, Milena stroked Francine's cheek.

'Tell me more about the south, mi amor,' she cooed at Francine.

'There's a blue like nothing you've ever known, Mile mi amor,' she said, stroking Milena's back, grazing her neck and collarbones with her long nails. 'It's like Havana, but the beaches are rockier. It's quiet, and Yves Klein learned his blues there. I live by the eternal sea. I eat breakfast on the rocks every day as the waters crash against them, un petit déjeuner de pain, marmelade, et café. Paris is seasonal; I spend most of the year in Nice.'

That night, after much cajoling and multiple little deaths, Milena packed her meagre belongings into Francine's small car. It was impulsive but felt right, like the choice to leave Cuba for France. She didn't bother to wish Saturno goodbye because he would likely have a heart attack, and she wouldn't be tied to this town because she killed that geezer.

She went to Club Mannequin one last time, to quit and say goodbye to The Madame in-person. Minerva was sad to see her go but knew what it was like to be young and infatuated and free. She gave her a necklace she'd had made to give her on her sixth month anniversary as a dancer, a small gold necklace that said 'muñeca' in gold script. They hugged, a street mother watching another sparrow learn to fly.

The drive to Nice was long, but when she put her head out the window and smelled that sea breeze for the first time, watching Paris turn small behind her seemed less and less painful. The Côte d'Azur smelled like Havana or a piece of it, she thought. Watching Francine speed down the highway, a manicured hand chain-smoking out the window while the other gripped the steering wheel, she felt warm. Milena Ronveaux felt, for the first time since she left Cuba for France, that she'd found a semblance of home.

Thursday, December 16th, 1990

Katherine Mann

I wake up to the sound of ravens cawing outside. I'm too hot under the blankets, overwhelmed and panicked. I throw off my covers and lie like a corpse, the sheet beneath me clinging to my sweaty skin. The panic eases, but the relief from shifting the blanket wears off. My head aches under the tight skin of my brow, with the feeling of the quickening heat of the day. The birds are making a gasp of it outside because soon it will be too hot for anything. My sash window is thrown open. The dusty fly screen, flecked with holes, is not much more than gnarled wire the insects fuss over. Tiny flies form an endless spiral of black beads near the ceiling. Uki snaps at a blowie. She's stretched out in her usual spot under the window, her tan Kelpie coat has shed enough hair to form a fine mat beneath her. She glances at me and spits the dead fly onto the floor.

I sigh and rub my sweaty face on the pillow slip. We are facing morning four of the heat wave, bursting, waiting for the cool change to blow over the mountain to the West. The summer has only just arrived and already the firies are worried, whistling air through clenched teeth. 'You mark my words,' they say, 'this year we will burn.'

I can smell the soil where the sun hits it. As one, the cicadas commence their roar.

I roll out of bed in search of water and make my way up the dim hall, bare feet slapping on dusty lino, past the bathroom where the shower runs. I push open the kitchen door and stop suddenly at the sight of Dad, who is shirtless and leaning over the sink full of dirty dishes. With one hand, he holds the awning window open while he smokes, blowing a trail of smoke through the gap at the bottom of the window frame. A dainty porcelain teacup rests on the sill. He keeps his back turned, sparse hair marches across his bare shoulders. He is between me and the kettle.

I hesitate. I always make tea first thing, but Dad is there and I don't like to ask him for anything. 'Will you put the kettle on?' My voice sounds too loud, too demanding, so I hold my breath after asking.

He grunts, doesn't look up. He responds to my request with his whole body, a reluctant shoulder slump, an impatient glance back at me. Instead of doing what I ask, he takes a sip from his cup, abrupt, economical; he has no time for wasted movement, or for me. His cigarette ends in a sagging cylinder of ash between his fingertips. He doesn't want me here.

I cast around, the heat, my thirst, impatience building. There's a jug of water on the table. I seize it, putting the wide lip straight to my mouth and gulp with such relief, I spill water over the side and down my naked chest.

'Christ,' Dad says, 'clean that up.' He throws a tea towel. It sails through the air and lands flat on the tabletop.

I scrub at my chest, wipe the seat of the chair, then stand there, staring with the towel clutched in my hand.

'Put some clothes on, would you?' His voice is a growl.

I drop the towel back onto the table and nick off.

'I don't want him burning like yesterday.' Mum breezes past me in the hall. Her fresh smell holds me there, clean hair, polished shoes.

'You hear me, Kit?'

'What?'

She has stopped at the top of the hall, one hand on the front door's timber frame. The stained-glass kookaburra set into the top of the door lets in shards of light, a white block of glass by the brown beak. Turning back to look at me, Mum's face is in shadow, permed hair lit like a halo around her head. Glasses glinting.

'Where's Dad?'

She nods towards the bedroom.

'Dad's gone back to bed,' I say flatly, thinking of him flung across the rumpled sheets, waiting for me and Chris to bugger off to school. 'No work today,' I add. There is a pause I can count in. I begin to rehearse the seven times tables. I get to four sevens are twenty-eight.

'Do your job properly, Kit.' She opens the door. 'Get dressed. Help your brother.'

'Bye, Mum.'

The screen door screams as she slams it shut, wooden frame rattling, as she steps outside.

I go back to my boiling room and throw myself on the bed, burying my face in the sheets. My door opens and closes. Running steps and Chris clambers onto the bed beside me.

'Don't touch me!' My voice is muffled.

Hard, skinny limbs press up against me.

'Gettoff!' I push Chris away with one hand, his body heavy. I sit up and back away against the wall, cool for a moment through the crisp cotton of my school dress. The dog has followed him, nosing open the door, she prowls around sniffing at the corners of the room. The kookaburras start as the sun shoots through their tree. Their calls clamour, cackles laid down, one over another.

'My face is hot.'

I look at him, burning red cheeks, forehead pale where his fringe sat. 'I won't let you burn like yesterday,' I say. I pat his hair, push the front down again over the pale skin, touch his red cheek with a fingertip.

'Did Dad go to work?'

I shake my head, fall back on the bed, see again the ash of his cigarette nodding its way into the ashtray, the chipped teacup on the sill, the delicately curved handle too small for his thick fingers, his shaking hand.

Chris sits up with urgency.

I lay a hand on his arm. 'No. Don't.'

'But I want—'

I grip. 'Leave him be.'

Chris relaxes under my hand and I say it again, 'Leave him.' I pull Chris back into the bed, try to ignore the heat radiating from him. 'Let's turn the fan on. I'll read.'

'Yeah?'

Winnie the Pooh is on the floor halfway under the bed. I cut the sun with the heavy curtain, switch on the fan. The head whips around like a snake's and I recoil. It catches its groove and begins to gently oscillate.

Chris presses his lips to it on a close pass. 'Exterminate. Exteeeerrminaaaate.' He laughs at his Dalek voice, cups the fan to hold it steady so he can speak into it again. The fan clicks, attempting to turn.

'Stop it!' I swat at him with the book, which clips his arm.

We read the chapter where Christopher Robin takes all the animals on an expedition to find the North Pole. Chris gets caught up on Piglet blowing on a dandelion.

'What does he mean?'

'He's just making a wish.'

'But he says, "This year, next year, sometime or never".'

'Yeah, for a big thing to happen.'

Chris flops onto his front, face turned to the fan, arms dangling like a rag doll. 'Well, it's never, isn't it?'

The toaster pops and the kitchen smells of burned breadcrumbs. I layer my two slices on my plate taking the butter dish from Chris' side of the table. He's left his knife point-down in the block of butter.

The front door opens and closes.

Chris drops his toast, turns to the window, cranes this way and that. 'I can't see.'

I put his half-eaten toast back on his plate. Melted butter and jam marks the tabletop where it has fallen. I stare at the mess instead of distracting Chris from whatever Dad's up to. Dad never leaves the house early unless he's working. Mum said he wasn't working.

The screen door bangs as Chris rushes outside. I go to the window where, leaning out the way Dad did earlier, I can see the two of them by the ute. Chris is bounding after him excitedly. I put my hand in Dad's teacup and it slips out the window. The delicate handle breaks off as it clips the sill, landing in the scrubby bushes below. A thick blackberry cane arches to the height of the window ledge, the knotted spines tangled in ropes of jasmine vine. The white flower-stars have all died back to a brown lichen.

The car door creaks as it hangs open. A box sits on the passenger seat. There is a thud and metallic scrape as a toolbox is loaded onto the ute's tray. It slides into place beside another box. The dog whines, stays close to Dad. He steps back into her, pushes her away with a leg.

'Stay there.'

'You're not taking Uki today?'

The rope he usually ties to the dog's collar to keep her from hurtling off the tray trails over the mitre saw. The tray door slams shut. Dad scrubs sweat off his forehead with the back of his wrist. He flips his wide-brimmed hat onto his head, pinching the crown tight. It is sweat stained where it presses into his scalp, a dark line in the felt. The brim cuts a wedge of shadow across his face. He pauses there, looking over the dancing dog. His eyes rest on Chris, who is waiting to see what he will do. There is a backpack at Dad's feet.

I bump it and the ashtray falls out the window with a clatter. Ash and cigarette butts burst out, fireworks style.

'Don't you climb out that window, Kit! I've told you kids a hundred times.'

His raised voice a trigger, the dog starts to bark, keeping a perimeter around Dad. Her hair bristles on her neck.

'Shut up, Uki,' he bawls.

Her barking intensifies as she positions herself between the two of them, her nervously waving tail backing up into Chris' thighs in an effort to protect him.

'I'm not—' But, my voice is drowned out by the dog, which darts forwards and takes a nip at Dad's ankle.

'Get-out-of-it!' he snarls, kicking out with his boot.

It connects and the dog lets out a horrible yelp, scooting out of range.

'No!' Chris shrieks, his face twisting up as he tries not to cry.

The cicada roar starts again, adding to the clamour.

The dog keeps barking, high pitched.

Chris starts to howl.

'Shut up!' Dad bellows at all of it, but none of it stops.

I hesitate. Dad might go in the time it takes me to get to the front door. He has his thumb and forefinger pinching the bridge of his nose like putting out a candle, or a fuse. A weird shout escapes him, wordless, eyes squeezed closed.

Chris' crying has moved past the first bit, he's now producing a wail that's building to a crescendo. I count three cat-and-dogs. Then it bursts out of Chris like the end of the world. He face-plants and howls into the gravel.

The dog stops barking, and sniffs at the side of Chris' wet face.

Dad puts his hands on his hips, eyes darting. He sighs, chest collapsing as he looks down at Chris. 'Come on, son. Get up.' Dad squats down beside Chris, gives him an awkward backrub. 'Eh? It's alright, mate. I wouldn't belt Uki.'

It doesn't work. Chris keeps crying like he's never going to stop.

Dad looks around, rubs his face so hard his hat lifts off his head. 'Come on now, mate. I've gotta go.'

'Where are you going, Dad?'

He looks up at me, half hanging out the window. He stares for a good few seconds, eyes sliding down the wall and away. Then, he says, 'Kit, come out here and get your brother.'

I pelt through the house, but the engine starts up just before I reach the door. By the time I stand on the front verandah, the ute is reversing fast. It swings around and heads down the drive. The toolboxes slide around in the tray, but the heavy stuff is secured behind the cab. He is taking everything, like it's the first day of a big job. What big job?

Uki creeps up and licks at Chris' ear. He flails at the dog, but takes a shuddering breath and sits up, hiccupping sobs.

La Bohème

Thomas Hamlyn-Harris

The Australian flag, worn superman-style around his neck, did little to protect the boy as he crashed through the front window of La Bohème Mid-Century Showroom and Café. He landed on an Eames sofa and matching ottoman upon which a Johnny Cash record, a Chinese puzzle box and a pineapple-print one-piece pantsuit had been placed by the proprietor Cameron Bird a short time earlier. Locals only ever referred to La Bohème Mid-Century Showroom and Café as 'La Bohème' and if it weren't for the shattered front window, customers might have thought the half-naked teenager with the Australian flag cape was one of Cameron's esoteric window displays – a postmodern tribute to *The Death of Marat* by Jacques-Louis David or a reference to an obscure Peter Greenaway film.

Cameron prided himself on La Bohème's window displays and used the term 'intertextual references' at which customers nodded eagerly without understanding. Behind the shirtless boy stood a collection of antique absinthe bottles, a ceramic cardinal, and a stuffed goat. The boy's delicate sandy curls escaped from below a promotional beer cap – the kind you get from a bottle shop when you buy a carton. The cap was golden yellow and matched the pineapples on the pantsuit. A trickle of blood drew Cameron's attention to the white shadow of fluff on the boy's cheek. Too young to shave.

La Bohème was not open today. It was the 26th of January and a mid-week public holiday. A day without customers meant Cameron could reorganise the front window display. He also wanted to avoid the Australia Day barbecue that Laney, his ex-wife, had planned. Cameron and Laney had remained friends since the divorce. They had no dependents – furry or otherwise – and their inner-city Queenslander had recently sold for a ridiculous price, allowing Cameron to rent the run-down carpet store that he transformed into La Bohème. Laney was involved in the business. She did the accounts and sometimes helped in the café but referred to La Bohème as Cameron's 'baby'. The boy's friends had fled, all underage-drinking and shit-scared. Blood soaked through the boy's jeans leaving his groin black and shiny. The stuffed goat avoided looking directly at the blackened groin. A distant siren wailed.

The Johnny Cash record cover was trodden into the shards of glass on the street in front of the showroom where a crowd gathered. Cameron picked it up and held it to his chest as a policewoman asked him questions that he struggled to answer: 'What were you doing in the shop? ... Do you know the boy? ... Why didn't you call the ambulance? ... Have you been drinking?'

The policewoman informed Cameron the paramedic had seen him taking photos.

'I'm going to need your phone,' she said.

'I took a few photos for insurance purposes,' Cameron said.

The officer took the phone and walked over to her partner. They scrolled through the photos and glanced at him a few times. She returned his phone, advised him to delete them and wrote down his details in a spiral-bound notebook.

'Why so many photos?' she asked.

Cameron shrugged and showed her the phone screen as he pressed delete.

Cameron watched the news that night but there was no mention of the boy. In the Australia Day montage package, there were several images of young shirtless men wearing Aussie flag capes. They were pudgy and sunburned which made Cameron angry; he was unsure why. He turned off the television.

La Bohème was closed for a few days while the window was repaired. Cameron moved the goat, now sporting the yellow beer cap, into his office. The paramedic had removed the cap to check the boy for head injuries and placed it on the goat's head. When La Bohème opened, the story was told over and over to the regulars. Cameron expected follow-up phone calls from the police or enquiries from various media outlets. There were none.

It was a slow Thursday afternoon, so Cameron shut La Bohème early. Based on the fluff on his chin and smooth chest, Cameron placed the boy's age at no more than fifteen so he had most likely been admitted to the children's ward of the public hospital a few blocks away. He walked around for a while, bought some daisies, then threw them in a bin. He went back to the shop to retrieve the cap from the goat. The cap gave him a clear sense of purpose as he walked to the hospital. He was returning the cap, that was all.

The nurse at the front desk knew the details. Cameron explained he was the proprietor of La Bohème and wanted to pass on his best wishes. The nurse had heard of La Bohème but not yet found time to visit. She smiled, told him the room number, 4E, the boy already had visitors. He was welcome to go on up. In the lift Cameron realised he'd forgotten to ask the boy's name.

Cameron sat in the hallway outside the room on a row of plastic chairs with the cap on his lap. The door was half open, allowing a truncated view of the end of the bed. The boy sat cross-legged on the bed with the blanket flat and smoothed down in front of him. A few teenage boys with their backs to the door stood, laughing and talking. Cameron moved to the next chair for a better view. The boys were playing poker. Through the door Cameron could see the curious choreography of the boy's hands. Cameron could see two jacks in the hand of an older boy who stood with his back to the door. The older boy pushed imaginary poker chips into the centre of the blanket.

'All in!' The shout echoed in the hallway.

The players folded to a great roar of laughter and pantomime protests. Cards were thrown onto the thick, pale-blue blanket and a hand swept them into a pile. Cameron watched, smiling at the anonymous hands as they shuffled and dealt and gestured. The hospital blanket was like a safety net below the acrobatic hands. Cameron knew the feel of the blanket. It had been burnished by a thousand sickly hands and was now transformed into something else – a stage, a casino, an ocean.

A nurse appeared in the room and the game was over. The teenagers moved towards the lifts and past Cameron who held the cap like a dove with a broken wing. He waited for the nurse to finish in the room. She wrote on a chart, checked the blipping machines, and walked towards the nurses' station. Cameron stood as she walked past and he handed her the cap. 'This belongs to the boy in 4E.'

Laney and Cameron had met in chemistry class at high school, but it wasn't long before Cameron carved their initials into the *love tree* at the far side of the school oval. Laney thought the gesture was cute in grade nine, but by grade eleven they were both a little embarrassed by it. Laney's family moved to Sydney in the final year of high school and Cameron wondered if he would see her again. A few years later, they ran into each other on an express bus to the city. Laney had moved back to Brisbane to study accounting and Cameron, stretching the truth, said he was a documentary filmmaker. He did want to be a filmmaker, the kind that travelled to rugged places and captured some kind of chaotic truth. He told Laney his plans to visit Canada to film Inuit ice fishermen.

'I'm just waiting for Arts Council funding,' he said.

'Right,' Laney said. 'You should totally do that.'

Cameron knew he wouldn't go – he hadn't even submitted the application.

When Cameron got home that night, he found a mixed tape he had made for her after she moved to Sydney. He hadn't sent it. A few days later Cameron picked her up for dinner and they listened to the tape in the car – Depeche Mode, Echo and the Bunnymen, David Bowie – they didn't make it to dinner.

On their wedding night Laney told him the real reason her family had taken her to Sydney.

Since the accident, Cameron had slept on the single bed in his office at La Bohème. A coffee franchise had opened next door and a discount chemist franchise emerged in place of the second-hand bookstore across the street. The windows were painted yellow, and a hat stand full of sun hats replaced the water bowl left out for local dogs. As if to distract the pundits of hat stands and dog bowls, a photograph of the chemist's face was printed the size of a drowned giant and stuck to the inside of the front window.

The gentrification of the inner-city back streets where Cameron grew up was now overseen by the giant face of the chemist. From behind his desk at La Bohème, Cameron watched the unblinking chemist and the unblinking chemist watched Cameron. He was not surprised when the landlord came into La Bohème one day and lamented about the numerous and generous offers she had received for the run-down building. With Laney's help, Cameron and the landlord came to an agreement, giving him three months to vacate and a fair payout for the remaining lease.

Sleeping in his office at La Bohème, Cameron dreamed he was ice fishing. He could see a school of fish swimming below the ice under his feet as he walked in wide arcs, trying desperately to find the fishing hole. Below his feet, a wild-eyed goat stared up at him. Cameron clambered up from the frozen lake, away from the goat's silent scream, to an ice hut. It was shaped like a yellow promotional beer cap – a piss-coloured igloo. A flume of smoke rose from the centre, but Cameron could not see any windows or doors. He removed his gloves and traced the shape of the yellow bricks of ice, bloody fingers trying to find a way in.

The following day, Cameron wheeled the goat out of the office and put it next to the industrial bin in the alley. A group of teenage boys were digging through milk crates of scratched records that Cameron knew he couldn't sell but didn't want to give up to the finality of the industrial bin. Cameron nodded to the boys, signalling that the goat, like the scratched records, was now fair game. Cameron thought about his group of friends when he was sixteen and imagined the goat as the ultimate stoner's trophy. It would finally be given a name, cigarettes would be placed in its yellow teeth, it would be sat upon, talked to, dry humped and dressed up for the remainder of its life in a teenager's garage.

Back in his office, Cameron turned on his computer to make a few signs to print out for the front window. He hit print with a sigh and shuffled through the papers on his desk. Under a pile of invoices was a manila folder he'd been deliberately ignoring. He opened the folder and read the documents again and the note from Laney explaining the legal process for biological parents to contact an adopted child.

Later that day, Cameron stood inside the empty front window of La Bohème. The goliath face of the chemist smirked as Cameron taped a sign to the window – EVERYTHING MUST GO! 50% OFF! A car honked and there were shouts and laughter from the street. A boy in a yellow cap and his friends balanced the stuffed goat on a skateboard as they zig-zagged across the street and headed towards the park.

On the Boat

Linda Godfrey

By the time Harriet and Louise arrived in Weipa, they'd been driving for a week. A phone call from Charlie, and Harriet had been able to hear the desperation in his voice. He needed a cook and a deckhand, or he'd be losing money he didn't have. 'As an owner-operator, I can't afford to have the boat sit in the dock!'

On the wharf, Harriet's brother, Charlie, was standing with his hands on his hips, the same as he had when he was twelve, all bluff and bluster. His hair was a bit darker, his skin a bit redder. 'Put ya bags on board.'

He turned his back on them. Before Harriet stepped on board, she picked two frangipani flowers from a tree flourishing near the greasy water and put them in her hair. Louise threw their bags onto the stern. Charlie ordered the crew to cast off; none of them looked at the two women.

'*Prawn Star*? The name of the boat is *Prawn Star*?' Louise said.

Harriet shrugged. They lifted their noses into the sea breeze. Even before the boat had left port there was an overwhelming smell of dead fish.

They took their gear and stowed it in a cabin, no more than two bunks and a cabinet. Harriet's hands and knees were shaking, she attempted a steadying breath before anybody could notice it.

Louise tied her blonde hair back in a bandanna; Harriet's was in plaits down her back.

Charlie didn't introduce them to anyone. He showed them the galley and the deck where they would work.

He took them along the walkway. 'This boat's a floating prawn factory. The catch is sorted and graded here,' he said, pointing to stainless steel tables. 'Some are cooked, and some are packed raw into cartons, and then they're stored in the freezer over there.'

As they left the harbour, there was a steady hum under their feet from the motor. Harriet said goodbye to the land, threw the frangipanis overboard, one for her and one for Louise, and prayed that they would return to solid ground soon.

She was standing on deck, watching the water, when she heard footsteps nearby. It was one of the crew. He had a big belly, and was wearing grey jockettes and blue plastic scuffs. Half-closed eyes peered at her as he slid past.

Harriet decided the crew would be friendlier after the first of her fabulous meals. She and Louise climbed up white steel steps to the wheelhouse. Charlie saw them out of the corner of his eye, but rather than acknowledge them, he tried to look impressive by peering into his instruments. Charlie adopted a serious tone, talked on the radio, then authoritatively handed the wheel over to the mate.

'Darryl.' Charlie pointed.

Darryl had a red nose, stout legs. His arms were overdeveloped with clawed paws that had rubbed raw and then healed into leather casings. His face was burned brown, white in the creases at the corner of his eyes.

'How you goin'?' Darryl asked.

'I got in the same stores as last time,' Charlie said to the two women. 'Be on deck by 16:00. You'll work through the night. We have a cooked meal before that, at 15:00. We eat plain. No fish. Coffee while the nets are going back into the water. You'll need to work fast.' He looked over their heads to the nets behind them. 'Right. Stay out of trouble. Get down to the galley and put on the coffee. I have white, two sugars. Darryl has black with three.'

'Hang on, how many are we cooking for?'

'Karol will eat in any weather. Full contingent on a calm day is seven men plus youse two.'

Darryl was at the wheel and Harriet gazed past him out to the sea. It was calm and yet the boat was bucking and twisting with each swell.

In the galley, there were rails to keep the equipment and produce on the benches. All the cupboard doors had latches on the outside. Louise strode about the lurching boat with a firm foothold, anticipating each wave as she ran the drinks up to Charlie and Darryl on a little tray.

Harriet bumped around the galley, looking at supplies and equipment. With each lurch, there was a twist and a pause. In that one small pause she stood erect and breathed out, her throat relaxing. As she regained her balance, the sickening sequence started again.

At 16:00, both women went up on the deck. Charlie ordered the lowering of the trawling gear. The boat had two main nets, one on each side plus a smaller sampling net at the stern. The main nets were suspended from two six-metre-long metal booms, fixed with trawl boards that took the net to the bottom. A metal chain attached to the sampling net scraped the sea floor, stirring up the prawns and everything else. This was raised every half an hour or so to get an idea of what the catch might be.

When the main nets were winched up, load after load was dumped onto the tables to sort prawns and discard the seaweed, fish, crabs, sponges, sea cucumbers, snakes and even sharks, dolphins, and turtles. Louise was on the table separating banana and king prawns into baskets, and throwing the tiger prawns into a drain between the tables. Harriet's job was to sort the tigers by size. All the prawns were washed with a preservative, weighed, and boxed ready for export. Dark and wet, there was the stench of dead fish and barely enough time to stretch and relieve sore muscles. Harriet's hands were shredded from pulling ropes and her fingers were sore from handling prawn spikes.

By 04:00 Harriet and Louise were exhausted. The murky brown sea around the boat was full of floating fish carcasses. Harriet had no idea how she was going to sort all night and cook as well. They wouldn't be able to fall into bed until 07:00 came around.

Two days later, after Louise had taken coffee to Darryl and Charlie, she came back with stains all down her shirt.

'What's up?' Harriet asked as Louise stood over a basin washing coffee off her arms and neck.

'Karol's up there ranting and raving on at Charlie about us being on board. And Charlie told him to shove it, that we've been pulling our weight and the food's never been better. After that, the bastard came bursting down the stairs and spilt coffee all over me. Look what he's done. It stings like hell.'

Harriet stepped forward and peeled the shirt off Louise's arm. 'You need ice packs.'

Harriet unpacked the first aid box to find gauze, retrieved ice from the cool room and applied the packs to Louise's arm, hand and neck, careful not to break the skin.

'That feels better already.'

'You can't work like that. I'll go and tell Charlie.'

'Think I'll lie down for a bit.'

Harriet climbed the stairs to the wheelhouse; Charlie was looking cranky. Before she stepped through the doorway, he growled at her, 'Come to have your two bob's worth have ya?'

'What? Assault not reason enough for you?'

'What the fuck do you want? I'm fuckin' busy makin' a fuckin' livin'.'

'Calm down. No need to bite my head off, Louise has been badly burned and is taking the shift off.'

'We need everyone on deck!'

He turned away from her and said to Darryl, 'Take over here, get the nets out. I'll go and see the invalid.'

He stormed off to the galley. He poked his head in and bellowed, 'Louise, where the fuck are you?'

From behind him, Harriet said mildly, 'She's lying down.'

He turned around and crashed into her. They cracked heads and stepped back.

'Jesus, Sis, get out of my way.'

She pressed herself against the wall. He went to their cabin, walked in without knocking. Louise was lying down with her arm propped up on a pillow. It was red and had begun to swell.

'You right?'

'What do you think?' Harriet said from the doorway. He turned and gave her a foul stare. Shut up, he mouthed at her.

'I'm not sure about working tonight,' said Louise.

'We'll see how you are tomorrow. It doesn't look that bad.' He ruffled her hair.

Before Louise had a chance to answer, he was out the door.

Harriet could see in his eyes that he had to stop himself from throttling her. She stepped back. She had an enlarged bit on the cartilage of her left ear where he whacked her once when she was thirteen.

Harriet left Louise in bed and went back to the sorting table. Nobody said a word, they were all at their stations working hard. When the final call came for the night and they were cleaning up, Darryl came over to Harriet and said, 'Don't take it personal. You'll never change 'em by cooking goor-may food.'

'You're as a big a prick as them, you fuck,' she said with a smile.

He nodded. 'After Karol's cooking I had to conclude that pricks have a special diet – lamb chops, mashed potatoes and peas.'

Harriet laughed. It confirmed her plans for dinner that night.

When she got back to their quarters, Louise was sleeping, her arm still propped up on a pillow. Her skin was blistered but the burns weren't too deep.

The two women woke about 13:00 and staggered out into the bright sunshine. Around them the sea was a glittering blue. Both were in cozzies and carried sarongs. They went to the top of a storage area at the prow, applied sunscreen, pulled hats over their eyes and lay back to soak up the sun.

Harriet lit two cigarettes. She turned to hand Louise one and caught sight of Darryl staring down at them from the wheelhouse. She rolled over onto her stomach and said to Louise, 'They can't stop perving on us.'

'Wouldn't you think they'd appreciate us for our minds?' Louise said.

Harriet wrapped her sarong around her. 'I think I'll cover up my mind.' She stubbed out her cigarette roughly. 'I'm going inside to shower,' she said, looking up one more time at the wheelhouse. Darryl and her brother were watching. She gave them the finger. They looked at each other and laughed.

The shower was no more than a rose over the toilet. Harriet locked the door with a sigh of relief and stood over the bowl. The non-slip white tiles were like marble under her feet. The water was salty. A moment later someone banged on the door.

'Don't take all day!' Karol rattled the door. 'I want to use the head.'

She turned off the shower and wiggled her toes in the overflow. It slopped back and forth. There was a tiny piece of seaweed, a skerrick, caught on her toe.

'You're supposed to be cookin'.'

'I'll be out soon, Karol.'

'Fuck me. Hurry up.'

By the end of the first week Harriet could barely manage to concentrate on the type of prawn she was sorting. The coffee break, while the nets were out, made no impact on the torturous routine of the sorting tables. Some mornings she was surprised to see the sunlight, other nights she was watching the horizon willing the sun to come up. Most times she was too tired to care.

Harriet received compliments for her cooking and made fresh desserts. There were biscuits for coffee breaks.

Despite Charlie's instructions, she couldn't help herself. She made a fish curry, so fragrant it didn't taste of fish. The crew were halfway through it before they realised it was seafood. It was complimented too, some even had seconds. Harriet was relieved; it meant she could use some of the fish that came up with the prawns.

But fish curry was not enough for her; she wanted to try another dish. A risotto with cuttlefish cooked in its own ink. It may have been in the cookbooks and on restaurant menus for a long time, but if Harriet could get this crew to eat it, it would be a personal triumph.

Day ten, after a good catch, and Charlie was beaming; it was the best haul so far this trip. The decision to return to an area that was left to regenerate last season had paid off. He pulled out steaks from the bottom of the freezer for a big barbecue. Harriet made a satay sauce, potatoes marinated in oil and chillies cooked on the hot plate and a stir-fry with vegetables and noodles. Bottles of ice-cold beer were welcomed.

When Harriet woke, Louise was already up. Harriet turned over to sleep for another hour, then joined Louise in their sunbaking spot. Louise was topless.

'Giving the boys a thrill, are we?'

'Give me a break, I couldn't pull my cozzie over my arm.'

'Could've asked Karol to help you,' Harriet said, all sugary.

'He's offered, don't worry. He asked my breasts if my burns were all right.'

'And they said?'

'They said, fine. See?' Louise had her sarong over her arm so it didn't get sunburned.

'Those burns are looking much better.'

'He did apologise for accidently spilling coffee over me, said he slipped.'

'Prick.'

'Thank you, sweetie, for looking after me.' Louise squeezed Harriet's arm.

Harriet put her hand over Louise's and looked into her eyes.

Louise shifted her hand away. 'But I'm going to have a tan line on one shoulder,' she said.

'Poor baby.' Harriet unfolded her towel beside her. Louise was looking so good, Harriet wanted to reach over and rub in that bit of white sunscreen on her thigh that Louise had missed.

While she was thinking about it, she looked up. Charlie was glaring down at her.

With everyone in such a good mood, Harriet decided to cook the risotto for dinner. She rescued two good-sized cuttlefish. As she took them off the sorting table, a suspicious Karol asked her what the fuck she was doing.

'Risotto in its own ink.'

'Fuck me. That stuff's shit.'

'Try it.' She knew he liked her cooking. 'It has to be a change from sauerkraut, doesn't it?'

He spat at her feet. 'Why not do the work you're meant to and suck my cock.'

She turned away and busied herself at the sink, but she would have cried if she let herself. That bastard. Pity the prick liked salt and chilli too much for her to use it to spoil his food. She could cut the crutch out of his underpants, but he might like that too. Instead, she thought of all the rhymes about cold vomit pies and cats' noses in custard that she could and sang them to herself until Charlie called a halt to the sorting and the nets went back into the water.

About half an hour earlier than usual, Harriet wandered down to the galley. In the fridge the two cuttlefish were waiting. She hoped no one would come in.

She cleaned the cuttlefish, careful not to break the sacs of ink and put them to one side. Karol walked past but she made sure the onions and garlic that she was dicing required all her attention. She fried those until they were translucent, added the cuttlefish, salt and pepper and cooked it for thirty minutes.

The dominant smell was garlic; the aroma in the kitchen was pungent, seductive. She didn't eat a lot of her own cooking, she was not hungry after she had cooked it, but her mouth was watering. She added the rice and stirred. Poured in some stock, the ink, and then ladle by ladle, the rest of the stock. She turned down the heat and stirred and stirred until all the liquid was absorbed and the rice was cooked.

She tasted it, added salt and pepper. This dish was creamy and unctuous with a touch of rosewater taste from the ink. Gorgeous.

They would either fall at her feet in adulation or it would start a fight, the risotto was that good. She called everyone to dinner.

They sat at the table. In the electric light, white laminex lit up their faces from underneath; through the portholes the pattern of sunlight and ocean played over their arms.

Harriet served the black risotto and put the plates down in front of the crew. Everyone was dumbstruck.

Harriet slid into her place and said, 'Please start, you didn't have to wait for me.'

'Mm, it's good,' Louise said.

Charlie threw a forkful into his mouth. He chewed, swallowed, and stared straight ahead.

'Not bad,' said Darryl.

'They charge top dollar for this in restaurants,' Harriet said.

'I'm not fuckin' eating it,' Karol said.

'Chops tomorrow. I'll make you an extra big batch,' Harriet said while under the table she stuck her finger up at him.

From the corner of her eye, she could see Darryl picking chunks of the cuttlefish out of his rice.

'Saw ya sunbaking. Ya got nice tits.' Karol nodded in Louise's direction, just as Harriet was beginning to think they were getting on so well together.

Charlie put down his fork and rubbed his fingers along his brow line.

'So?' Louise said, looking down at her plate. She pulled her trousers away from her waist where they had been rubbing on her sunburn.

Karol sat back, his weight making the chair creak. 'What about that head job?'

Harriet chased a piece of cuttlefish across her plate; it was a bit resistant, and she jabbed at it, skewered the fat white blob with her fork.

'In your dreams,' Louise said, with a curl of her lip. She stared at Charlie.

Karol idly scratched his forearm with his knife.

Charlie ran his tongue over his teeth and said mildly, 'Back off, mate.'

'What were they doin' sunbaking out there, if they don't want it?'

'We're getting a tan, der,' Harriet said to him.

'Other girls come across, what's wrong with you two?'

'Nothing, you fool, that's why you'll never get anywhere with us,' Louise shouted.

'Ya musta fucked Charlie to get on as crew,' Karol said as he pushed his chair back and reached over to get some bread and butter. He turned to Harriet. 'I don't have a knife, oh and the butter. Get them for me.'

Harriet had had enough. She stood up and cracked her plate over Karol's head. 'Shut up and get them yourself, you bastard.'

Karol slumped; his face landed in his plate of black risotto.

Darryl retreated from the galley with his hands full of biscuits and a beer from the fridge.

Karol lifted his face out of the risotto and wiped it with one hand. 'You two'll keep. You've gotta sleep sometime.' Swearing under his breath, he stood, rubbing his head, stumbled out the door and knocked over the chair near Louise.

Charlie turned wearily to them, 'You two are more trouble than you're worth.' He eyed Louise as if she was an idiot. 'Clean this mess up,' he said, and left.

The two women retreated to the deck to smoke cigarettes in the fresh air.

'What'll we do?'

'Pricks. Charlie's always been like this. Doesn't want to upset his mates, and happy to push me around,' Harriet said. 'What do you want to do? Leave or stay?'

'I don't want anyone bursting into our cabin in the middle of the night.'

Harriet said with more confidence than she felt, 'I'll make sure nothing happens to us.'

Closed-Circuit

Kerry Greer

The only night Tom came to Lena's house, he caught the last bus from the city, walking along an alleyway to reach her cul de sac. He didn't drive, and when Lena had mentioned her address, he had a list of bus times ready on his phone. 'I could get to yours at 8:50 p.m., or 9:36 p.m., depending on which bus I catch,' he'd said.

'Catch the last one, just in case I'm not quite ready,' Lena had replied.

It was June in a city built for heat that cracked the roads, for sun that split the land into fissures – but not for winter, not for wind. From her open window, Lena took in the southern hemisphere at night, the sky wide, blue-black. The city stretching like it knew there was nothing beyond but miles of scrub, and then – the end of the continent, sea, ice, white space. The wind moved along the streets of the city, shaking the doors and windows, checking entry-points. Lena stood at the glass door which led to her small garden – a few kumquat trees, a bougainvillea bush, and her washing line. She could see the fence, and the street beyond, beams of gauzy yellow where the streetlights lit up the dust, between pools of deep-grey night. A storm was blowing in off the coast, picking up sand and scattering it far across the city. Earlier, it had been warm enough to wear shorts on a winter's day. Lena had felt the stillness in the air, as if the sky held its breath. Now the wind was taking her apart just like the trees in the garden – quickly, carelessly. Anxiety swirled somewhere high above her, disconnected from its source.

Lena watched the street for Tom's arrival. It was 9:30 p.m. She turned out the electric lights and left the blinds open, then leaned back against the couch. At 9:33 p.m., Lena saw him: a smooth shape darker than the surrounding night, moving along the path towards her front door. She bit her lip, held her breath as he passed the fence. Then she could hear his footsteps.

Lena let Tom knock before she walked to the door and opened it. His face was as pale as the dust blowing along the street. He had his hood up, and when he moved to kiss her, the wind came into the house with him. 'I need to use your bathroom. Sorry,' he said, letting her go.

He was in there with the water running for almost ten minutes. Lena waited for him at the other end of the hallway, listening. Once she heard him turn off the tap, she moved closer to the bathroom door. She met him in the hallway when he opened the door. Tom's shirtsleeves were damp. The skin of his hands and forearms was red. He pulled the bathroom door closed behind him, trapping in steam and the fragrance of Lena's cherry blossom soap. She didn't ask him what he had been doing. He was here in her house, on the wrong side of the locked front door.

Tom stepped forward as if he might want to kiss Lena, to break the tension between them. 'I've made tea,' Lena said, moving back, unwilling to let him mask his embarrassment with any part of her body. She returned down the hallway towards the living room. The room was lit by citrus candles and a lamp with a wicker shade, so that Lena felt she was walking through orange air.

Tom was carrying a large backpack that looked like it came from an army surplus store. He brought the backpack into the living room and pulled an old thumb-drive out of a pocket. 'I have some music and movies on here. The only problem is – I need to ask you something. I think I'll need to stay the night. I don't have enough money for a taxi home. I get paid tomorrow, but I'm stuck until then.'

Lena's expression was blank. She looked at Tom's backpack. 'I guess that will be okay,' she said, turning towards the kitchen counter. She could feel Tom behind her in the room and, when she turned back, it was as if the room had contracted around him, so that he was everywhere, setting up his laptop, asking for her Wi-Fi password, closing the blinds. There was nowhere she could go.

Outside, the wind lifted the leaves of the bougainvillea bush. Lena could almost hear the fuchsia blossoms falling across the pavement, if she was very still.

Lena met Tom on a dating app. She made the mistake of talking to him on the phone for weeks before they met in person. They believed they had a real connection. Tom would hint at his feelings: 'I dreamed of a woman like you. She was blonde and fair. I'd taken DMT. I don't usually go for blonde women, but I think I was looking for you. If I tell you I have strong feelings, I mean they are as strong as they can get.' Then he would go silent, and Lena would wonder if he meant he had an erection, or if he was talking about love. Her hair was no longer blonde – it had only been blonde for a few weeks, during which time she took a lot of photos – but it was flattering to think he had prophesied their relationship.

The first time they met in person was at an Irish bar next to a hotel in the city centre. Above the entrance to the bar, the name 'McLaverty's' was displayed in curling gold letters, lit up night and day by a strip of flashing lightbulbs. There was a plastic shamrock above the sign, the paint peeling off in long, green strips. Tom was seated at the bar when Lena arrived, his hand sliding a glass of water backwards and forwards. He stood to greet her, and she realised she was taller than him, that he'd lied about his height. Tom's photos on the dating app had all been black-and-white selfies, taken from slightly below his face, accentuating the sharp line of his chin. In the background of the photos, an electric guitar leaned against a wall, and a T-shirt hung from a hanger on a hook in the centre of the frame.

At first, Lena thought his photos were artistic, stylised. She sent screenshots to her best friend, and, when the friend responded favourably, to her mother. Now, standing before Tom, she felt there had been a deception. Something was off, though she couldn't pinpoint it. The person she'd imagined on the other side of their nightly phone calls was confident and commanding. He played bass guitar and had creative goals that correlated to his aesthetic sensibility. Of course all his photos were black-and-white. Of course he was busy in the daytime because he volunteered at a community radio station. But here in the same room at last, Tom couldn't hold her gaze for long. He was pale, as if he'd been indoors for months or years. Even his voice was not the same. Perhaps it was just nerves. They were both nervous.

Lena ordered a drink, then Tom led the way to a table outside, near the wall that adjoined the hotel. Over the wall, kids could be heard screaming as they dive-bombed into the swimming pool, the sound of water sloshing onto concrete. The smell of chlorine mingled with the yeasty odour of beer and sweat-stained collars, relics of some past that couldn't be washed away. Everything felt damp, especially the air.

Lena studied Tom, trying to match his appearance with the image in her head. He had a faint scar which ran down his cheek under his right eye. The scar ended above his lip, but there was another scar across his collarbone peaking out the open collar of this shirt. Later she would find that the scar continued across his right shoulder, angling towards his bicep and down his arm, so that it seemed he had been stitched together. For Lena, the scar was the most striking anomaly in Tom's appearance – not because it was there, but because it was absent from any of his profile photos.

When Lena went to the bathroom, the image of the real Tom immediately floated away, as if it wasn't attached to him. Instead, she remembered the Tom from the photos. She returned to the table to sit in front of him, and he grabbed both of her hands, leaning towards her in a posture of earnestness that allowed him to keep her close.

'You're skittish like a horse that wants to bolt,' he said.

Lena felt dizzy. In her mind, she'd fallen into the gap between the two images of Tom – the imagined and the real. 'Oh, great,' she said. 'I'm coming off like a horse on the first date.' But he didn't laugh or realise the blunder in his comment.

A strange look crossed his face. Then his eyes studied her lips, and he leaned closer.

Lena didn't know how anyone could kiss with passion on first dates. She had seen it happen between people who were drunk. But to be cupping another person's cheeks, stroking their ears, the nape of their neck, taking their tongue into your mouth – as if in love so suddenly, and not at all drunk? She froze inside, forgot how to move her hands like a normal person, wanted to hold them close to her body. Anyone watching from far away would see she was uncomfortable. This telescoping sense of herself made her try to relax, to move in the ways other people did with ease. But she felt like a puppet, jerky and unreal.

Tom's neck smelt like sour milk as he kissed her. She let it happen. She held her breath, and parted her lips, trying not to think. When Tom pulled away, he said, 'You're a good kisser.' He put his hand to her chin. 'You're like a doll. Your face, your little mouth. Even the way you move.' She felt he was trying to re-write what had just occurred between them – an awful and forced proximity, that might become less artificial through repeated contact.

Lena wanted to leave the bar and go home, but she let Tom kiss her again, and she continued to pretend everything was fine. To be out in the night air after long years alone, lonely – she might be anybody, listening to the background noise of the city streets, people passing by, music drifting from the bar, as she was kissed.

If they only talked on the phone, Lena could persist in believing they were falling in love. Tom's voice had a hypnotic effect on her, dulling her senses to the outside world, and calling her towards some shared sense of destiny. His voice was deep, commanding. She'd do anything he asked – over the phone.

What did they talk about, all those hours alone together, in separate rooms? Sometimes Lena wasn't sure. Tom seemed to know her in a way that few people did after such a short time. There was a familiarity with her manner of thinking, rather than the substance of what she thought about. It cut through the need for small talk or explanation. This short-circuited something in Lena, so that she overlooked other needs, like similar values, or attraction.

'Do you like the cello?' he asked her once, and Lena couldn't breathe.

'Yes, I played the cello. In school. I could still play it,' she replied.

'I found this piece of music that made me think of you.' Tom texted her a link to the Elgar cello concerto, the one which she had loved since childhood. 'I'd love to listen to it with you. Here, I mean. In the same room.'

Every time Lena visited Tom at his apartment, she told herself she'd never return. His place smelt like turmeric and unwashed clothes. Tom said the previous tenants had spilled oil in the pantry and covered the evidence with laminate sheets. He kept his bedroom like a kingdom of all his possessions, which were displayed in an incongruous mix on his bedside table: an ouroboros pin, an antique anthology of Celtic fairy tales, a postcard featuring a lotus flower, a collection of foreign coins, a bent toy soldier, a set of keys with a PO Box number written on the key ring. The most expensive thing in his apartment was his record player, which he put together himself. He'd taken a short course in electronics not so long ago. 'I need to know all about audio and video recordings for my music,' he had said.

Their relationship might have continued for years over the phone. Lena liked the part where she dialled Tom's number each night, after the whole long day was over. Tom would pause for a moment when he answered the call. Then he'd say, 'Ah, it's you,' as if she was a pleasant surprise. It could have been a long-distance relationship from the same city, if things had continued this way, in the innocence of half-light, a sort of true love expressed only in voice and mind.

But Tom always wanted to arrange to meet Lena. In person, he would put pressure on her to follow through on the actions they'd discussed the previous nights. He was like all men in his needs, shattering the façade of a future, a thing of glass built in the altitude of Lena's optimism. Before they had sex the first time, he cleaned himself meticulously, then he supervised as Lena showered. He dried her off with a dark red towel that left fluff across her stomach and legs. He kissed her like she was one of the treasures from his bedside table. Neither of them talked. Lena studied the walls and cornices, the flat span of the ceiling. She moved around the intensity of Tom's gaze. He wanted her to make eye contact. She could feel that every time he looked at her. But it seemed impossible for her to do this. Eventually, she closed her eyes. She let him touch her everywhere. He said, 'Can I put my hand on your neck,' and she nodded. Lena's voice was floating far from her, a mist across the ceiling. Maybe this was how it had to happen – it always going to be awkward, the first time together, but perhaps only one person was ever aware of that, and the other kept on pushing, pushing.

When Tom guided her to the bedroom, she felt very far from her body. Only as they were having sex did she become aware of what she was doing. She wanted to leave, to have her body back. Tom was rough in a way that scared her. His apartment was on the second floor of a narrow high-rise near the city. Lena could hear a baby crying through the wall of his bedroom. As Tom re-positioned her, Lena pictured herself driving home alone, stopping her car at a traffic light on the ramp to the freeway, pulling out three tabs of gum to mask the taste of Tom's tongue. Hooked around this image, she managed to pretend she was alright. Then it was happening – she was in her car driving away, arriving home and showering again, using her own towel on her own body, talking to Tom on the phone before she went to sleep, saying, 'Yes, I had a good time. No, I'm not free this weekend, but maybe on a weekday.' She fell asleep talking to him like things were the way they'd always been – he was far away but available and she could see him anytime she wanted.

The day Lena decided to end things with Tom, she had been waiting to see her doctor. She needed to get a prescription for the Pill. In the background of the clinic, there was an old television – the sort that looked like a death-trap, positioned as it was above the magazines and toys. An anti-smoking commercial was playing on the television, and Lena watched it, to avoid the eyes of the other patients in the clinic. The actor in the commercial had skin the shade of paper left in the sun for days. His jaw was narrow, his teeth stained, and he exuded the opposite of vigour or good health. Immediately, Lena thought of Tom, of how he'd taken those black-and-white photos from below, and staged a version of himself that never measured up. But it was impossible for Lena to point a finger and say he'd done this deliberately, without making herself appear superficial. She'd been lied to, and she'd never be able to call attention to it without reflecting criticism onto herself.

The ad came on again during the next commercial break. The more Lena watched the crepe-paper face of the actor, the more annoyed she became with Tom. There were large gaps in his past that didn't add up. Lena's mother asked where Tom worked, and Lena said he volunteered at a community radio station. 'So, he's on the dole,' her mother had replied, without any hint of a question. 'Do you know where he was before you met? Can you find anything concrete?'

When the ad came on a third time, Lena began to feel unwell. The camera zoomed in on a tumour buried hypothetically in the actor's body, pulsating with blood and, it seemed, the death impulse. Lena typed Tom's name into a search engine and tried to find some trace of him. She searched using his email address, his home address, nicknames she had heard him mention. But there was nothing she could identify as relating to him. No social media accounts, no news articles, no court records. As far as she could tell, Tom didn't exist on the internet. Someone without a past – there were only a certain number of explanations.

Lena had walked up to the receptionist then. 'I'm so sorry. I have to go. I'll need to cancel my appointment. Can you apologise to Dr. Sharma for me? I'll still pay. I'm so sorry.'

Back inside her car, she started typing a text message to Tom, but there was nothing she could write that might stop him from trying to find her. She typed her own name and address into the search engine and scrolled down.

Lena started the car and headed home. She watched the rear-view mirror and the road. It would be possible to change her phone number, to leave that part behind. Tom told her once he kept an encrypted file on his computer with every photo she had ever sent him. He said, 'You don't need to worry. Nobody will ever see my photos of you.' She hadn't sent any photos she'd be embarrassed about, and she wasn't worried about him showing photos of her to friends. It was possible he'd found other photos of her, somewhere. Tom's past stretched behind him like an inaccessible shoreline. He knew how to encrypt files, but he said he'd never used social media.

At home, Lena made chamomile tea. The flower buds leaked out of the strainer into the water, and she watched them form a flocculent mass. She tipped the tea down the sink. It was late afternoon and the sky outside had gathered all the light of the day. Everything was orange; everything was golden. And above it all: a ceiling of cloud, broken only by the setting sun. The wind was picking up. Lena dialled Tom's number. He answered quickly, as if he was holding his phone.

'Hello, you,' he said. 'You're calling me early for once.'

'Hey. Yeah.' His voice made her feel heavy. She had the sensation of leaving something behind, in order to move forward. 'I was just thinking about you.'

'Funny that. I was thinking about you too. Did you see the H.G. Wells story I emailed you?'

'Not yet. I'll read it tonight.'

'Is something up? You sound very far away.' She could tell he had an eyebrow raised, and his mouth turned down, as if he was actually saying, *Come now. Sit here on my lap; tell me all about it.*

'Aren't I always far away?' Lena tried to laugh. 'But no, it's not that. Or it is that. I keep thinking – this isn't what I wanted – to be so separate all the time. Maybe there's a reason for that. For us being apart after months—' She stopped, letting the last thought hang in the air between them.

'But it's you who insists on this. I've wanted to be together a lot more. It seems like every time we see each other, you go cold, and then it takes weeks for me to bring you back around.'

Lena was silent. She wanted to say, *I'm not attracted to you. You're not attractive to me, Tom.* But she wasn't sure how to say a thing like that to anyone, let alone Tom. She thought she might say it if backed against a wall, if he wouldn't listen to other reasons. Maybe then. Maybe face-to-face.

'Can I come round? Please?' Tom asked, like he could hear precisely half of her thoughts. 'This is silly. You know we have something different. Please, Lena? I love you. I'm not going to leave you. Don't do this. Not over the phone.'

'Okay,' Lena said. 'Okay. Yes. Come over.' Lena gave Tom her address, and as she spoke, she wrote his address on a pink legal pad, then circled it several times.

Lena lit candles and turned off the overhead lights. She put on shorts and a singlet. The rain hadn't started yet, and the air in the house clung to her. She moved from room to room. She studied her face in the bathroom mirror for a long time. She watched the street outside her window: the clouds moved quickly east into the night. Then Tom knocked. Lena opened the door to him. He wore a black sweatshirt with the hood pulled up. He carried a backpack over one shoulder. Lena noticed how it weighed against his body as he moved.

'Hello, you,' Tom said again, holding Lena for a moment. It was good she couldn't see his face in the half-light coming from the living room. She liked him when he held her – when he was just a body, pressing into her. 'I need to use your bathroom for a minute. Sorry,' he said, letting her go. He walked into the bathroom, backpack still over his shoulder, shutting her out in the dark.

She walked down the hallway and listened to him in her bathroom. There was nowhere to for her go.

A View of the Gully

Michelle Jäger

I was reading a story when Mum told us the news. I was staring at a word I'd never seen in print before – tenterhooks – and I was struck by how wrong it looked there on the page. I had always thought it was 'tenderhooks', so I was convinced it was a mistake. I didn't know what a tenterhook was. I didn't know what a tenderhook was either, but tenterhooks seemed meaningless. It's not a word. *Tenderhooks*, I thought, *now that makes sense*. Hooks piercing tender flesh – that's how a person might feel when they were anxious.

I sat there, thinking about this. Trying to make sense of it. Mum was saying: 'Grandpa is dead.'

Every day, Grandpa takes a walk along the gully behind his house. On Tuesdays and Thursdays, I walk with him because these are the days he picks me up from school. Me, running ahead and then back, taking his hand to tell him about something I've found or seen – a feather or beetle or strange lizard – him, puffing and wheezing.

Mum says it's because he smokes too much: 'Filthy habit. It'll be the death of him.'

But Dad says Grandpa is as strong as a bull: 'He'll outlive us all.' Dad never smiles when he says this. But I do. I imagine Grandpa as a bull sitting on Dad's grave, eating the flowers. If I had to leave flowers on a grave, I'd leave daffodils because they are my favourite, yellow and happy.

I agree with Dad though. When I hold Grandpa's hand, his grip is firm and strong. I feel callouses from gardening, and scars that are much older. It's very rocky along the gully. When I was small, I would sometimes slip on a loose stone, but Grandpa would pull me up, so I never touched the ground. Grandpa made me fly instead of fall.

I know I'm safe with Grandpa.

Grandpa's body was found in the gully. A woman walking her dog found him.

I thought about asking Mum if she could get me some daffodils to put on Grandpa's grave when they buried him, but Mum was crying. Aunt Shonee was there with my cousins Anessa and Alex. We were at Grandpa's house sitting around the kitchen table.

Anessa and Alex are identical twins. They're five years old. I like to look at them and spot the difference – like those puzzles you find in kids' books. But their differences are less obvious. Anessa's nose is slightly more upturned than Alex's, her face a little longer. Alex's eyes are a bit smaller, a bit closer together.

Aunt Shonee told Mum that Uncle Wilf called and would be over soon. Anessa and Alex watched Mum.

Alex looked at me and said, 'Auntie's sad.'

'Grandpa's dead,' I said. Their eyes widened; they looked like big moons in their little faces.

'Guess what?' said Anessa.

'What?'

'Our dad's dead, too.'

Aunt Shonee squealed, 'Nessie, that's a terrible thing to say.'

'For real,' said Anessa, not caring. 'We ate him.'

I laughed and Aunt Shonee looked cross. But I saw Mum trying not to smile. I liked this. Mum was one of us. Aunt Shonee wasn't.

Aunt Shonee asked where Dad was.

Mum waved a hand. 'He's at home, making dinner.'

Aunt Shonee scowled. 'Surely being here's more important?'

Mum shrugged and wiped her nose with her hand. If I did that, she'd tell me off. She'd tell me to use a tissue. I don't say anything, but I try to remember it for later.

Anessa and Alex were using tea-towels for capes. They were running around the table chasing zombies, karate-kicking and chopping the air.

Aunt Shonee told them to be quiet.

'We can't! We're the Loud Girls,' Anessa told her. They roared and ran away.

Mum pulled me to her and asked, 'Are you okay?'

She smelled like perfume and garlic. I saw snot on her cheek where she'd wiped her hand. Bright green, it glistened. I pulled away.

I said, 'You've got snot on your face.'

Mum didn't say anything. Her mouth got very tight and straight so that her lips disappeared. But Aunt Shonee said something. Aunt

Shonee said, 'What's *wrong* with you, Anya?' She said 'wrong' and shook her head in a way that made me angry. I bunched my fists and stood very still not looking at anyone.

My hands are like Grandpa's. I have short stubby fingers and bitten nails. I have hard callouses on my palms from playing on the monkey bars.

We compare hands, putting them side-by-side to inspect them.

'You have good, strong hands like me,' he says, patting my cheek with his rough palm.

Grandpa likes to laugh at Dad's hands.

He says, 'Pretty hands. You don't know what hard work is.'

Dad goes very red when he says this.

Mum says, 'He's hardly going to get beat up old hands like yours doing tax returns, is he, Dad?'

Grandpa laughs and says, '*Faultier.*'

Dad mutters, 'Nazi.'

Mum said, 'Come with me to Grandpa's room.'

On the mantelpiece, Grandpa had a bust of Winston Churchill. Churchill was his hero.

Mum said, 'When you were little and we stayed with Grandpa for a while, you used to tell me you heard Winston Churchill bouncing down the hall at night.'

'I remember,' I said, smiling at her.

I didn't remember. I just remembered her telling the story. She'd told me many times. I liked when she remembered things that I did when I was little, too little to remember myself. It made me feel important. Special. She remembered the things I did and made them into stories.

'You loved staying over at Grandpa's. He'd get those variety packs of cereals just for you.'

'I remember,' I said, and this time I did. 'The Frosties were my favourite.'

'That's right.'

Grandpa would eat them, too. We'd sit together eating our cereal and he'd give me a small sip of his coffee. Dark and bitter, I hated it, but I accepted a taste every time.

Coffee. That smell was the smell of Grandpa.

'Can I have Winston?' I asked.

'We'll see,' said Mum. Her face looked hollow, like there were little bits missing. Bits that you'd only notice were gone if you really looked, if you really knew her.

Looking at Mum, I thought, Looking at Mum, I wondered who would tell me stories about myself when she was gone.

Grandpa's house is very neat and clean. Grandpa always tells me that there's a difference between neat and clean.

'Neat means things are orderly, in their proper place. But they might not be clean. I like my home to be both,' he smiles. 'I'm a good little *hausfrau*.'

I try to be like Grandpa, but sometimes I find that my things have escaped from their proper places. Or there's a mouldy bowl or cup under my bed.

Grandpa just laughs when he sees my room: 'It's because you are a creative one. Too many ideas and thoughts going on for cleaning or tidying.'

Dad thinks Grandpa's house is too big for him: 'What does one old man need all those rooms for?'

I hear Dad say that Grandpa should be in an old folks' home. That he should let us have the house because we can't afford to buy. I don't like when he says these things. The house would be all wrong without Grandpa. It would be an empty place.

'It's the right thing to do,' says Dad. 'We could get ahead.'

And then Mum and Dad fight.

When we went back to the kitchen, Uncle Wilf was there. His face was long and grey. His eyes were red. He looked like Mum.

Anessa and Alex jumped up and down and grabbed his legs. 'Daddy! Daddy!' He smiled and patted them on their heads.

'Liars,' I said, grinning. 'Your dad's not dead.'

'That's because we pooed him out,' Anessa said, and they wiggled their bums about, squealing with laughter, before running into the lounge room to be lions.

Uncle Wilf gave Mum a hug.

'Did you see him?'

He nodded.

'What did they say?'

Aunt Shonee said, 'Anya, maybe you should go to your room.'

'Why?' I said, not wanting to leave.

'Just do as I ask.'

'Mum—'

Mum held up her hand and said, 'Please, Anya.'

I felt bad about saying she had snot on her face, so I did as I was told. But I didn't go to my room. I stood just a little way outside the door and listened.

I heard Uncle Wilf say, 'They think he slipped and hit his head. They think it was instant.' I heard Mum sob.

Grandpa likes the gully because he thinks it's quiet and peaceful: 'It helps me to clear my head.'

I don't think it's all that quiet. I think it's noisy, but a good kind of noisy. You can hear birds and the wind in the leaves. It's funny how the wind can sound just like the sea, like there is water rushing through the leaves, not air.

But today, walking along, we hear a horrible grunting, snorting sound. I stop dead-still and won't go any further.

Grandpa says, 'C'mon, Anya.'

'Pick me up, Grandpa. Pick me up.'

Even though I'm eight and too old to be such a scaredy cat, I try to climb him like a tree. I'm sure it's a beast from one of the books Grandpa reads to me. The Minotaur come all the way from Knossos, or Gmork from Fantasia.

Instead of picking me up, Grandpa squats down, puts his arm round me and points to the top of a tree.

'There,' he says. 'What do you see?'

I squint hard into the leaves and branches. 'A koala,' I gasp. 'I thought it was Gmork.'

Grandpa laughs, and this makes me laugh. The koala growls.

'What are you doing skulking in the hall?'

Dad stood there staring at me. I could see he was in one of his moods. He looked at me as if I wasn't a person, but something horrible. Like a booger. 'Why are you snooping?'

I looked back at him but couldn't speak. I was trembling.

'Why are you *always* snooping?'

I ran out of the house.

'What are you doing down there?'

Dad looks down at me. Dad's face carved up by light and shadow.

I'm supposed to be in bed.

The lounge room is light, the hallway where I'm crouched down, dark. I see Grandpa behind Dad, sitting on the couch, head in his hands.

Mum's out because it's Wednesday evening. On Wednesdays she runs a group called 'The Circle of Security'. Her special group. I like the sound of it, it sounds magical. But I cannot go. It's for adults, not children. Mum tells me it's to help adults be better parents.

I wish I was there now.

Instead, I've been sitting in the hall listening to Grandpa and Dad argue. It's not my fault. I heard Grandpa arrive and wanted to say hello, but when I got to the door, I couldn't open it; their voices were too angry. Grandpa's never angry.

'Why are you asking Grandpa for money?' I ask.

Dad doesn't answer. He pulls me up and drags me to bed.

I lie there in the dark, cross and sad. I didn't get to speak to Grandpa. Staring into the darkness, I hear their voices – low, muffled. A door slams. Grandpa leaves. I close my eyes.

Drifting off to sleep, I hear someone crying. It can't be Dad. Dad doesn't cry.

I ran along the gully until I couldn't hear any people sounds. I sat on a rock, picking up stones, feeling their hard edges. Some sharp, some blunt. The ground around me was covered in mossy stuff, but it was cracked and dry. There were lots of ants moving about. The air felt still and heavy. The ants might've been busy because it was going to rain.

I thought about how Grandpa and I would hunt for hitting rocks.

'A good hitting rock must have some weight and edge to it. But you also want it to fit neatly in your hand.'

We would make a collection and then each pick a favourite.

'Who are you going to hit with your rock, Grandpa?'

'Ernst.'

'Who's Ernst, Grandpa?'

'A boy who used to tease me for being poor.'

Grandpa mostly chose people from when he was a little boy. He said those hurts still stung like fresh wounds. I liked the way he said that. As if he were an old warrior remembering past battles.

'Who are you going to hit, Anya?'

And I'd say, 'Evette' or 'Matthew' or whoever was upsetting me at school.

Matthew said I was weird. Evette would say I'm a starer. 'Why do you always stare at me like that?' she'd ask. 'You're a real stare bear.

A creepy stare-bear.' But I wasn't staring at her. I was thinking and she just happened to get in the way.

Sometimes, though, I'd say, 'Dad.' And Grandpa would laugh.

Grandpa tells me that when he was a little boy, he and his brothers would go hunting for treasures in the remains of bombed houses. Just like us, sifting through for-hitting rocks.

'We thought it was a magical playground made for us.'

I ask him what the war was like. I want him to tell me about it, make it like one of the stories we read, but he doesn't. All he says is, 'I was a little boy. Littler than you. I had to go to a school where they told you Hitler was good. A great man. Imagine that? But I remember everyone was fearful. Fearful of the enemy. Fearful of each other.'

He goes quiet for a while.

'You'll never guess what we had to eat,' he says.

'Fish guts on stale, old bread!'

He claps his hand to his forehead and laughs. 'How'd you guess!'

'Because you've told me a million times!'

We stand on the edge of the gully, holding hands, looking out over the trees. The sun is low and the light golden. It's very steep and, at the bottom of the gully, it's very dark.

I sat at the bottom of the gully. Here you couldn't see any houses or fences. Here was the middle of nowhere even though it's somewhere in the suburbs. You could do something bad or silly and no one would know. No one would see.

I thought about how many years Grandpa was alive without someone who knew him when he was little. Without someone to tell him stories about himself. Now that he'd gone, I had one less person to tell me stories about myself.

Grandpa's favourite stories to tell of me were about my tantrums. He told me that one day I didn't want to leave the park, so I threw myself on the ground and began to bellow. People from the houses around came out just to see what the noise was. When he strapped me in my pram, I freed my arms and stood bolt upright and bellowed all the way home.

'That shows a strong will. You were small but determined.'

I especially liked these types of stories. Stories of me being loud and determined. I was quieter now.

Dad said I was a little shit when I was small. Dad did not tell good stories.

Though it was still light, I saw that the sky was turning a darker blue. I wished I'd known Grandpa when he was little.

When I got back to Grandpa's, Dad was sitting on the couch watching TV.

'Where've you been?'

'Down at the gully.'

'I don't want you going down there anymore – not by yourself.'

His face was very white. I could almost see through him. I wanted to say that I'm eleven now and don't need his help, but instead I said, 'Where's Mum?'

'Mum's gone home; she's gone to bed.'

'Oh.'

'She's very upset.'

'Yes.'

'What about you? How're you doing?' His tone was a bit softer, his face less white.

'I'm sad.'

He patted the seat next to him, but I didn't move. I felt stuck. And I realised that what I'd said was a true thing. Sad. I saw the word clearly in my mind and tasted it on my tongue, salty as tears. I wanted to cry, and this was why I felt stuck. I knew I would cry but not now. Not in front of Dad.

Instead, I turned away from him, went to the bookshelf and took out the dictionary.

'Tenterhook,' I said. 'A hook used to fasten cloth on a drying frame or tenter.' I frowned. 'I don't get it. What's that got to do with being anxious?'

Dad held out his hand, I gave him the dictionary.

'Tenter,' he read. 'A framework on which fabric can be held taut for drying or other treatment during manufacture.'

'Oh,' I said, sitting next to him.

'Like you're pulled tight, pulled in different directions, waiting for something to tear. To break.'

'Yes,' I nodded.

Dad took my hand. I ran my fingers over his palm like I used to do with Grandpa; he flinched.

'What did you do?' I asked.

'Nothing, I just had an accident cooking.'

There was a red welt, nearly a cut but not quite. It would scar.

'What did you make?' I asked.

'Goulash.'

'Is that why you were late?'

'Yes.'

Dad looked away as he said this, and I wondered if he felt sad too. Goulash was Grandpa's favourite. I thought that was nice of Dad.

'My favourite,' I said, which wasn't true, and Dad gave me a squeeze.

I smiled, holding Dad's hand, looking at the wound. Because I couldn't help but think it was a bit funny that this should happen after Grandpa's gone, that Dad waited until now to show that he was a little like us, when Grandpa couldn't see.

Hanging: The Young Man and the Sea

Dean Kerrison

Kale always sat alone on the rocks at the bay, just hanging.

I'd see him further down the beach when I was with friends or on my own. Kale and I would wave or nod, then dive in the water – full or low, royal blue or turquoise, or brown from farm runoff. Across the bay, fishermen with reverent patience for forces out of their command would surrender to the fate of the ocean.

Years earlier, I saw him at big high school house parties. No salutations between us in a sea of those we knew. He'd smile in groups, hanging around, his face warm, a flame torch in a cave. Chatting up girls with his practised grin, like the rippled waves in the bay, he'd lean in and away to pique their interest. They'd shuffle together in front of the DJ and skip off hand-in-hand to his car in no time.

A few days ago, I thought I saw him driving out. No waving or eye contact, just heading down to where snorkellers kick their fins amongst the marine life and fishermen trust the process.

Kale's housemate came home to echoes. Creaking.

Anyone home?' She called, entering Kale's room to find the kitchen stool, sideways on the floor. Bare, hairy feet. She blinked, convinced for a second she was dreaming.

I attend the funeral at church. Open casket but I don't want to see. I keep the distance we've always had. The full spectrum of humanity is on display. People whelping like sick dogs. Screaming as if someone's thrown acid in their eyes. Rubbing backs and holding onto each other close, as though all love is equal. Being dead can't be too hard. Only for those hanging on, scarred from the Angel of Death but refusing to surrender. Why *can't* someone just prematurely submit? Why even prolong living? Kale might say we're just insignificant mammals floating around the universe, stopgaps between the dinosaurs and the robots, a freckle on the face of time, hearts beating for a few cycles around the sun and returning to the earth, replaced by fresh life springing from the soil. No reason to be sad for Kale. He's making room for the new. His flight from the Angel over. Lungs relaxed. Itch relieved. I'm sure he's jumped out of his skin, drifting past us down the aisle, wafting in the clouds that deliver him to the bay. Breathing underwater through his gills, hanging with his kind, having the last laugh with the fishermen.

Really, Truly Fiction: A Ghost Story

Laura Fulton

Listen. My house is haunted. I know because my son has talked to the ghost.

I realise this is a strange confession to make, you know, this late in human evolution. Farfetched. Not the sort of thing people go around confessing in public. It's the kind of confession a sane and savvy person might only make in a work of fiction. A thinking person could never say something so ridiculous in a memoir and expect to be allowed to continue to drive.

Even in a work of creative nonfiction, this sort of nonsense is likely to raise eyebrows. 'Is this author being serious?' the reader might wonder. A reader is apt to see words like 'haunted' and 'ghost' in a work of not-fiction and question, 'Is this piece of writing true? How much is true? Which parts, specifically?' But, of course, *you* don't need to concern *your*self on *my* behalf, Reader. This story is *fiction*. Really. Truly.

Because it can't be true, in the factual sense, an outlandish confession like 'my house is haunted'. Not now, in this modern world of stem cell research and spinal reconstruction surgery and virtual reality and 5G. How could something as archaic as believing in haunted houses coexist in the face of such progress?

I don't know.

Except.

There are over two million moving parts in a human eyeball, in a space only two centimetres wide, all working together to make sight – incredibly – happen, almost effortlessly. There are forty-two bones in each of my hands, another forty-two joints, plus thirty-four muscles and hundreds of ligaments, tendons, blood vessels and nerves, all synchronising – remarkably – to get these words out of my head and onto this page. Even now, no one is entirely certain why we dream, although there is evidence to suggest that we learn – amazingly – to cope with stress, handle our moods and even consolidate our daily memories while we sleep. And while all of these highly complex and elegant processes are, probably, the result of several millennia of evolution, the fact that my eyes can see and my hands can write words that my mind has imagined and my psyche can dream is, if you think about it, kind of like magic, kind of extraordinary and awe-inspiring compared to something as insignificant and inconsequential as a house that is haunted.

I'm not delusional. According to one legal dictionary, a person is 'insane' when they cannot distinguish fantasy from reality, or conduct their affairs due to psychosis, or control impulsive behaviour. By this definition, I believe I am sane. I'm an educated, homeowning, employed taxpayer. I enjoy several healthy, stable relationships. I demonstrate self-control and reasonable levels of ambition. I am not addicted to anything but stationery and making lists.

I almost never rave.

I am a creative person, sometimes even a victim of my own imagination. I have, in the past, felt undue anxiety, envisioning an abundance of possible (but improbable) outcomes that may derail me. I am often late for appointments, irrationally believing I have more time than I actually do. I can be hopeful to an unrealistic degree. But I'm not crazy. I just know my house is haunted.

Here's how I know.

First.

When we moved into our house ten years ago, it had been sitting empty for a few months. The previous owners were eager to move to the coast, so they left before they had a buyer. I doubt they ever noticed the ghost. My own family and I were living in a rental house down the street. We had just arrived in Australia from overseas and much of what we owned remained packed in shipping boxes. When we closed on the new house, we were still adjusting to this haphazard half-life.

One afternoon, as the kids watched television in our rental house, I went to the empty new house on my own. I was in the back bedroom – moving, unpacking, organising – when I happened to glimpse movement in the corner of my eye, definitely a form. I didn't get some eerie sixth sense that someone was watching me. It was the movement of a shape, a child, I was sure, that caught my attention. When I looked, all I saw was a wisp, a shimmer of a figure.

But he was there. I knew it.

I was so certain that, for a moment, I thought one of my own two boys had walked down the street on his own, which scared me.

They were only four and six years old at the time, too young to go wandering. They should have been parked in front of cartoons in the care of my partner. I ran back down the street, slightly panicked – imagining one of them gone, missing, lost forever – but I found both boys right where I'd left them.

It's important you know that the 'new' house was only new for us. It's been here since the 1970s or 80s, we think, maybe longer. The old man who used to live next door once told me his house was the first one built in our area. For years, he said, for decades, his house stood alone, surrounded by wide open paddocks, empty land waiting to be carved up and sold. He died a couple of years after we moved in.

But people have been here for centuries. People of European descent have lived in this region since the 1800s. Two of the oldest homesteads in Victoria stand within walking distance of my house. And then there are the Wurundjeri people of the Kulin nation who have been the traditional custodians of this land for thousands of years, plus whatever other tribes and wanderers have traversed this place with (and without) their permission. What I mean is, people have been crossing this patch of land since long before my house was built. I have no good reason to think so, but I feel like the boy who haunts this place died a long time ago. A long time. And I think he knew I saw him. I think he wanted me to know that we had seen each other.

Because.

We had only been in the new house a couple of nights when I heard a bang. It was a warm, pleasant evening, the end of summer, and we had left all the windows open. Our metal fuse box is situated on the walkway that leads to the front door of the house, on the wall outside my sons' bedroom window. This night, the boys were playing with their Lego in the back room while I sat up reading alone, my partner not yet home from work. In the quiet of the evening, I heard a metallic clanging sound, as if someone had opened the door of the fuse box and slammed it shut again.

For a moment, I thought it might have been the wind.

Except.

No one had opened the fuse box all day, maybe not since we'd moved in, so the wind could not have blown it shut. I wondered if maybe someone had crept up to our house – past the windows of the playroom, past the windows of the office space, right alongside my sons' open bedroom window, nearly as far as the front door – and whacked on the fuse box, just to scare us, just to be an asshole. But I really don't think so.

Finally. And this is the main reason.

My son has talked to the ghost.

Now, what you need to know about my son is that he's not like other kids. He has always been naturally kind and honest and brave and just. He has always defended those weaker than himself, helped others when they needed it, given of himself. He is the peacemaker among his friends, the fearless warrior who is not afraid to stand up to bullies when they pick on kids who cannot defend themselves. Once, in Grade Six, he went to the principal when a teacher made a joke at his friend's expense. He would not have done it for himself, but his friend was in tears and my son insisted on seeing right done.

That's just the sort of person he is. At nine, he donated the fifty dollars he got for his birthday to the Royal Children's Hospital. At ten, he sold his bike so he would have money to give to homeless people when we went into the city. He has more empathy, more emotional intelligence than anyone I've ever met, adult or child.

He instinctively knows how to heal others, how to fix things between people. What I'm saying is that my son is special. I think he might have been chosen from the heavenly host before he was born and sent to me to teach me everything I never knew about being a good and strong person. I think he might be an angel, or something like it.

Which, again, is the sort of bizarre admission a person can only make in a work of fiction. If I were to call this story 'memoir', you would wonder about my mental state. If I were to call this story 'creative nonfiction', you might be tempted to pick it apart, wondering which parts really happened and which I have invented. You could be willing to believe the details about the bullies and the teacher and the birthday money and the bike (all true, by the way), but this nonsense about angels and ghosts? The person writing this story must surely be incapable of distinguishing fantasy from reality. And who would publish the ravings of a lunatic? No one. That's who.

Unless the author doth protest too much? Would an author lie about the genre of their story, just to cast doubt in the mind of the reader? Seems a bit cruel, doesn't it? Dishonest.

Only.

No one expects a fiction story to be true. That's what makes it fiction.

For the record, there are hundreds of stories about what seems to be evidence of things unseen: children who recognise people they have never met and places they have never been, toddlers in their beds who appear to be conversing with people who are not there, animals who find their way home across hundreds of miles of terrain against impossibly improbable odds. Are none of the people who tell these stories able to distinguish fantasy from reality? Or are they simply reporting what they have seen with their own eyes and heard with their own ears (sometimes captured on film or video)? A person who believes in things like ghosts and angels and eyeballs and dreams could see where I'm going with this piece. A person who doesn't ... well, it's just a story. A *fiction* story.

So. Maybe some or none or all of this story is true or not true or some version of true. Believe whatever makes you feel good. All I know is that my son talked to the ghost who lives in my house.

More than once.

To be honest, it's been a while since it last happened, almost ten years. I think the ghostly boy has regressed or gone into remission or fallen asleep in that space between the floorboards and the earth, or else he's floating in the rafters of our vaulted ceiling, watching the chaos, listening to the daily cacophony of a modern Australian family: the PlayStation, the dishwasher, the washing machine, the shouting. Once upon a time, he came right up close and got to know one of us well.

It began with the screaming. Night terrors, I guess you'd call it. When my son was very little, barely talking, long before we lived in the new house, when we were still living overseas, he would have very vivid dreams. They'd often wake him, send him pattering down the hallway to crawl into my bed under the doona in between me and my partner.

But the screaming was like nothing we'd seen before. Only a few nights in the new house, and I woke from a deep sleep to the sound of his cries. We couldn't fathom how they slept through the noise, both he and his brother in the bunkbed above him. His brother – who was evidently chosen from the heavenly ranks of past heroes, Achilles perhaps, for whom he is distantly named (but that's another story) – his brother, the hero, sleeps like a soldier at the watch, lightly, ready to spring. It seemed quite unusual that both of my two boys could dream on, though my angel son shrieked with the full force of his lungs. It was the way a four-year-old might reasonably scream upon meeting a ghost through the thin veil of sleep. Even at six, his brother is the type who remains calm in the face of danger.

At first, I didn't connect the screaming with the ghost, even though I'd already caught the wisp of a figure in the corner of my eye outside the back bedroom, I'd already heard the inexplicable bang on the fuse box through the open windows.

It was the laughing that convinced me.

I spent a couple of nights running into the boys' room to find them both sleeping soundly while my angel son screamed – like he was falling, like he was terrified – waking him to find he had no memory of the dream. When the screaming stopped for a few days, I wanted to believe that all was well: that my vision was unreliable, that some asshole was just fucking with us, that my son was simply adjusting to what had been, in fairness, an epic move, from one country and culture to another. Every certainty in his young life had been upended, replaced – different weather, different people wearing different clothes. Everything was weird now, for all of us. I understood. More than once, I felt like screaming. Besides, who wants to believe in some sort of outlandish, farfetched reality in which a person's house might actually be haunted? Plenty of people. But not an educated, taxpaying homeowner like me.

Except.

A few days after the screaming stopped, I heard my angel son again. I was up late watching tellie in the lounge room when I heard his voice from his bedroom. I leapt up, determined to rescue him from his nightmares.

But.

When I got to his room, he wasn't screaming. He was laughing. Not a gentle mumble. His was a full, rolling belly laugh. Something was, in fact, hilarious. He was shaking, he laughed so hard. In the bunkbed above him, his brother, the hero, slept through the din.

And then. The laughing turned to talking. I couldn't quite make out what he was saying, but it was obvious he was telling – someone – a story that was so funny he couldn't help the laughter bubbling over into his voice. He could barely speak the words. And in the bunk above him, his brother slept the sleep of a soldier who knows his watch is secure. I couldn't tell you exactly how many times this happened – the laughing out loud, the happy chatter, the talking through the laughing – but it was more than once. Two or three times, at least.

I don't know what's happened to our ghost since then. Eventually, it all stopped – the talking, the laughing, the screaming. For good. In nearly a decade, he's never done any of it again. I wonder if maybe the phantom boy, stuck in some spectral childhood, has turned his attention somewhere else or if he watches over us quietly from the hidden places in our house. Maybe he's finally found a way to rest.

Or maybe I've imagined the entire affair, or I'm unable to distinguish what is real from what is fantasy. But I don't think so. Either way, *you* don't need to worry about it. Because this is just a fiction story.

Drift

Brooke Maddison

On the horizon you see the island: the sharp jag of the headland, the wild scrub of the national park overtaking the eastern flank. As you get closer, you see beaches, too. The coffee-coloured rocks of Back Bay, the shifting sands and drag of the waves. You see the island's secret wet places, lagoons and swamps and springs, mossy ferns and rainforest. Hear the hum of insects down by the lake, ticking like a hidden language.

On the island, a town. Hemmed by bush and rock and ocean. In the summer there is a slow trickle of tourists from the mainland, but for the rest of the year the island is known by few.

On the island, a girl. A woman, who still feels like a girl. A woman-girl: not yet old, no longer young. Her body soft and round, her hair a muted blonde. Alice. She has lived her whole life within the island's borders.

The woman-girl lives in a fibro shack on the far reach of the island. Walk out the kitchen door and you will find a knotted path leading directly to a secluded beach. It is the one place where she feels she belongs, where the limits of her life are wider and uncluttered. She likes to feel the way the sand welcomes her when she slips her sandals off, the way the water makes space for her body when she enters the surf. The ocean gives her the space to ignore the tightness in her chest.

The sun has risen, but Alice wants to stay lying in bed, in the slant of light that streaks across the blanket. The whine of the alarm shakes her from her dreams. Eyelids crack open, sunslant coming into view. The possibility of the day is framed in this moment. Reality has not yet taken over.

The feeling doesn't last. Before long she will be consumed by the day, by the island and the smallness of her life. Pulled from the cocoon of her bed and launched into the daily routine. She measures the passing of the day in the time it takes for the dregs of cereal to solidify and become stuck to the bowl. For company she has the drone of daytime television or the hum of the little portable radio that she keeps in the kitchen. She works at the front bar of the Royal Hotel three nights a week. The same people come in night after night, ordering the same drinks and having the same conversations.

She knows that she has drifted far from who she could be. There is another life that could be hers, if she knew how to let it in.

Away from this – the island and its people, away from the smallness of their lives – there is another woman. Frankie. She is driving towards the island. Radio up, windows down, hair whipping around her neck. She has little baggage, carrying only what she can fit in her van. So much has been abandoned: her job, her people, her nice apartment in the city with its bright lights. She has done this before. Whenever she feels the need to push against the borders of her own life, she packs up and leaves.

She stops at towns and beaches along the coast, sleeping in her van on the edge of national parks or perched high on headlands. In the morning she drinks coffee and watches the whales migrating to warmer waters. She swims in the ocean every day, and the changing temperature of the water as she moves from south to north tells her that she is heading in the right direction. She knows that she has stayed away for too long.

As she drives with the wind against her face, she notices how the light changes. It becomes rich and viscous, like honey. Golden hour. It has always been her favourite time of day, when the light catches the land and moulds it into something new.

Soon the sun will begin to fade. She's looking for a reason to stop, to stand still.

The two women meet at the Royal Hotel. Alice is soft, sensitive. But she has learnt to hide her softness, to mask it with indecision and idleness. But still, it shows on her body, in the roll and vastness of it, like the ocean. And her face, round like the moon.

The other woman, Frankie, is different. Harder. Not just on the outside, but on the inside too. Don't believe that she is cruel or swift or unthinking, she is none of these things. She is spontaneous and free, quick to spend a few days in someone's bed or on the periphery of their life. But it is never more than that. Something always pushes her to leave. It is a different type of guarding when you render your heart into stone.

When they meet, the borders between them shift like a tide on the turn. They both feel it. Little waves that will ripple throughout the rest of their lives.

Out the front of the pub, the faded red lettering of the *Rooms For Rent* sign sways in the breeze. A dog waits quietly for closing time, and the breeze winds its way through the network of streets that crisscross the island. In the rows of dark houses, people sleep, their secrets shut behind closed doors. Beyond the houses there is the bluff of the headland and the brace of the ocean, the deep pull of the unknown.

Alice is working behind the bar. It is not busy – a Tuesday night in August, towards the end of a wet winter. The tourists and seasonal workers have long left the island. As the locals order their drinks and drift over to the television which always plays the same things – the footy, the dogs, the horses – Alice lets the sounds of the pub wash over her.

'Wouldya getta look a' that—'

'Carn, Robbo!'

'If she pulls that shit one more time—'

'Nah, that's fucked, mate!'

A portrait of the queen looks down on them from its position by the door, watching as Frankie walks into the pub. The locals look her up and down, trying to register how she has come to fit within their lives. She doesn't have the kind of body that belongs here. Life on the island is slow, giving people a haziness to their bodies, as if rendered by a polaroid filter. She is hard edged – toned muscular legs under denim cut-offs, cropped hair accentuating the firmness of her face.

One of the men by the television can't help himself. 'You lost, love? Mainland's back that way.' He jerks his head towards the door.

'Shut up, Ray. Leave her alone,' says Alice. She's not putting up with their shit tonight. Her eyes meet Frankie's. Someone brays from the backroom, where the pokies are kept. 'What can I get you?'

'Schooner of Old, thanks.' There's a quick smile – a flash of brilliance. A million-watt glow. She leans forward, her arms resting against the smooth wood of the bar. 'What do people do for fun around here?'

'Depends what your idea of fun is.' Alice pours herself a beer. This is not the kind of pub where people care if the staff are drinking.

A cry goes up; someone has won big on the dogs.

'You ever ride a bike downhill so fast that you saw your life flash before your eyes?' Again, that smile. White teeth with a hint of gum.

'Yeah, I grew up here,' Alice laughs, caught off guard by the question and the steadiness of Frankie's eyes on her. She is used to people looking away. 'There's an old BMX track down by the jetty; I used to ride there when I was kid.'

'Well, I think we are all chasing that rush. All of us,' Frankie indicates the men gathered around the television, the couple who have sidled up to the bar and the smokers out the front, 'are searching for that feeling when the bike bottoms out, and you hit the dirt. When you think you're gonna shit yourself but discover that you can fly. When you think you might die, but somehow you don't.'

Alice's pulse quickens, and her words fall out in a hurry. 'I know what you mean. Sometimes I do dumb things, dangerous things, just to make myself feel something. I like the rush.' Her voice has gone very quiet. She's aware that there is very little space between them. 'I'm Alice.'

'Frankie.' She sips her beer as she watches the cars hoon down the road outside. Closing time. She takes out a rollie.

'You know you can't smoke that in here.'

Frankie ignores her. 'What are you most afraid of?' Her hand inches forward, brushing against the soft flesh of Alice's arm.

Alice imagines what it would be like to find herself in a place with no bearings. Her arm feels warm from Frankie's touch. 'Not being able to feel that rush ever again.'

At closing time, Alice leaves the heated closeness of the pub and the stillness of the night wraps around her. She shakes her head, as if trying to dislodge something from her brain. At home she finds that she can't settle. She calls Luke. A familiar pattern.

He is at a mate's house, and they drop him off twenty minutes later. She hears their screams over the screech of the tyres as they tool off up the road. *Fucken get in there, Wilko.*

She answers the door in her underwear and a t-shirt, no bra.

'Special delivery.' Luke holds a bag of hot chips in one hand and a small baggie of weed in the other.

Alice opens the screen door for him without saying a word.

The chips are good, the weed better. They sit on the floor in her lounge room, backs leaning against the sofa. The radio is playing in the kitchen, and Luke goes in to flick the dial to something more upbeat. Alice stretches back on the floor, the rug bristling against the back of her legs. She knows that she needs more than the smoke haze to take away the heat she had felt when she met Frankie. Being with Luke is something she doesn't have to examine.

She rolls towards him and feels his body go hard against hers. He lifts her t-shirt up, biting at her neck. They remember what to do, fitting together. It is quick. It has been this way between them for a long time. When it is over, Alice rolls away, feeling a flush of hot tears pressing against her eyelids.

The sex is as far as the intimacy extends between them. Luke stands, pulling his shorts back up.

She sits up, crossing her legs in front of her chest.

'It's good to see you, Al. I hope you're doing okay.' And then he is gone, the screen door swinging behind him.

He *knows*, she thinks, *he knows that* something is going on.

She can feel him rushing from her now, and all she feels is a hollowy emptiness that runs down her legs.

The next morning, Alice wanders down to the beach. It is empty, apart from a lone swimmer out past the breakers, who is lifting their arms in wide strokes that slice through the glassy surface of the water. She stands on the shore, watching as a strand of seaweed rolls in the continual rise and fall of the water.

In summer she usually strips off, leaving her clothes in a messy pile that she scoops up on her way back to the shack. She doesn't care if she isn't wearing her swimmers. No one is ever there to see her anyway. And fuck them if they are, she thinks to herself. This is my beach. On days like that she never showers, preferring to leave the lick of the sea on her skin all day. In a way, this is her one bodily rebellion – swimming naked or in her underwear, spending the rest of the day braless, her dark brown nipples showing through her cotton dress.

But she will not go into the water today. This morning it is enough for her to feel the slip of the tide against her ankles, to sink into the sand a little and to imagine, for a moment, that she is not bound by the island's coastline.

The swimmer is coming in, and as they stride through the water, she realises that it is Frankie.

'Hey.' Frankie's voice sounds far away against the crash of the waves. She flicks wet hair away from her face.

'Hi.' Alice can make out the curve of her breasts under her black swimsuit and her eyes sweep downwards before she looks away.

The women fall into step alongside each other, walking towards the scrub where their paths will diverge. They reach the soft sand, and even though it is autumn it holds enough heat to irritate their feet.

'Do you want a coffee? I live just up there.' Alice indicates the cluster of rocks and, beyond them, the path that leads through the scrub. And then, quickly, before she can stop herself, 'I've never done this before.' She's spoken the thing between them into existence, the mess of her hot breath making it real.

Frankie looks past Alice, taking in the track and the overhang of the headland. 'I should go. Maybe tomorrow?'

Alice watches her walk away. Sees the way her neck tapers up from her spine, the ripple of movement that passes down her legs. The little skip that she does as she steps over the last of the warm sand.

Alice is left with the roar of the waves and the squeal of the gulls overhead. The tide is receding, reaching back on itself. Whatever it has concealed will slowly be revealed, altered by the drift and heft of the water.

Coda: His Final Solo

Anita A. Thomas

How Do We Remember?
recollection

is a fractious conversation with oneself

with a disproportionate emphasis on petty details,

denying this, amending that,

veering off course,

stalling at remembered amusements,

buoyed by past elations,

crippled, at times, by a sorrow so engulfing

you find yourself on your knees

We think it's old age … till it isn't.

My father, a retired airline pilot, takes ill with vascular dementia. His physical and cognitive abilities shut down in progressively incremental missteps as the blood vessels in his brain suffer a series of strokes and his mind re-programmes itself capillary by capillary.

The initial symptoms begin slowly, unnoticed, after his retirement, but the end arrives suddenly, with no warning; vindictively unforgiving.

His first fall – he has no recollection how or where – opens up his forehead; blood flows fast and bright. The gash is stitched up by a neighbour's daughter, a medic.

Mum says his flowing *mundu* probably caused the fall. 'Have you noticed he has recently begun shuffling instead of walking?' she asks as she stows his starched and mathematically pressed *lungis* and *dhotis* on a very high shelf, out of reach. I purchase shorts by the dozen.

The hallucinations begin at night, starting slow and small, building up to all-night conversations, almost entirely on flying, between pilots, and with air traffic control. Tangled and jettisoned bedsheets bear witness to take-offs-and-landings-from-the-bed.

Mum, trying to sleep beside him, is almost always awake, tired, stressed, confused, and aggravated; she makes no sense on the phone. We absorb her outbursts of fury, however inconsequential they seem, however detrimental they are to us. Combative and fierce in her complaints, she is much like a snapping turtle with a crumbling carapace. Vulnerable, angry, fragile.

'Impossible to live with,' she mutters. 'I'm seventy-five years old. Trying to cope on my own.' Implicit is the rebuke that we have abandoned her. 'He now accuses me of stealing his money! Won't let me go to the bank. Has locked up the passbooks and chequebooks! Says I'm having an affair with the neighbour downstairs!'

Explosive tantrums, sheering mood shifts and messianic eruptions – together with an arrogant contempt for social protocol – become

Dad's response to the increasingly baffling, confusing minutia of his daily life. Mum becomes his reflexive interface. Explaining the world to him, explaining him to the world.

Religion, naturally, becomes her solace. As Dad implodes, Mum suffocates, but finds strength in prayer. Hour-by-hour, day-by-day, a fierce, desperate, stubborn faith keeps her going.

On a visit, I gift my parents a projection clock; time conveniently displays on the ceiling in a dull, inoffensive digital red.

Dad now takes umbrage with it. Leaping out of bed at 4.00 a.m. one morning, he repeatedly hurls it at the wall, splintering it, dismembering it as Mum cowers under the sheets.

She is fraught when I ask, 'What happened? Why?'

'Ask your father,' she sighs.

Dad has always been considered a maverick, an *enfant terrible*. His estranged family, a couple of whom stay in touch, regale us with stories of his eldest sister; mad they say, shrew, virago. The tales are varied and absurd: her blind husband thrown out on the street, her eldest son fleeing overseas, healthy young goats she glared at through a window fell dead. Her children, a nun and her brothers, consult the church and ecclesiastical consensus hem and haw about 'the sins of the father'. They perform sanctification rites for their mother; special masses, prayers and hope they have secured expiation with the precise monetary acknowledgements.

It's Dad's turn now, the nun says, even if it is just 'dementia'. The gods must be appeased. Dad must be exorcised.

Mum gratefully embraces this abstraction of cause, effect, and reparation. It is an evil family spirit, therefore not Dad's fault, or hers. He can be 'exorcised' back to normalcy. The Church says so, the nun says so. Her mission impossible need not be impossible.

The nun directs her to the parish priest, who gives her a letter of introduction and the contact of another priest, known for his work with evil spirits.

Weeks pass, and Mum calls the number repeatedly but the exorcist will not, does not, pick up his phone. She explains this, anxiously, repetitively, phone call after phone call till she finally resorts to default.

It is now my responsibility; I have to make the exorcism happen.

Dad's memory and comprehension deteriorates, becoming ragged, tattered, treacherous. That terrifies him. He begins to sleep a lot, grows suspicious, anxious, angry. He forgets names and words, withdraws from people and social interaction. His behaviour turns abusive, fuelled by mistrust and depression. His paranoias, sudden and mercurial, convince him everyone is an adversary; they must be vanquished, annihilated. An unwarranted, unprovoked rage festers; a continual simmering infused with occasional flashes of sanity.

It leaves him – and us – dazed and confused.

A friend suggests I indulge my mother. Visions of Linda Blair, spinning heads and unmentionable acts materialise.

'A blessing by a priest, some praying over the person; that's all it is,' she says mildly. 'If it gives your mum peace of mind, where is the harm?'

The flight is delayed; I reach home past midnight. I am unable to sleep, the mind a foment, much more than the usual Monday morning ramble of thoughts.

Five-thirty a.m. The house is quiet, hushed; my parents, asleep in their separate bedrooms. The first blush of day is a tentative hovering on the cusp, an almost spilling into stillness, yet not into light. I lean gratefully into this transcendence; the beginning of each day, this perfect moment of quiescence before bedlam commences.

Much to be done, and no plan, but ... this *could* be the right time to snag an unsuspecting priest. Carpe diem.

He accepts the early morning call from my unknown number, suggests I bring my parents across at noon. Calls back. 'Don't forget to bring the letter of introduction.'

Mum knocks on the door. 'Coffee?'

'We have an appointment,' I tell her, at which she bursts into tears. 'Thank God! *Thank* you, God.'

I grab the mug as it tilts, hold her in amazement as she hugs me tight.

She sincerely believes a miracle born of unwavering, steadfast faith will surpass science. That all of this will go away; one visit, and Dad will be a transformed man. Cured of whatever ails him.

This painful illogicality rooted in desperation beggars belief.

Dad is no fool. I mention in passing – casually – that we have to meet a particular priest. Today.

'Why?' he demands.

'Because Father S suggested it.'

I could tell him we are going to perform an exorcism on him because Mum believes he is possessed by an evil spirit because of something *his* father did, but I don't.

And he knows better than to ask because we never 'visit' priests. This is no ordinary day.

I look him in the eye. He sits very still.

We are playing a game – we don't know the rules – we make them up as we go. He knows he is unravelling; we know something is terribly wrong, but we all ignore the elephant in the room. For now.

A couple of years ago, a summer evening, the susurration of wind amidst the orange-red *gulmohar* blossoms a hand's breath away. A rare moment of amity. Dad and I leant against the wrought iron railing of the balcony.

'I am a very sick man,' he said.

I laughed. 'You? You're as strong as an ox.'

We were both quiet, distractedly attentive to home-flying birds, the slow sunset and a posse of little boys playing noisy cricket below us.

'If you feel you are sick,' I asked, 'why don't you see a doctor?'

'I'm scared,' he replied quietly. 'They might put me in a mental hospital.'

'You're joking,' I said then, and we left it at that.

And now, here we all are.

Mum runs his bath in a frenzy of anticipation; lays out his clothes, gets him ready two hours before we need to leave. He sits reflective and distant, surrendered.

I sit opposite him in taciturn kinship, wishing Mum would shut up, stop her fussing and prattle. And exactly how long are we going to sit around, dressed, staring at each other, waiting to leave, before something – or someone – explodes?

We set out earlier than is required or planned. It is not far, Thiruvanmiyur, we find it easily enough.

A watchman bars our entry with the sniggering authority of the browbeaten. 'Reverend Father *not* available.'

But I am firm. 'I have an appointment.'

The place – a seminary – is large, sprawling, completely deserted. An open door in a building nearby leads to a parlour of sorts. I get Mum and Dad comfortable, switch on a couple of large dust-coated fans and open the windows wide before I venture forth in search of the Reverend.

It is a Jesuit institution of classrooms, corridors and courtyards, much acreage, banana plantations, coconut groves and termite hills. Not a soul around; perhaps it is a day off for seminarians.

A small door, ajar, seemingly in the middle of nowhere. I approach carefully. There is no clue as to who, if anyone, inhabits the room; it could be a toilet with a couple of unsullied seminarians inside, but it turns out to be the Reverend's, fortunately, *with* the Reverend in it, counselling a despondent couple.

I wait for the couple to leave, patiently, idly glancing at a small termite hill nearby, distracted, until I feel movement. Termites, in an unsteady ascent up my jeans. I squawk with an involuntary leap; some drop to the ground, a few do not.

I recall and rapidly execute – from leached memory – a vigorous Irish jig, taught by strict Irish nuns, habits a-whirl, instructing: kick-leap, rise and grind, hop, hop, hop, foot in the air, now shift your weight. It works. The termites find little purchase. When the Reverend Father comes to the door, I catch his bewildered gaze mid-leap.

He crooks a finger, cautiously.

'Enter,' he says, gesturing to the rusting blue-paint-flecked aluminium chair across his small table. '*What* were you doing?' he demands. 'And *who* are you?'

'The early morning telephone call?' I remind him.

At his urging, I describe Dad's symptoms, Mum's anguish, the extended family's insistence that Dad be exorcised and the nun-cousin's intervention leading to the parish priest's letter, which I ceremoniously hand over.

'Hmm,' he murmurs as he reads. And again, 'Hmm.'

He looks up. 'Your parents. What is their background? Their relationship with each other?'

'Love and hate in almost equal measure,' I reply. 'They cannot live with each other. They cannot live without each other.'

He hmms a bit more. 'All your father's symptoms indicate dementia and senility. This is only to be expected with old age.'

I am so tired of hearing this, so very, very tired.

'The dementia will worsen; there can be no reversal. Their problems are rooted in their relationship, and his dementia makes it worse, especially the violence towards your mother.'

I privately disagree. Dad never intends Mum harm; in fact, in his 'normal' periods, he is demonstrably affectionate towards her even though she never sees it. 'Indira, have a biscuit, a toast, do you want a banana, a cup of coffee?' Indira this, Indira that. If he cannot chauffeur her, Indira should never walk alone, never take an autorickshaw alone. Indira. Indira. The leitmotif of his existence. I once found a card, dated 1957, deep under his papers, mostly old bills; he had written, *'My darling, sweetheart Indiramol.'*

'Bring your parents to me,' the priest says, but Dad can barely walk, and I blanch at the vegetation and termite hills to be negotiated. I suggest the Reverend Father take a walk with *me* instead, to the parlour. Reluctantly, he heaves himself from his chair, leaving me in no doubt about the enormity of the favour he is doing us.

He introduces himself to Mum and Dad, chats easily, asks about their daily routines, sleep and eating patterns. Holds their hands, takes their pulse. Sits back, stretches his feet.

'Your problem is the lack of a 'buffer'. You love each other, yes? But you are all by yourselves, solely focused on each other, to the point of provocation and exasperation.'

He turns to me. 'One of you should look after them, live with them, be a shock absorber for their personalities. They are getting old. How else will they manage?'

He wants us to live with them, primarily to deflect their every irritation – ongoing, eternal and endless. This is no exorcism.

The Reverend lifts the cross hanging around his neck, prays over them and blesses them both. 'Hand me the oil,' he says without turning his head, stretching out a hand as he continues to mutter-pray. Exorcism 101. No one had given me the instruction manual.

I rush out with terse instructions to the hired driver, who in turn dashes past the curious watchman to a small provision store outside the gate, and speed-skates back in a whoosh of perspiration, holding high a litre of cooking oil, coconut oil in a shiny pink plastic packet, grimy with sticky fingerprints while the priest has managed to keep the solemnity of the occasion going with breathless reverence, sans oil.

He now waves the disreputable packet over my parents, blessing it as it crackles noisily. He withdraws rose petals from his cassock and distributes them amongst us. 'From Medjugorje,' he pauses to inform, 'a small village in Bosnia-Herzegovina.' He hands me the oil with the directive to boil it, cool it and immerse the rose petals in it. 'Apply some oil to your father's head – or any part of his body – every day. He must say, '"Victory of the blood of Christ" and your mother must respond, "Mother Mary is with me, I fear nothing".'

And that is the end of it.

Mum asks, carefully disingenuous and vague so as to not alarm Dad, 'Isn't there some "family" influence on the "current" situation?'

'If there is,' the Reverend assures her, 'I will take care of it. Leave it with me.'

It does not please her one bit.

She wants to be told there was an evil spirit, it has been cast out and everything will go back to the way it used to be.

'Walk me back to my room,' says the Reverend Father, and I do. We stroll practically arm-in-arm.

'Did you see any evil in Dad?' I ask. That makes him smile for the first time.

'Your father is not evil, my dear. He is an honourable man, a man of character and principle. And a perfectionist. He does what he thinks is right. People may agree with him or not but he will not be swayed. Understand this, discipline and rigour defined his job – there were no margins for error. He could not afford to make one single mistake. He has been "in command" every day, every hour of his working life. Respected and obeyed. When he comes home, he expects the same. Implicit obedience, no arguments. Does he get this from his wife? Your mother is strong, independent, capable. She rules the house. Her nature is to give of herself and more of herself. People are important to her. They give her what your father does not. Both strong personalities. With strong egos. Your mother needs help and understanding as well.'

No evil spirit materialised from Dad's head and escaped through the window. This 'exorcism' is a clear-sighted explanation of personality and relationships. Nothing else.

Yet I need to make something clear, to myself, if not the priest. 'I don't believe in spirits and possession. I'm doing this primarily for my mother's peace of mind, and because the parish priest recommended it.'

He ponders that. 'Every family has a "family spirit" passed down from generation to generation. Many things defy "rationality". We don't know everything my dear.'

I ponder that, science and religion. Different ways of knowing? Discrete, yet overlapping?

He does not elaborate; I don't ask him to.

'Anger is often misunderstood as evil,' he reflects. 'And anger has many causes.'

Back in the parlour, bathos reigns. The sun is still blazing; the parents are silent. The plastic packet of cooking oil rests against the leg of a chair. I take both their hands; we walk out, carefully down the steps to the cauldron of the hired car and the perspiring driver who exudes that familiar malodour, so ubiquitous in South India.

Nothing has changed.

It feels necessary to acknowledge this ceremony with some recognition of higher powers at work, so we drive to the Velankanni Church.

Ma sits in the pews, eyes closed, palms raised in a supplicant's despairing entreaty.

Dad staggers and stumbles around the periphery, making his way to the altar. Hand on his heart, he stands a long while before the statue of the Virgin. He stands newly exorcised without his consent, stripped of every vestige of pride and ebullience, humbled, reduced. Not negotiating. A silent pleading for strength. He lurches unsteadily to the statue of St. Antony. His patron saint.

It breaks my heart.

We definitely need earthing.

I offer to take them to Buhari's for lunch. Food. Dad's eternal panacea.

Closed for Renovations says the sign outside.

'Home then, for leftovers.' Looking at my parents, eighty-three and seventy-five, I have an epiphany of sorts. In the end, all that's left of life are leftovers, vestiges, dregs, flotsam, ashes. A knowledge I have come to too late, so accustomed am I to my circumscribed little world.

The exorcism is forgotten in the subsequent weeks. Dad begins a tumultuous descent into madness. He demands knives, shreds possessions, sheds clothes. Nights coalesce into an endless nocturnal feral roaming as he battles unseen obstacles preventing him from returning home – his childhood home in Irinjalakuda, Kerala. He cannot, will not be solaced.

Fear reigns unchecked at home – fear, suspicion and anger.

He is corralled and injected, medicated and tied down.

He begs to be set free.

His speech grows guttural, he has trouble swallowing. He is aspirated regularly; a tube is inserted down his throat, His hands are bound by silk scarves so that he cannot pull out the tubes.

He follows us around with his eyes.

It is a rapid descent into a suffering that is unbearable to witness, much less endure.

Nine months become a blur of phone calls, messages, innumerable flights to Chennai from Singapore, Gurgaon and Dubai; emails and updates, often multiple times each day. Helping Mum understand, withstand. Comforting her as we restrain and confine him. Juggling multiple hospitalisations, nursing changes, doctors, and medications. Each decision discussed and micromanaged through confusion and unease. We foresee nothing, can control nothing. We learn humility in the most painful way imaginable.

Our sibling world of dread and assimilation, taken one day at a time, is soldered by moral, practical and ethical considerations;

our blind support of each other is leavened by embarrassing doses of gallows humour.

In the last month of his life – before he is intubated – Dad lies quiet, waiting to die. His last coherent words, steadily uttered are: 'Nitu, Dillu, Sanju, Daddy is going.'

Daddy?

We have not called him 'Daddy' in decades.

Her Scented Walk

Deborah Huff-Horwood

It's a beautiful autumn morning. Twists of sunlight dance beneath the elms. She cuts beneath them, leaving the footpath, not wanting to catch anyone's eye, smile, say 'g'day'. She just needs to breathe.

The oval is watered and lush, an all-you-can-eat feast. Kangaroos graze here at night; she steps around their droppings. Cockatoos screech on the wires. Hidden in the branches, young galahs gasp and rasp in unrelenting asthmatic agitation. Precisely four seconds of silence and the feathered frenzy starts again.

She crosses some asphalt, passes through a wire gate in the fence. Concrete squares are set in the dirt, a metre apart, facing the wild grass field. The first time she found this place she imagined a swimming pool erased and pictured herself diving in. Instantly, she recalled the flooding, the slipping, the frisson of bubbles and lush loveliness at going down, down, down, held by the water's embrace. She longed to stay underwater forever, enraptured in its watery grasp.

Now she walks beneath pine trees, brown needles a blanket underfoot. The air is different in here, her movements cautious, as she navigates her dark, secret woodland. She attunes to the *crunch* of twigs and draws in the warm pine scent. It's a comfort, like wrapping herself in fleece, like soaking in a warm bath. She recalls a painting of a Roman woman bathing with a female slave applying perfumed oils. Closing her eyes, she imagines the slide of hands, firm and sure, tracing her curves.

The forest ends. Marking the next corner is her running tree, her *Alice in Wonderland* tree, with its invisible cardboard-tag-tied-with-twine message, 'smell me' where she mustn't pause, mustn't falter but instead answer the call of ritual. Here she needs to reach up, take a handful of eucalyptus leaves and squeeze tenderly, then hard. Her fingers savour their suppleness, cherish their fine curvature. She places the bundle beneath her nose to deeply drink in the scent. Six steps, four steps, two steps, and now she runs.

Her feet pound the earth. She's inflamed by the rich, sweet scent in her chest. Her hand stays cupped as she smells the oil. She moves freely, swinging her arms, her steps growing surer. Beside her, a spinney of silver birch blocks the arterial road. Yellows and oranges, gold and rust, dusting on the breeze and feathering the path. She inhales, fixing her mind on the sensation of those young gum leaves, imagining their sighing crush as they come together within her grasp, oils released in one swift brutal moment.

She's endured that herself. She has made it through, so far ...

Powerlines stretch like a musical score above her. Once, she sang to birds, sang the tune they made while sitting, fatly black, on their wires. There are no birds today. She hears the sound of water trickling down the stormwater drain, another marker. She's run this route so often she could trace it on a warm, oiled back.

She's beneath old oak trees. Sequins of sunlight break through the canopy, casting sparkling discs on the damp dirt path. Leaves lie littered – plums, purples, browns. Here it is cool. Lovers should walk beneath these trees and picnic under their mighty boughs. The bark of these oaks is gnarled and thick. Their skin cannot be pulled or peeled. They let their leaves fall without crying. Several spiral slowly, landing untouched.

This is a place for tender words and honesty, and she came here once, shared this place – but he left her, just like all the others, taking another layer with him. She's learnt this now: men try to find their lost selves in plundering. And she misses feeling so alive, but wants softness and suppleness in her future, yearns for it, if only she could reach out.

Onwards she runs, approaching the final corner, then rounds it, loving the curve. She moves into the sunlight and the world opens a little; already she's lighter in her soul. She slows to a walk, heads up the rise to meet the footpath and arrive back at her gate.

But home isn't home. Even softened as hers is with plants, carpets, art, this concrete and metal built-by-men world abhors her. Home is where the heart is, and her heart isn't here. It's adrift, riding a wave of eucalyptus oil, seeping between trunks in that deep dark wood. She's lost, and all she can do is step and crunch and smell and run, weaving her way until whatever she's searching for is close enough to grasp.

Should she go again? She vacillates, battles herself. Could she slow herself, drink in the dark pine forest, lose herself in the fantasies of its lushness? What would happen if she stopped at the running tree – might it whisper to her, detect her breath?

Metal gate, rusted latch jars her velvet heart. She's in her courtyard and smells her hand again but the scent is gone. She pulls out a chair, brushes red maple leaves from the calico and sits lightly, trying for gratitude. All around her plants bear seed pods and blossoms, and in a tree hangs a little brass temple bell. Glass-jar candles wait to be lit. She closes her eyes and places her hands in her lap.

Fat, warm tears drip down her face. She doesn't wipe them away. Her hands are open, accepting. This keeps happening and she hopes it helps. Mornings are good; sun is good; she is safe and alone. A survivor.

She wipes her nose on her sleeve and heads inside, pulls off her clothes and tosses them in the wash. The carpet of the stairs is soft beneath her toes. Under a warm shower she sloughs off the layer risen bitter outside. Her hands smooth her shoulders, curve her breasts, shape her hips. She is moist inside, silky and luscious, her finger finding home in the valley of her folds. Then she towels herself dry and decides what to wear. Pale jeans, white shirt, sorted for the day now and ready to—

But there are no *have-to's*, no appointments or meetings and she has that knot in her stomach again, fear of a wasted life. She cannot eat, but coffee, there's an idea, and she grabs her bag and keys and is out the door in a flash. When she comes back inside for her sunglasses, she pauses, surveying her home. Here are her creature comforts, white sheepskins on the couch, houseplants, the drinks cabinet with its beckoning gin and whisky. She shuts the door against the noise of such silence.

Girl in Corner

Sarah Giles

The courier packs my bubble-wrapped paintings into his van, sandwiching them between a couple of boxes and the back of the passenger seat. I hand him an envelope and ask him to deliver it to Evie, explaining that she's the gallery owner. He gets behind the wheel without saying goodbye.

Back in the studio, I open the window for some fresh air. Clair's sketches catch a breeze and skitter across the floor, blowing up against the walls. I collect them. They're all the same. Versions of the clockwork figure she scraped across our lounge room wall in ash and charcoal. Frightening. Heavy dark eyes deep-set in a skeletal clock face. The same face waits to be completed on a canvas on her easel – a head without a body. It's not unusual for Clair's work to be at least a little miserable, but I've never known her to draw something repeatedly like this. How is it that Clair hasn't drawn a thing in weeks then produces a figure that looks like it might jump off the canvas and rip my oesophagus out of my throat?

People say my paintings are subtle. What they mean is my paintings are boring. I take the fistful of drawings to her desk and place a glass paperweight on them.

My phone screen glints in the dappled sunlight. I call Evie, telling her what she already knows: the paintings are coming. It takes me less than a minute to make the conversation all about me.

'I'm seeing Birdy today,' I say.

'Oh,' Evie says, the sound of typing falls silent on her end. 'That's huge.'

I move a jar of brushes to a higher shelf and slide a book of cold-pressed paper to the back of the bench, clearing my throat. 'Might invite her ... to the show.'

'Good for you,' Evie says.

'She won't come.'

She pauses. 'Maybe not.'

I wonder if Evie's remembering how we met, how Birdy took her in.

'Don't know what she'll do, haven't seen her in years myself.' She exhales the last few words, her voice getting a little higher with each syllable.

I grab the jar of brushes again and move them back to the benchtop, putting a roll of paper towels in their place on the higher shelf. 'Well. It's whatever.'

Evie's quiet. I know she's waiting for me to say more. If she still smoked this would be the moment she'd light a cigarette. I think of the portrait of Birdy I painted for Evie's exhibition. I drew her in profile with a light hand and a graphite pencil. In a single line, never letting the pencil tip leave the page, I made swirls and lines that overlap in curls like a cotton thread dropped on the floor. I traced the line with a narrow, ink-coated brush.

Pressure rises in my chest. It's the feeling that makes me want to ignore texts and hide in the studio from Clair.

'Why haven't you told her you're back?' I say.

Evie sighs. I imagine she's sitting at her desk, cheek leaning against her fist.

'Suppose it's the same reason you haven't mentioned the exhibition,' she says.

'What reason is that?' I wanted her to tell me because I wasn't exactly sure why I'd stayed silent on the subject.

'Scared of Birdy's reaction.'

My turn to sigh. 'She's just so—'

'I know, darl,' Evie says.

I feel hands on my waist. Clair rests her forehead on my shoulder. 'Anyway. Gotta go.'

'Call me later if you need,' Evie says.

The tires dip in and out of puddles, spraying orange mud up the sides of the sedan as we venture up the long driveway to Birdy's new digs. Clair parks next to a green skip bin full of splintered wood and greying plastic. I step out of the car and peep inside the bin to see what Birdy's tossing. It's mostly full of old smashed-up furniture along with ancient VHS tapes and a few yellowed novels, but tucked inside a cobwebbed pram is a folder of loose papers. I slot my foot into a shallow groove on the side of the skip and lean in to grab it.

'Get out of it, Candy,' Birdy says.

I swing myself upright and see her marching down the front path.

'Why are you throwing this out?' I let the folder flop open to reveal a bunch of Birdy's drawings.

She yanks open the wide wire fence and storms toward me. 'Get out of it.'

Birdy tries to grab the folder, but I turn away, jumping out of reach. Clair frowns.

'I want them,' I say.

Birdy pauses, sweeping thick cherry-red hair back with open hands, only it falls in her eyes again. Gravel crackles under her boots as she heads back to the house, throwing a dismissive wave. Clair smiles at Birdy as she passes. I put the folder in the car, then jog to catch up with Birdy.

'Why didn't you get rid of all this stuff before you moved out here?' I ask.

'A lotta that shit was left behind by old tenants,' she says. 'Close the gate.'

Why does she want the gate closed when the house is in the middle of an empty paddock which is surrounded by more empty paddocks? I fasten it with a piece of galvanised wire that hooks onto the fencepost beside it.

'This isn't very secure,' I say.

Clair hovers by my elbow.

'Okay?' she whispers.

I shrug, pulling a hair off her shoulder.

'Go easy,' she says.

She kisses my forehead, then my mouth. I've been clenching my jaw. I relax a little, pulling Clair in for a hug and taking a few slow breaths.

'Are you going to tell her about the exhibition?' Clair says.

'Maybe.'

Clair tightens her arms around me the way I like. I breathe her in: she smells like the orange she had for breakfast and the coffee she drank in the car on the drive here. We head up the cracked concrete path together. She kicks her sneakers off at the door even though Birdy wore her boots inside.

The first thing I notice about the house is the huge bay window in the lounge room. It's the kind with a bench seat that you see in American movies where girls sit with a loose-knit blanket reading or talking on the phone. Birdy's window is missing curtains, the seat has long black scuff marks on it and the varnish is peeling. I sit down.

'This'll do up nicely,' I say.

'It's a huge space,' Clair says, standing next to Birdy.

'That lot's yours,' Birdy says, pointing to a stack of boxes by the door. 'You can load it up and sort it at home.'

I pop open a small box on top of the nearest pile. It's full of waxy crayons, knife sharpened pencils and a handful of chipped marbles. Clair peers inside and smiles. She picks up a marble with yellow and pink waves set in the glass.

'Mum never let me have these,' she says.

I open another box and find dozens of issues of *Total Girl*. I pick up a copy from 2003 with Delta Goodrem on the cover – it's the 'Best Friends' edition with stories on *The Saddle Club*, craft ideas and tips for hosting the best sleepover.

'Can't believe you kept these,' I say, smiling and picking up another magazine.

'Chuck them,' Birdy heads into the kitchen off the lounge room.

Clair picks up a box, nodding in Birdy's direction before taking it out to the car.

The kitchen lino is covered in pieces of crumpled newspaper. I pick them up as Birdy unwraps a dinner plate, letting another sheet float to the floor.

I clear my throat. 'How've you been?'

'Busy with all this,' she says, gesturing to the boxes.

There's a small square canvas on the table next to an ice cube tray with paint squeezed into the holes.

'You've been painting.' I drop an armful of newspaper into an empty box.

I learned to paint portraits watching Birdy. But this canvas is nothing like the pictures she drew when I was growing up. It's a smudgy painting of an open mouth with rotting teeth and holes in the gums. The throat looks like a deep swirling pit.

'This is different,' I say.

Birdy's at my side unwrapping another plate.

'It's ugly,' she says.

'Amazing detail.'

I hold the canvas up to the sunlight and examine the fine brushstrokes forming black and yellow teeth and cracked lips. Birdy huffs, turns around to put the plate in the cupboard. Something shatters.

'Fuck,' she says, pressing the heels of her hands against her temples.

I bend down to clean up the broken dinner plate.

'Stop. I'll do it,' Birdy says.

She tries to take a spiked fragment from me, but it slips between her fingers and slices the webbed skin that connects her thumb and forefinger. Birdy hisses then sucks the first drops of blood. I grab the roll of paper towels from the bench above us and tear off a couple of sheets, pressing the bunched-up paper to the cut. Her warm fingers rest on the back of my hand as I apply pressure. I watch Birdy surveying our hands – she pushes the wild strings of curly red hair pushed behind rosy, pointed ears. There's a round peachy sunspot on her chin that I'm sure wasn't there last time I saw her and suddenly I feel very young.

'Does that hurt?' I say, watching the blood soak through.

'I'm fine,' she says.

Clair kneels down beside us. 'Shit. Do you have any Betadine?'

'I'll do it,' Birdy says, pulling her hand away.

'Tell me where, I'll get it,' I say.

She steps around us, disappearing down a hallway. I go after her. Clair follows, reaching to take my hand but I pull away. The hallway is long and dark except for the yellow bathroom light at the very end. I approach the doorway and peer inside. Birdy's rinsing her hand in the sink.

'Mum,' I say.

I watch a dark swirl of blood slip down the drain.

'Go home.' She kicks the door and I stumble back into the hallway, bumping into Clair as it slams shut.

I pinch Birdy's folder under my arm, unlocking the front door. Clair backs out of our driveway on her way to work with my boxes still on the backseat. The house is dim, but I don't bother opening the curtains or turning on any lights. Instead, I make a gin and head to the studio, opening Birdy's folder on the coffee table. Birdy has drawn me holding my teddy bear under my chin. My own eyes look up at me, shiny full moons. The bear was a wire-haired terrier with one missing ear. In the drawing, Birdy made a thin inky line with tiny stitch marks to show where she had sewn the hole.

I spread Birdy's drawings across the floor. The sheets come together like mismatched panels on a quilt. I count fourteen portraits done in watercolour and ink or sketched using a blue pen. In the bottom right-hand corner of each page, in Birdy's uniform handwriting, are names and dates. Without the names, I don't know that I would have realised who the faces belonged to.

> Lucile (Luce) 14.12.2010–22.12.2010
> Jayde 05.09.2011–07.09.2011
> Celine 23.05.2007–26.05.2007
> Evelynn (Evie) 02.06.2008–13.02.2009

After I started high school, Birdy set up a single bed in the corner of our small lounge room next to a chipboard bookshelf. The bed was for strays, mostly women or kids who needed a place to sleep for a few nights. Evie stayed for almost nine months; she was in her twenties and an aspiring painter. I was fourteen and got in the habit of making extra of whatever I was having for breakfast. We would sit on the concrete verandah outside to eat and talk.

'Kill for a ciggy,' Evie said, chewing on a hunk of sausage.

The cement was warm. I was sweaty behind my knees.

'Your mum's a top lady.'

'Yeah.'

'My mum's a bitch,' Evie said. 'Kicked me out when I was still in school. Reckoned I was too much for her and blamed me squarely for my dad leaving. Did it ever occur to her that maybe he was just a cunt? Deserved each other.'

I move a rock out of the marching line of some ants.

'Your mum takes care of you though,' Evie said.

'Yeah ... but I don't think she likes me very much.'

'What makes you say that?'

I scooped a forkful of scrambled eggs into my mouth, hoping Evie would get bored and change the subject but she waited for me to finish and answer the question. I cleared my throat. 'She's mean. She doesn't yell much or hit me or anything.'

'But?'

I felt the heat gathering behind my eyes, wetness building in my nose. Evie was rubbing my back and that's when the sobbing started.

'I'm invisible to her. That's all. Think she'd prefer if I wasn't around.'

'Aw, darl.' Evie smiled and pulled me to her chest. 'Your mum loves you, how couldn't she? You're kind and generous. You're a good kid.'

I let myself sink into her, wrapping my arms around her middle and squeezing. When I pulled away there was a wet patch on her t-shirt. I put my hand on it.

'Don't worry, love. It'll dry,' Evie said.

She took my hand and squeezed. A puckered redness crept up her neck. Tears trickled down her cheeks too even though she was smiling, and she wiped them away with the heel of her hand.

'Need a smoke,' she laughed.

That afternoon I came home with a half-full box of smokes I'd stolen from a girl at school. Evie lit one on the stove and inhaled slowly.

'Legend.' Evie pushed the box toward me.

I wanted Evie to like me. I wanted us to do something together. The cigarette slid out of the box and felt like a hollow pencil in my hand. Evie's smoke gathered in the kitchen and stung my eyes. I blinked quickly to stop them from watering.

'S'pose we should take it outside?' Evie said.

Sitting in our usual spot on the verandah, I lit my cigarette from hers and inhaled. My lungs felt hot. Evie laughed as I coughed. I thought about the time Birdy rubbed Deep Heat on my neck after I hurt it trying to climb on top of the monkey bars at school. The cream made my skin tingle, then burn. It felt like Birdy had poured hot water over me and I begged her to let me wash it off. 'Stop sooking,' she said.

I decided I didn't like smoking, so only pretended to inhale and flicked the ash into the garden. Evie must have noticed because she didn't offer me another cigarette. She smoked three in a row while we watched the sun sink behind the houses across the road.

Stacking Birdy's drawings back into the folder, I down the rest of my gin and suck on an ice cube as I pour another. I cradle the ice in my tongue and press it to the roof of my mouth, letting it sting until the ice melts. Then I take a swig.

My head swirls as I reach for my phone. I ignore a text from Clair, searching, instead, for Birdy's phone number, hitting the call button before I chicken out. The call rings out. I call again.

'Hello?'

She sounds blurry, like she was sleeping. I feel my courage ebbing away, water down a drain.

'Mum,' I say. 'How's your hand?'

'Fine.'

'That's good.' I close my eyes. 'Did you know Evie's back?'

'No,' Birdy says, brightly. 'How's she going?'

'She quit the smokes.'

Birdy laughs. 'Good girl.'

'She's only back for a bit, curating an exhibition in town.'

'You've been in touch then?'

My palms are sweaty. I switch to loudspeaker, drying my hands on my pants. 'Found her on Facebook a while ago.'

'Right.'

'I should've told you.'

It's quiet on Birdy's end. I push my fingers against my eyelids until I see sparks of white.

'I'm in Evie's exhibition. Maybe, if you wanted to, you could come.' I hear clinking, shuffling. I think I hear her moan, or maybe that's my mind lying to me.

'You don't have to,' I say. 'It was Evie's idea for me to be in the show. Don't think it really counts for me, but I wanted to help her out.'

'It counts,' Birdy says.

Another stretch of silence. I break the spell. 'Anyway, show's this weekend. Doors open at ten, close at five.'

'Where?' Birdy says.

'The old textile factory. I'll text you the address.'

I breathe slowly, controlling the part of me that wants to cry. I scrape my thumb nail over a small scab on my chest, finding its edge and peeling it back, feeling the sting.

'I'll try,' she says.

I press my hand to my throat, massaging the tension loose. 'Thanks Mum.'

'Okay. Good night.'

'Wait,' I say. 'Why do you paint?'

I sit on the cool concrete floor and stare at Clair's clockwork man, her canvases packed like books on the shelves. My paintings hang on drooping lines of twine strung up on my side of the studio. Face after face, stone eyes and worm mouths, hair like weeds. Faces of people I've seen on the street or just imagined. Looking at my drawings now I see a little bit of Birdy in all of them – soft lines and round edges, pressed mouths and restless eyes – pulling away.

Birdy sighs. 'It's all I'm good at. Used to be good at. I thought.'

'You're great,' I say.

'Why do you paint, Candy?'

'Because of you.'

Something crackles down the line.

'Mum?'

'It's past my bedtime, kid,' she says.

Cherries

Emily Gray

it is hard to believe when I'm with you that there can be
anything as still as solemn as unpleasantly definitive as
statuary when right in front of it in the warm New York
4 o'clock light we are drifting back and forth between each
other like a tree breathing through its spectacles

~ Frank O'Hara, 'Having a Coke with You'

There's an eagle hitching a ride on the updraft, eyeing the clifftop
for prey. I'm sitting on the deck of our holiday rental, mouthing a
wine, watching the bird and reading an old *New Yorker* magazine.
The cabin is a bit rustic, according to Marc, but it suits me fine. A
few metres away, wallaroos are grazing on a rocky outcrop, native
grasses sprouting up between the sandstone and granite. Beyond is
a sheer drop down to the flats of Lambs Valley and Torryburn, miles
of undulating countryside that stretches all the way to Barrington

Tops, rising up from the flats like a sleeping giant. I glance towards the girls' bedroom to make sure they haven't snuck out to explore the cliff face.

I chose this place because I wanted an antidote to the hemmed in feeling that comes from living in the city for too long: the views into other apartments, the constant hum of traffic, the etiquette of the co-op and minimalist cafes, the army of Lululemon mums championing salad for breakfast and natural immunity, and the city-lawyer life – scrutinising the million stupid decisions of strangers.

We are staying at the Wedgetail Wilderness Resort – a lot of wilderness, not so much resort – a few ranges over from the Hunter Valley. Although our cabin is one of twenty or so strewn across the mountain ridge, and the shuttered restaurant, Kumbaya lodge, and empty recreation area make it seem like an abandoned Christian camp – the view, at least, is worth it. I feel my spirit swoop into the valley and tumble across the flats. I let it linger there, meandering over the paddocks and hillocks and creeks. It is quiet save for the sound of wallaroos nibbling the grasses, a light wind rustling the clifftop trees, and the thump thump of the odd kangaroo passing through.

Marc squeezes my shoulders, kisses the top of my head.

'They asleep?' I ask.

'Took a millennium but, yes, they're down. Had to listen to Julia recite the entire lyrics to "Shake it Off", and Annika wouldn't close her eyes until I'd asked her ten maths questions.'

'Jesus. Thanks.'

'Easy as,' he says with a grin, settling into the chair next to mine. He pours his own wine, and I wonder whether all men make the quotidian tasks of parenting so performative.

'This is alright, isn't it,' he says, taking in the view, exhaling loudly.

'Do you reckon we could live somewhere like this?' I ask.

'You're not serious, are you?' He looks at me over his tortoiseshell glasses.

He's a handsome man – a light stubble, aquiline nose and speckled brown and grey hair quiffed back from his forehead. He could pass for an academic, or a surfer, though he is neither of those things.

'Humour me for a moment,' I say.

'I think you'd be out of here faster than you could say snakebite.'

'The kids though, they'd love it, wouldn't they? So much space.'

'Sure. So many cliffs to fall off, so many rednecks to befriend,' he says, with a sweeping gesture.

'Country towns aren't like that anymore.'

'Aha. Tell that to the blackface minstrel figurine in the Paterson General Store. Speaking of which,' he says. 'I'm going to brave the descent to stock up on groceries. Anything you want?'

'More wine. And cherries, if they have them.'

With a nod he gets up from the chair and heads back inside to grab the car keys and shopping bags.

'People are moving to the regions in droves, you know,' I say, hands cupped around my mouth, even though he's almost out the door.

'And I salute them for it. Will give us a bit more space in the city.'

The front door closes and the car engine starts. I settle in to read my magazine but find it hard to latch onto a story.

In the quiet and the stillness, I feel your absence like a pain. I think of our weekend in the country, twenty years ago now. Do you remember the old ladies in the tearoom? I say ladies because their hair was short and grey and curled tight to their heads, paisley blouses buttoned up to their necks, and lips so small and mean that their mouths were like lines drawn with a pencil. At first, I thought their stares and tuts were because of our laughter, flowing and unconstrained like water over rocks. Or that maybe we weren't eating Devonshire tea like interracial lovers in a country town are supposed to.

'Is it the jam or cream that goes on first?' you said.

'Can you spoon the cream on like a cloud or is a schmear more appropriate?' I said.

We laughed at the word 'schmear'.

Maybe you weren't supposed to lean over the teacups and the lavender sprigs to wipe cream from my lip with a smile before sucking it off your thumb.

We were young then. And what did I know? I saw the hardness in their eyes and their lips close like sea anemones and I realised their discomfort was that you dared to be joyful and unrestrained in your skin, not small and quiet and apologetic. I don't think they liked our absorption in one another either, batting happiness back and forth like a tennis ball, the smiles they couldn't wipe off our faces, not even with the starched napkins, stiff and white as a nun's habit.

'Fifty bucks they're a pair of old dykes themselves,' I said, leaning in.

You bristled at the word 'dykes'.

'Oh, come on, it's our word now. Didn't you hear? It's been reclaimed, we can use it how we like.'

'Your word maybe, not mine.'

You were fine so long as we were just two people in love. You'd countenanced the possibility of being gay, but you said 'lesbian' like it was a medical condition; 'queer' was beyond the pale (back then). Besides, you reminded me, your parents wouldn't let you date women forever.

I told you I didn't need a label, and that I thought everyone was on the spectrum anyhow. Funny how 'on the spectrum' means something different now.

I remember that weekend in Young as one of the best. Do you? Not because of the tearoom but because of the cherry orchard. The day before, we'd picked cherries and ate handfuls along the way until our tummies ached and our teeth gleamed red – cherry drunk. We ambled up and down the rows of cherry trees in the sun, a bucket apiece, your hand in my jeans pocket. You kissed my neck when no one was looking, and I felt utterly enveloped by your love, like I could float down a river on it. We found a spot without any creepy dads or shrieking children and smiled at each other in the silent slanting afternoon light, kissing until our lips were sore. With you there between the cherry trees as the sun sank, we were living like we were supposed to, sucking the marrow out of life, scouring every corner for joy and mopping up the dregs with crusty bread. I still have a photo of us from that day, arms around each other, smiling into the sun, you bending over with laughter, our lips red. Something loosened in me that day, an unfurling into abundance.

The tearoom was our last stop before driving home. The tension of returning to the real world, of your parents and colleagues who had no idea about us, seemed to fracture things, make the air between us brittle. It started with me marching over to the tearoom ladies all indignant, telling them that you were training to be a doctor, that you were born here, and how dare they look down on you.

'I don't need you to do that,' you said as we paid for the bill and walked to the car.

'I didn't want them to get away with treating you that way.'

'It's a tad paternalistic,' you said, slamming the car door.

You were right, of course.

'Sorry babe. But I reckon behaviour like that needs to be called out.' I turned the key in the ignition.

You glanced at the skin on my arms, the colour of cream.

'How about next time you're the subject of racism you can speak up about it.'

'So everyone for themselves, hey?' I felt humiliated, as though you failed to see I was trying to do something good. A gear shifted inside me, like I needed to hound you until you felt bad about something too. I don't feel good about it now, just so you know.

'That's not what I meant.'

'Is that why you don't vote, too? Think you'd be meddling too much in the body politic to actually have a say?'

'Ouch.'

You pulled down the visor in the car, looked out the window, and we were silent for a long while as we drove past the granite boulders and brown hills and drought-ridden paddocks.

After an hour or so you reached across to hold my hand. '"A brown grass love",' you said, nodding towards the mountains.

I squeezed your hand and smiled.

'"They were beckoning mountains with a brown grass love",' I said. 'Wish I'd thought to write it.'

You'd given me an inscribed copy of *East of Eden* for my birthday, the last birthday, as it turned out, we'd be together.

'You will one day, I know it.'

I'm reading now on the deck, Marc is still out and the kids are still asleep. It's an article you'd love, I think. It's got it all: cherries, New York, the peculiarities of bees and the peccadilloes of the human heart. It's about a guy called Arthur Mondella, the 'Cherry King of Red Hook'. Arthur owned a sprawling maraschino cherry factory in Brooklyn. Typical tough guy, connections to the Brooklyn mafia, had a stint on Wall Street before returning to take over his father and grandfather's business.

The hipster apiarists of Brooklyn started noticing that bees, flying back to their rooftop hives, had turned red, and that their honey was approximating red cough syrup rather than the real thing. Turns out they'd been feasting on the maraschino cherry syrup leaking out from Arthur's factory. The authorities' suspicions were raised when they visited his factory to investigate the bee saga and noticed an overpowering smell not entirely disguised by the cherries. Once they solved the bee problem, six years went by with no further visits from the Feds. Meanwhile, our man Arthur was living life larger than a maraschino cherry income might provide – walking into clubs with twenty grand in each pocket, amassing a garage full of luxury cars, a yacht, a suite of Rolexes, a *Penthouse* magazine model, and snorting bucket loads of cocaine while he was at it – y'know, nothing dubious.

When the inspectors finally turned up with a warrant, they found a secret moving bookshelf, behind which stairs led down to the basement, and New York's largest ever marijuana crop. Arthur excused himself to go to the bathroom, yelled at his sister through the bathroom door to look after his kids, then shot himself in the head with the .357 Magnum he'd worn in an ankle holster. Apparently, no one, not even his family, knew about his side hustle. Had it not been for those greedy bees, they may have never known, and Arthur could still be spreading his beneficence, still supplying those hipster apiarists with the best weed they ever had. I wonder if Arthur, having tasted abundance, couldn't let it go.

I think that's what appealed to me about this place – all the unbounded sky, the space between things, the feeling of being unconstrained by people, by concrete, by the minutiae of life. Yesterday we all went for a roam around 'the Resort', taking with us the sticky laminated map from the kitchen top, which promised so much – a restaurant, a bar, a spa, even a babysitting service. We strolled down through the brown grass and untended paths to the Black Lagoon and Snake Swamp. The lagoon had a sorry-looking clump of upturned kayaks on the shore, but the water itself was black, thick, covered in lily pads. We walked along the jetty into the middle of the swamp. Marc had been approximating a relaxed holiday schtick before he screamed at the girls to stay away from the edge. It wasn't entirely uncalled for. If they'd fallen in, we wouldn't have been able to see them under the water, and who knows what slippery, knotty beings might be lurking underneath.

The Snake Swamp looked like a small dam, with a dilapidated gazebo on its shore. Inside, a young couple edged towards sex, which made the girls giggle and shriek. It didn't put the pair off, enveloped as they were in one another.

I think about Arthur Mondella, how he longed for freedom through excess, abundance; but all that money, the drugs, the sex, in the end, just highlighted where the cracks were, let the wind blow through faster and stronger, illuminating the absences within.

All this space and sky here is letting me unfurl for the first time in a long while. Still, when the wind blows up from the valley, I can feel that little seams have started to form, that some air is sneaking inside.

Car tyres crunch over the gravel in the driveway, Marc clanks the keys on the kitchen top.

'How was the drive?' I ask.

'Like the Wild Mouse ride at Luna Park. Not fit to be a road. A goat track maybe. Experienced goats only, mind.'

He walks out onto the deck and places a bowl of cherries in front of me. I clasp my hands together in delight. I peek inside and count twelve cherries in the bowl.

'Are there any more, or is that it?'

'That's it. Absolute racket. Thirty-five dollars a kilo.'

I feel cold from the wind and there's a roiling in the pit of my stomach. I bite into a cherry. It's sour. I wonder, if you were sitting with me, whether I'd be warm, whether the cherries would taste sweet.

Diamond and Pearl

Kristen Dagg

Gloria shoved the last of her grandmother's moth-eaten dresses and coats into the garbage bag. This one contained mostly fur coats. One of them was a fox stole with a fox's actual face on the end of it, and a clasp that attached to its pointy little mouth. It hooked onto the other end, so you could have a beast's head sitting right on your clavicle. Its poor, sad, dead eyes had been replaced by black shiny marbles.

Gloria shuddered. It was truly hideous.

She tried to imagine her gnarled up gran in her prime, wearing one of the lace dresses with court shoes and seamed stockings, with the fox stole slung over her shoulders, but it was difficult.

The gran she had said goodbye to a month earlier was a tiny, shrivelled up skeleton, with a wisp of white hair and sunken eyes.

She was gone now, and Gloria was a practical woman. She was not a vintage lover and thought jackets that had once been fluffy animals were plain awful, so it was to the Charity shop with the lot.

Pearl switches on the lights and they all buzz to life, revealing a huge boutique with racks of colour-coded heaven. She loves surveying her handiwork. She sees that Diamond has placed the vintage ball gowns a little closer to the doors, with the Givenchy belted maroon waist dress positioned at the front. She approves. It really pops.

But Diamond has gone a little rogue and done a whole rack of Glam Rock looks. Furry waistcoats and spray on shiny jeggings with a lot of animal print. It is fun, but they hadn't spoken about it.

This is what happens when I leave early, thinks Pearl.

She is well aware that Diamond plans things and waits until Pearl isn't there before executing them.

They would talk about it later.

Even though she likes the Glam Rock rack, Pearl wheels it closer to the Povo racks, as they call them. Just to make a point.

On cue, Diamond pushes open the double glass doors, which bash against the wall. The sound makes Pearl nearly roll an ankle. Her silver strappy platforms are a little small and rather precarious.

'Jesus, Diamond! You gave me a heart attack!' Pearl clasps her pearls and limps over to the cash register to see what paperwork Helen stuffed up last night.

'Morning gorrrrrgeous!' Diamond sashays over to the counter, not noticing the rack change yet.

She's wearing a leopard body con dress with hot pink fishnets and low zebra ankle boots with a red fake Chanel quilt bag over her shoulder and pink Ray Bans that are almost certainly from Bali. She looks fabulous.

'You're wearing the shoes!' She lowers her sunnies to reveal the matching pink eye shadow. 'I love them on you!'

'You look amaaaze!' Pearl purrs.

Diamond does a little catwalk turn to show the full glory.

Travis comes in from the back warehouse holding two gigantic lattes. He looks a little red-rimmed and glassy in the eye area, but the girls say nothing. He comes to work and drives a forklift stoned, but he brings them coffee every day.

His reflective vest does nothing for his sallow skin, and Pearl tries to think of something flattering to say about his appearance but draws a blank.

'Oh, Travis, baby! Thank you, sweetheart! You're a lifesaver! This guy!'

'I know, he's the best! Travis is the best!' Diamond holds out her multi-ringed hand and takes her coffee. 'Vanilla syrup?'

'Yep. How's it going?'

He always seems so bored. Which is odd to Diamond and Pearl, because there's nowhere else they would rather be. The Divine Bleeding Heart's Charity Megastore is Nirvana.

'Jackie, a lady just came in with a whole stack of stuff. You might want to check it out. It looks old and it smells like dead animals.' He hands Pearl her coffee. She snatches it and purses her lips.

Pearl ignores him.

'It's *Pearl*, Travis.' Diamond gives him her well-practised stink eye look, and Travis does everything within his power to halt a deep sigh.

'Okay, sure. Well, *Diamond* and *Pearl* ... some lady's grandmother died and there's heaps of shit to go through. Plus, the charity bin guy from Bay area has unloaded his bins.'

Diamond claps her hands together and the bangles sound like Christmas bells. 'Ooh, we love a dead old lady don't we, Pearl!'

'That we do! And Bay area always has good stuff. Thank you, *Travis*.' Pearl takes a sip of coffee, which is actually a vanilla chai latte, but today is not the day to complain.

Travis walks back to the warehouse to sneak in a quick cone before the women take over his space.

'Oh my God. When can we do it?' Diamond is jumping up and down, a little coffee splashing onto her front and she frowns, wiping it away.

Pearl is examining receipts and mutters, 'Soon, D. I just need to sort out this mess.'

There is no mess. Helen used to be an accountant. She is meticulous with balancing the till and reconciling receipts, but Pearl sometimes has trouble understanding how the system works and can't let on.

'Can I start?' Diamond saunters back towards the warehouse, where a mountain of wonder is waiting to be discovered and sorted. This would not usually be the manager's job, but Pearl and Diamond have style and recognise brands and trends, so no one else can do it.

'No!' Pearl considers, once more, that working with Diamond is much like working with a child. 'Who's going to manage the floor? Hello? We need to wait for Helen, at least.'

'Fine. I'm going to sort the skinny jean rack then.' Diamond completes an exaggerated turn and charges down to the high-end jeans section to weed out the tatty jeans that should be binned, not sold.

She stops suddenly. 'What happened to Glam Rock?'

Pearl looks up and sighs. 'Do we actually need a Glam Rock? It's not even party season yet and it just looked a bit like a rack of dead Muppets.'

Diamond tries to form the right words but the rage has taken over and then doors open softly and Helen shuffles in, head bowed, an anxious look on her face. A little brown mouse, ready to be walked over all day.

'Hi Pearl, hi Diamond,' she squeaks. She would never call them Jackie and Raelene. She would probably get fired.

They regard her as if she were a leaf blowing past in the wind.

'Hey,' they say in unison.

Helen deals with Povo. And the kids' racks. Diamond and Pearl have no interest in either section, and Helen is lucky to have a job.

What Diamond and Pearl don't know is that Helen has two Barbies propped up at home on the mantle and they're dressed as Diamond and Pearl in tacky, clashing colours with lots of skin showing. Helen likes to burn them with a lighter and then stick little dress pins into their faces. It makes her feel better.

After Pearl is done frowning at receipts, it's time to go through new stock. The women try not to look like they are racing, they never run. But they casually powerwalk like it's Tokyo 2020.

It's not easy casually powerwalking in ill-fitting 80s platforms and Diamond takes the lead.

In going through new merch, there are rules:

- If they love something, they can keep it.
- If they love it but it's small, it goes to Pearl.
- If they love it and it's roomier, it goes to Diamond.
- They are allowed to keep three times each, give or take a few.
- If it's a high-end brand, they need to plead their case because high end brands look good in store.

But they also believe they deserve nice things. It's the code. They are sisters in all things fashion and since the day they found each other, they share a deep, mutual respect for being fabulous and amazing. Although they would probably run the other one over for vintage Yves Saint Laurent.

These rules only apply to Diamond and Pearl. No one else is allowed to take anything. If Diamond and Pearl don't want you to have it, you don't get it, even if you offer to pay full price.

This forces Travis and the other warehouse workers to scavenge and steal whatever they like before the managers have access to anything. Then they sell the good stuff to other staff and friends at heavily discounted prices. This side hustle allows Travis to buy as much weed as he wants, which he also often sells in the warehouse.

Diamond and Pearl stop and take it all in. A literal mountain of garbage bags and boxes, chockers full of possible treasures. They squeeze each other's hand and know they are in exactly the right place.

They understand they could be one bag away from the leftovers of a rich, eccentric socialite with Dementia and a lifetime of mint condition Chanel.

So far, Pearl has snaffled away a Cartier scarf and a pair of black patent leather Betty Paige style stripper heels.

Diamond has a Madonna-like beaded conical bustier which looks way too small for her, an original Guns N' Roses tour t-shirt, which she will modify to a crop top, and a tattered Louis Vuitton graffiti clutch from the early 2000's, which she thinks can be salvaged with a little sugar soap and a toothbrush. It's real, or at least a very good fake.

She also finds a Peaches and Cream Barbie from the mid 80s still in its box, which will get her a couple of hundred bucks. But Pearl would want it for the shop, so she hides it in an old Sports Girl bag.

They watch each other closely over the piles of clothing and bric-a-brac. They ride a complex wave of emotions on a loop – fierce competition, excitement, shared joy, jealousy, suspicion, boredom, repeat.

It's a good haul and the girls emerge from the warehouse dishevelled but triumphant.

'Helen, there's some big piles for Povo to go through and tell Trevor there's rubbish to chuck,' Pearl barks, in Helen's general direction.

Helen scuttles towards the chain-link fence to the warehouse.

'Two days, Pearl. Two days for the shop to look like a bloody brothel. And not even a nice one. One of those places in the industrial estate, Lord have mercy!'

Diamond stalks around the displays throwing clothes on the ground and muttering to herself. How hard is it to make the store look good? It was her reputation on the line!

Helen is pleased to be sifting through clothes in the warehouse. She doesn't have to speak to anyone and could get lost in the joy of sorting by colour, size and type.

An old black wool coat has been tossed in her pile. It is very old and had once been quite beautiful. But the seams had come undone on the sleeves and hem. Helen could fix it. Shame to let something just shrivel up and die, even if it wasn't the brightest or prettiest. It has a little box in the pocket and Helen pulls it out to inspect. It's a small, black, velvet ring box. *Curious*, thinks Helen.

She holds her breath as the box opens with a creak. Helen's heart begins to pound hard. A little squeak escapes her mouth. Helen knows a real diamond when she sees one. It has an oval cut, with three perfect round sapphires surrounding it. Helen's mother had been one of those fancy women who loved diamonds, and she had many rings just like this. She dragged Helen and her sister into any jewellery shop they came across and drooled over princess and emerald cuts, explaining the differences in shape and colour of the precious stones.

Those diamonds were long gone now though, sold for a pittance and gambled away on the pokies.

This ring is probably a family heirloom. Helen toys with the idea of tracking down its owner and being a hero.

Selling it would have more benefit. The money would feel good for longer.

Helen has always wanted parrots. King Parrots, Lovebirds. But also Painted Finches too. She's so busy thinking and planning, she doesn't feel a presence looming ever closer.

'What's that?' Pearl's shrill voice snaps her out of her trance.

'Oh, nothing. An old ring box. A crappy old ring inside. Just glass, I'm sure.'

Pearl snatches it from her hand. 'Oh my god Helen! That is *not* a glass ring. Are you stupid? It's a bloody diamond and sapphire ring! This must be worth ... thousands!' Her eyes bulge out of her thin face and her breathing quickens.

'Holy shit! I can't believe I found it!'

Pearl tries on the ring, which fits perfectly on her engagement finger.

Helen can hear Diamond running towards them before she sees her, bangles jingling and Lycra swishing as her thighs rubbed together.

'What is it?' she squeals.

'I found a ring! A very valuable ring!'

'Let me see it!'

'No! You'll take it!'

'No I won't!'

They slap each other's hands and Pearl tries to get away. But Diamond shoves her, and with her delicate ankles and towering shoes, Pearl goes down hard crying out in pain.

Diamond isn't falling for it though and grabs Pearl's wrist with one hand and tries to yank the ring off. Pearl kicks her with her good leg.

Travis and Helen watch their managers fight. They're like two lip-sticked pigs rolling around in rainbow mud. They grunt and squirm, pulling at each other's hair and clothing.

Finally, Diamond is able to wedge the ring off Pearl's finger. It performs an Olympic quality triple somersault and flies through the air. There is silence in the moment, and time slows as they all watch the ring fly past.

It lands in a pile of Diamond and Pearl's Povo rejects, which spans five metres wide and at least two metres high.

They scream in unison and Diamond runs towards the pile.

Pearl drags herself along at Olympic medal speed and catches Diamond's foot, as Diamond falls head first into a child's Xylophone. Her head clangs with a cartoon sound effect but she keeps moving.

Helen and Travis have the same half smile on their faces. They daren't look at each other but stand together in solidarity.

Eventually, Travis helps Pearl to her feet. Helen thinks this is extremely brown nosey and she goes back to the counter.

Shadows in the warehouse grow as the women sift through old clothes and shoes, both with smeared eye make-up, dishevelled hair, shoes off. Diamond's leopard dress is twisted up around her stomach, and her spotty undies are visible through the pink gusset of her fishnets.

Pearl's ankle has swelled up the size of an eggplant, the colour too.

Initially, they hurl frenzied insults at each other, but after a while slip into a silent rhythm. They embark on a more systematic approach using a grid, starting from the top and digging to the bottom. They do everything together because trust is a thing of the past.

It's literally a needle in a haystack.

Except the needle is gone.

Travis, despite being ripped most of the time, has excellent eyesight and spatial awareness, and clocked exactly where the ring went. He snaffled up the ring while helping Pearl to her feet.

It's a two-pronged victory. One is, of course, having the ring to himself. But the other is seeing the women fighting over it. They are despicable creatures and deserve the agony they are experiencing.

By midnight, the women have all but given up.

They should go home, but they are so suspicious of each other they sleep on the pile of old, dank clothes.

Helen sleeps well in her warm bed with its hospital cornered sheets. Beside her on the pillow are two mangled Barbies with pins in their eyes and electrical tape around their mouths and ankles.

Travis sleeps with a smug smile on his face and a very sparkly ring on his pinkie finger.

Head management of the Divine Bleeding Heart's Charity Mega-store arrive at 9:00 a.m. to inspect the store and find two sleeping half-dressed managers asleep on a huge pile of clothes. Helen had let herself in and decided not to wake them, they needed their rest.

As Diamond and Pearl are escorted from the store, not without a fuss, Brendan from Centre Management speaks to Helen in a hushed tone. He praises her good work and level head in times of turmoil and makes her Store Manager.

The next morning, Travis brings Helen a large cappuccino and a black metal cage containing two green- and sunset-coloured Lovebirds. Travis is an enterprising young man and he knows a thing or two about ensuring one flies under the radar.

Helen is delighted with her Lovebirds. She calls them Diamond and Pearl.

Cockroach

Jane Cornes Maclean

Dolores eats pickled walnuts with her fingers. When she strokes my face they smell of nicotine and vinegar. If I sleep late, she raids my clothes cupboard and wakes me with tea and toast, dressed in my best suit.

Dolores is intuitive and calm. The bathroom cabinet is full of pill bottles and sometimes I count them, just to see. In the garden, agapanthus stretch and blossom in the shade of our lemon tree. I say *our* but it's hers since I am just a visitor who won't go home.

There's one bus a day out here and once I saw our neighbour castrating a pig. In summer the fields are blonde and spiked and I spend my days swatting flies and wondering when it will rain. In winter we walk along the gravel verge to the post office because I get to touch the trees and Dolores likes puddles. Most days there is a letter for Dolores. There is never one for me. The general store sells Blundstone leather boots in grey cardboard boxes which breathe dead cow into your face when you open them up.

Dolores collects things. The lounge is lined with glass cabinets filled with the detritus of her life thus far. These include a small Japanese mouse carved out of wood taken from the world's oldest tree, a relic from the gown of St Francis of Assisi, a stone taken from the Berlin Wall, a Madonna carved from volcanic ash, the tooth of a dinosaur, dingo bones, ancient Aztec jewellery and various crystals and rocks and stones, each arranged by colour. One of the cabinets features a bronze Buddha and all the other exhibits have been turned to face it. Another cabinet features Aboriginal embroidery and curling photographs of dark men and women in tribal costume.

I rarely get angry these days – getting older has taught me that it's a waste of energy – but I do sometimes get a bit tired of her talking about her things. Casualties have included a small porcelain milk jug decorated to look like a beehive and an ornately carved crystal candleholder given to Dolores by our deceased mother.

My father, also deceased, would have liked it here. He would say time away is good for the soul. Back home he spent all his Saturdays in a small shed he built at the end of our garden. It stood in a damp, neglected corner, backing onto a makeshift plank and chicken wire fence between us and the neighbours. The chicken wire was a relatively recent addition designed to put a stop to visits from defecating dogs and a fox that dug deep, ragged holes in our lawn and flattened my mother's flowerbeds.

None of us knew exactly what my father got up to down the end there except that, from time-to-time, the tell-tale sound of hammer against wood spoke of some unseen industry. If I happened to be in the garden, I'd sometimes catch the smell of a Gauloises or hear a cough nearby and remember with surprise that he was in there. He never showed us the results of his endeavours, silent or otherwise, and we never asked.

Mother, on the other hand, spent Saturdays in her room. Saturday was 'cut-and-come-again' day in our house. In other words, if it was in the fridge, you were permitted to eat it. This was a complete departure from the usual state of affairs. On weekdays we were forbidden to take anything from the fridge, bar milk for tea, and to help oneself to, say, a cold lamb chop or leftover rice, would be to incur the full force of my mother's indignance, usually on the back of the head. But on Saturdays Mother gave up the reins of culinary control and plucked her chin instead.

There was bounty to be had on Saturday mornings and, despite a reluctance to leave my bed the rest of the week, I was always first up. My father played guitar at a working club on the other side of Clapham each Friday night and, during the break, was encouraged by the manager to help himself to the supper buffet laid on for club members.

In our fridge each Saturday morning lay the spoils of his foraging – small sandwiches cut on the cross, sausage rolls, cheese and pineapple on sticks and, most prized of all, the occasional mushroom vol-au-vent, all of it rolled up into one untidy ball which, upon careful prodding, opened, oyster-like, to reveal its disparate treasures.

I didn't eat it all, of course, but took only my share. That my siblings rarely saw any of the nicer sandwiches – beef and pickle was my favourite – and certainly never got to try one of those wonderful vol-au-vents with the creamy chicken insides was down to their own laziness. A symptom, you might say, of things to come.

With Mother in her room and Father down the back, us children were left to our own devices. We were permitted to stray as far as the local newsagent. We still called the shop Fred's despite Fred having moved on well before my brother's birth. We had seen three owners since. The latest was a too-thin Pakistani woman who always looked cold. As an adult, I have often reflected upon this woman and wondered if my memory of her dark, limpid eyes and smooth skin is a figment of my imagination, but I think not. She really was something of a beauty. I was twelve and big for my age. Had I been a little older and more understanding of my own sexual tendencies, perhaps I would have worked at removing that chill from her face. Instead, I bought chewing gum and copies of *Smash Hits* and smirked at the way she held her sari tight to her neck. She was never so shy with my mother, to whom she chatted away merrily in that exotic burred brogue of hers, of husbands and who had done what on *Coronation Street* and had my mother seen the latest recipes for toad in the hole in the *Woman's Realm*?

To be an adolescent in London again! I was still too young for going out at night with friends, but I had begun to spread my wings in different ways. One Sunday, pretending we were off on some magical adventure, I persuaded by siblings to accompany me to the city. I had a friend – a boy from school, similarly bored to rashness – who had once been to Liverpool Street Station, he told me, in tones of hushed excitement. There, he said, for 80p a small booth recorded your voice onto a record. You could say anything you liked, he said, but demurred from revealing the details of his own performance a month earlier. As it turned out, he had sung 'The Cherry Tree' in a falsetto voice most unbecoming for a lad whose destiny lay, he told me once, in being the next Alvin Stardust. 'The Older Girls,' he whispered conspiratorially, '*love* him.'

The friend had also revealed that, nearby, stood The Monument, a monolith consisting of innumerable steps – but at least a hundred, he reported – leading to a lookout where one could see the entire city. The prospect of climbing such a beast and climbing it faster than my friend, a slightly portly lad who admitted he'd needed to stop for a rest halfway up, was too much for me.

It was the summer school holidays and I had already endured five weeks of sibling torture. I played 'Jeremy the Wonder Boy' and let them put imaginary coins into my hand to bring me magically to life. I allowed Dolores to comb my hair into waves most unbecoming and had Liam take rides on my foot up and down the garden until my thighs ached.

As soon as Mother left for church we set off, ostensibly for Fred's. Once we'd completed this first section of the journey, I told my siblings our mother wanted me to buy cakes for us all and had given me the money. The truth was less sweet. I had taken a handful of change from mother's purse that morning while she did her face, the smell of *Mitsouko by Guerlain* drifting down the hallway to where I stood in the act of theft, heart beating fast and hot. Liam was up for it straight away – my strategic mention of cakes did the trick – but Dolores was less sure. I was insistent, however, declaring I didn't know how disappointed our mother would be if we failed in this, her very first test of our maturity. Indeed, I said, our mother might never allow us such a privilege again if we failed her now. In the end, I had to walk on ahead a little with my brother, leaving Dolores alone and biting at her lower lip outside the newsagent's, one foot turned foolishly in as she rotated it back and forth upon the axis of her big toe.

I confess Dolores held out for longer than I expected. As we reached the pedestrian crossing on North Street she caught up with us, panting.

'If you're sure?' she said, in the insipid, bleating tone she uses in defeat even now.

'Of course I'm sure,' I said breezily, bending slightly to take her hand and giving it what I hoped was a reassuring squeeze. She squeezed back, as was our custom. It was a trick we'd learned at church. You could say an awful lot with hand squeezes when speech was banned.

My brother started crying when the tube train pulled in. I couldn't blame him. He'd never seen one before and they really do arrive with a terrible rush of noise and air. Add to that the fact that Clapham Common is one of the older-style tube stations with a narrow, central platform and trains that stop on both sides. Sometimes when you came down the stairs there would be two trains arriving at the same time, and even I had to work on the sense of panic that rose up within me.

I'd left Liam alone on the bench only momentarily while we waited for our train. There was a chocolate vending machine at the other end of the platform and I was keen to spend some of my mother's money. As fate would have it, it was just then the train happened to pull in. I could see Liam quite clearly from where I stood. From the look on his face, I thought he might make a run for it. Instead, he sat on the seat, more-or-less rooted to the spot by terror, knees pulled up to his three-year-old chin, arms clinging tightly around them, screaming my name. Not that you could hear him, really – the noise of the train saw to that – but you could see the panic in those little eyes of his. I rushed back, of course, and did my best to calm him. I put him on my knee, stroked his hair and even used my own linen hankie to wipe his snotty little nose.

It was just after 11:00 a.m. when we reached Liverpool Street station. It was more crowded than I'd imagined and we had to push our way through the people to reach the escalator. I was still carrying my brother at this stage. He seemed tired and kept putting his thumb into his mouth even though Mother always forbade it. I pointed out all the advertising posters for shows and concerts and books as we slid up towards the sunlight and this cheered him somewhat. But he was still rather quiet, considering what adventures lay ahead.

'It's a secret mission,' I said. 'Before we get the cakes we're going to record our voices for Mum, just like pop stars!' My sister piped up that she wanted to be Lulu and I told her we'd see. Then my brother said he wanted to be Lulu, too, and Dolores and I had a good chuckle.

The recording booth was just where my friend said it would be. We all squeezed in and closed the soundproof door behind us.

My sister said she now couldn't think of anything to sing and I said, 'What about "Lulu"?'

'I don't really like "Lulu",' she said.

I turned to my brother. 'You could sing "Baa Baa Black Sheep".'

He shook his head.

'We've come all this way,' I said, losing patience, 'and now you won't sing?'

They both just sat there looking at me. I gave Dolores a push on the shoulder and she fell backwards off the seat but you could tell she had done it on purpose, to make me feel bad. I looked at my brother and he started crying again. I must have shouted because there was a knock at the door and a voice saying, 'Everything alright in there?' I shouted back that, yes, everything was fine, thank you, and waited, but there was no more from the voice.

Dolores, meanwhile, had picked herself up off the floor and was pretending to cry. I told her to stop, that she'd only get our brother started, but she just went on crying. I really began to hate her then. Here I was, trying to give them a good day out and all they could do was whinge and complain. So, I put the four 20p pieces into the slot and waited for the red recording light to come on. Afterwards, we waited until a small, black record popped out of the side. I found it not long ago searching through my things and played it to Dolores. The label's pretty scuffed up but you can just about read it: 'Copyright Singalong Services, Illinois.'

My voice sounds oddly static – as if it's coming to us from somewhere deep in space. If you turn up the volume, you can hear my brother and sister sniffling. Then there's me, introducing myself and giving the date – 12th August 1971. After a bit of throat clearing, I start to sing, terribly I confess. Then another voice joins in, sweeter and more melodic than my own if I'm honest. It is my sister, who couldn't bear to miss out on the limelight. For a while our voices swoop and glide together then a third joins in. It is my small brother.

Dolores cried when I played it to her.

Once I went into Dolores' bedroom and she was having sex with herself. I saw nipples and wet skin. In my room there's a picture of Arnold Schwarzenegger and at night he comes out to play. His dick is as big as a child's arm. Any port in a storm, as my father would say.

I went to a Tupperware party with Dolores once. She won the melon baller and I got the red toothbrush protector. You clip it over the bristles to stop cockroaches.

The Last Person to Ever Read Henry James

Ned Hirst

The last person to ever read Henry James sits quietly in her living room. She would like to be outside on her balcony, but it is another smoky day and the radio has told her to limit her exposure. An hour in this atmosphere is the equivalent of smoking five cigarettes. Whether her thin walls and never-quite-closed windows actually do anything to protect against the carcinogens is not something the radio mentions and not something she wants to think about.

Her tea ration for the month has run out but she has brought her cup and saucer with her to the table anyway. The cup is filled with hot water, but if she concentrates, she can almost imagine the taste of Earl Grey. The other sensory experiences are comforting – the clink of the cup against the saucer, the sensation of the cool handle contrasting pleasantly with the warmth of the liquid, the weight of the cup as she lifts it. Her slow breath across the surface of the water to blow away the steam. Yes, she can almost believe that it's tea.

She turns the yellowed pages carefully. Some of them are stuck together. She has already ripped some trying to prise them apart, leading to little gaps in the narrative, but they are gaps without much consequence. It's not difficult to follow the plot because these novels move at a satisfyingly glacial pace. It's not the blanks in the narrative that she laments, it's the turns of phrase she has missed out on and the witticisms no doubt lost in the missing dialogue. The slow pace is a virtue, especially now. It is nothing like the frenetic entertainments of her youth, which seemed to want to pack in as many sex scenes, explosions and car chases as possible. We know you're busy, they had seemed to say, so here are all the highlights. The whole world was like that then, urgently jumping from one highlight to another. Now that everything has become more sedate, it seems better to savour the moments between the highlights. In her experience, anticipation is usually sweeter than whatever is being anticipated. It is tension, as much as anything, that makes life worth living. The golden bowl is going to break, that much is clear. It's just a question of when.

As she walks her dog along the cracked pavement, she wonders whether it is character that determines one's fate. She feels that she is a victim of her times as much as anything, her life being pushed from one event to the next by the vicissitudes of the zeitgeist, by external forces pressing themselves upon her. As if she were flotsam being pushed and pulled, dragged under and released, by the currents. But maybe this feeling is also a function of character. Maybe she is the kind of person who lets the world guide her along rather than one who would impose herself upon it. Maybe that's just the chemicals firing inside her brain, or the family she was born into and the world she grew up in. Maybe she couldn't have changed anything about her life even if she'd tried. Could anyone have saved Isabel Archer? Could Isabel Archer have saved herself?

They arrive now at the old burned-out gas station. When it was first ransacked, there had been talk of rebuilding it. There were vehement protests on both sides. She'd felt that the station ought to be left to disappear, to fade into the past that it had represented. But she didn't march in the protests. She was happy to read about them from home. To flick through articles on her phone, sitting in her old armchair, wrapped in a blanket. Is that shameful? We need to forgo comfort, the television tells her. We are the generation called upon to make sacrifices. And it's right to make them of course. But habits can be hard to break. So, she had sympathised with those who resisted too, in a way. Why should they meekly surrender the lives they had been promised? Sometimes history needs a push, says Lenin. Sometimes it does. But maybe sometimes it needs a break from being pushed in different directions all the time. Maybe sometimes it needs to be quietly watched, sympathetically observed, from an armchair.

The sun is setting now, turning the smog a luminous green. This is always a difficult part of the day – she loves the sunset but knows it is a dangerous neighbourhood and doubly dangerous after dark.

'Come on Charlie,' she calls.

He looks up from the busted parking meter he has been sniffing and cocks his head, as if reluctant. She has heard somewhere that for a dog sniffing is like reading. He's learning all about the past of the meter and who knows what narrative he is able to form. She gives Charlie another thirty seconds' reading time before she calls again.

'Come on,' she says. 'We really need to get back.'

He cocks his head at her again, this time rather quizzically. It is whimsy on her part, but she imagines he's wondering at her urgency. This isn't the first time they have needed to hurry back home. Charlie doesn't understand why, but he seems to know that it's not good to be out after dark. He trots towards her obediently and she gathers him up. Not knowing when he will next be able to take advantage of his new-found altitude, Charlie leaps from her arms to lick her face. This, as Charlie probably suspects, is pushing things too far and she promptly puts him back down. Nonetheless invigorated by the whole experience, Charlie races ahead of her, darting down a street to the right. This was not the way they came nor the way they would usually return, but the streets to the left and right are crescents which meet at a common point and, considering it will take no longer to get back, she decides to follow Charlie's whim.

As she skips across the road to join him, Charlie intently sniffs the kerb. His interest is partly feigned; he doesn't know this street and it is getting dark and he is afraid to venture too far ahead by himself. The leafless trees along the street look strange in the dying light, like contorted hands twisting up out of the earth. It is very quiet.

She is a little spooked and begins talking to Charlie, as much to break the silence as anything else. 'Come on, Charlie,' she says. 'We'd better get a move on—'

As she says this, a window slams shut behind her. Turning her head, she sees a flash of movement as a curtain is drawn. Her heart beats faster. She feels squeamish and grips Charlie's lead tighter. Her hand is turning white. The house from which the sound just came looks like any of the abandoned houses in the district. Paint is peeling off the door and the driveway and garden are overgrown with weeds. She is a little startled by the realisation that there are people in her immediate vicinity, but the slamming of the window was a defensive act.

The person, whoever it is, seems scared, not aggressive. But still, it is a reminder. After dark, it is appropriate to be scared. She calls Charlie who ambles towards her and licks her fingers as she connects the leash to his collar. Glancing about, she begins walking briskly up the street. As far as she can tell, no one is around, but she imagines eyes bearing down on her from both sides of the road.

After a few hundred metres, the houses begin to spread themselves out. There is a little green space with a disused swing set and an overgrown garden. Right behind is a concrete monstrosity that was once a multi-storey carpark. She stops to look at it. Cracks in the concrete have created an opportunity for grass, weeds and even small shrubs to establish themselves so that the structure looks as much like a multi-level garden as a relic of the car age. Its antiquity can be judged by the fact that it doesn't even have charging stations and she wonders why it wasn't ever pulled down. Still, at the time it fell into disuse there were more pressing concerns than the re-development or demolition of car parks. She is somehow attracted to the sublime ugliness of the building, which appears alien in the half-light. She walks up to it so as to take a closer look. Leaves crunch beneath her feet. She reaches a faded old door that once provided pedestrians access to the elevator. Charlie keeps pace beside her, careful not to stray too far ahead. He's no coward, but he's not foolhardy either. She pushes at the door and it swings open a few degrees.

'Hey! Who's there?'

She jumps out of the doorway. Presses herself against the concrete wall. Her chest is tight.

'Hey! What is it?'

'What?' A second voice. Another man.

'The door.'

'What about it?'

'Someone's at the door.'

'I didn't hear anything.'

Silence. She says nothing. Charlie proves his mettle now. No whimpering or barking. He sits at her feet. Or more precisely, on her feet, a technique he employs when he's anxious about being left behind.

She stands still for what feels like several minutes but is probably less than that. For a moment, she is convinced the door is about to burst open beside her but, as time passes, she gratefully accepts the likelihood that the men have decided there was no one there and become distracted by something else. Once she is certain it is safe to do so, she retraces her steps to the road, Charlie in her arms, careful this time to avoid the leaves. She does not put Charlie down until they are safely home.

A close escape, but she will never know how close it was. Quite possibly the men had been no threat at all. Perhaps even potential friends. The problem with living in dangerous times is that any chance encounter is risky. There is no opportunity for a serendipitous meeting of minds and, to that extent, life is insular. But this is perhaps not as big a sacrifice for her as it is for others. She is a naturally retiring, introverted person. Perhaps she was born at the right time. Most of her friends would call that an insane thought, but it is easy to romanticise the past. The Renaissance sounds appealing at first – but think of the smells. And the teeth.

She boils oats slowly – slowly is the only way to boil anything on her stove – then carefully carries her porridge over to the television. The news always conjures thoughts of chaos. In years to come, perhaps someone will distil these incidents and construct a narrative and perhaps others will learn that narrative and these times will begin to have made sense. But really, there is something awfully artificial about such a process. There is no story here, only a cacophony of events – dumb, loud, unorchestrated, and unconnected events.

She thinks it might be nice if life had a narrator. Even an unreliable one. But then that same feeling might be what led people to embrace demagogues. It is nice to be told what to think by someone who claims to understand what's going on. But ultimately, no one knows. Omniscience is a cop out. All narrators are unreliable.

There is a fire on the screen. Then police and the smashing of windows. Terrified faces. Having distracted herself for a moment, she no longer knows whether this is happening here, a hundred miles from here, or on the other side of the world. It could be anywhere.

She turns off the TV and goes to scoop out some tinned offal for Charlie. As she does so, she thinks about Henry James and his repressed sexuality. Would he have been different if had he been born later? Would he have been more extroverted? Or was his privacy a personal preference, unrelated to the era he was called on to inhabit? It can be hard to separate a person from their times. Impossible, in fact. Culture sinks in deep, almost to the DNA.

She leaves Charlie's bowl on the floor and returns to her chair in the living room. A siren is wailing outside, so she stands to shut the window. Charlie is curled in his kennel. The last person to ever read Henry James turns the yellowed pages. She is patiently waiting for a golden bowl to break.

Brandy Melville

Danii Jasmine

you had sent me '*Tomorrow's Gone*' amid an All-American
valentine's day
as the morning light crept across the ceiling like an approaching
predator
once again
—*you were trying to tell me something new & sweet*—
sweet needle-tip slick & inhaling honey—
penetrating the brain that had coloured it rose—
i was yours & you
were kind of mine ...

just a little more therapy before it turns pitch dark—
i wrote five paragraphs about neglect
& emotional rollercoasters without the thrill
& about *you*

still, no one on the forum knew how to help—turns out I couldn't
even take back the words.

i don't recognise myself anymore—
in these hazy days i'm worried the people around me don't either
or that they now recognise & have warmed to this resigned
sad version far more
& to change for the better would be too much of a shock.

i'll be silently idolising all the other sad-suffered drunks
who are still beautiful
& bound to get wet
wasting away in the fake-light of a tipped vodka bottle—prettily
poisoned over the years
—every day will scream nostalgia
but in a negative way
—tainted blood fuels future buzzed evenings
& self-loathing is ever the *adult theme.*

& you—the right-leaning cheap date—*heaven's sweet fallen mistake*—
angel eyes from another time & place that always remain exactly
the same
—while it decays & dictates
your diamond basement mind absorbs worlds—
if i could ever hurt you
my adoration would be your shame

—you star in my ice-cold midnight dreams of *car crashes*
lonely graves & *hospital beds*
—it seems you're not safe even in my unconscious head.

8 o'clock
steam rising from the drain—unexpected breakdowns in the shower
& dressing for a night-drive date drunken in a dream
—happiness is booze & a best friend for a lover
—hitchhiking in the lonely night
while a cold jasmine assaulted breeze slips down throats
& straight up to lovesick heads at the speed of light
—laying out picnic blankets
in the blackness of the neighbourhood park
while you show off your glock—hold me down flat & rough
whilst making love.

we'll pass by the local longing that emanates
from the abandoned house bordering the traffic
& ignore the long-buried cry for lonesome contentment instead
—i'll lean my heavy head on reverie's shoulder
   because the brain is petitioning a need for self-love through
metaphor
that only harms more than it helps.

& in reality ...
there are circle spells of fireballs & southern comfort

still i'm far from written off—

truth or dare where the questions not so elegantly

deep dive for the hell of it

still i'm far from elated—

turns out you floated exclusively on acid & stayed in touch with
mary-jane

—breaking expensive bass guitars just for fun & lighting morrison
wannabes on fire

supposedly by accident

while pretending to *like* music ...

at the dawn of my sick tired monday—*your slow depressive sunday*

you'll take your countless pills & regretfully spend your hard-earned
money

on *Brandy Melville*

—i'll drink till 4 a.m. again & find comfort in lonesome pretend

because this is the only way to live in love as far as i can tell.

Kingston and the Bush Woman

Allen C. Jones

People mistook Kingston for a bush. There was no explaining it. Perhaps he was a bit shy, and his hair certainly could have used a trim, but he never did unequivocally bushy things like grow leaves or set down roots. As far as Kingston could tell, he was as lonely and transient and human as the best of us.

For years Kingston lived in ignorance of this condition. He knew something was wrong with him but couldn't put his finger on it. His first inkling of a problem was the day two teenagers made love on top of him. He was quietly taking sun at the lake, as was his afternoon custom, and they crawled right into his arms. They seemed so happy, Kingston didn't dare interrupt, and he even tried to hide their coupling from passers-by. They pulled his arms tight around themselves, which seemed quite sweet, but it startled the birds from his hair. As he watched the birds flutter away, Kingston wondered if he might ever get the chance to kiss someone.

His suspicions regarding his bushy condition were heightened a month later when the plant lady at work watered him. He liked to perch on the windowsill during his breaks and here came Ludmila, dousing him thoroughly, even holding his arms up to examine for spots. She was so attentive, he thought she might be in love. He nearly found the nerve to say hello.

A week later, the landscapers picked him up when he was reading in the apartment garden area and threw him into their wheelbarrow. He thought this a bit excessive, but they were speaking Spanish non-stop. Perhaps they had kindly and thoroughly explained their aggression. There was certainly no anger in it.

The final straw came when his best friend, Wayne, nearly urinated on him outside the bar.

'Is that you Kingston?' Wayne yelled in the ridiculous Elvis voice he used when drinking. 'Pardon me. I thought you were a bush.'

Suddenly a lifetime of questions were answered for Kingston: there was his kindly grandmother who always tried to yank his arms off, that belligerent flight attendant who tried to cram him into the overhead compartment, and the time his father buried him.

Kingston knew there were only two ways to defeat a world that called you a bush. Either you rejected your bushiness outright, wearing smug, non-bushy clothing (a sleek turtleneck for example) and making diminishing comments every time you passed a bush (*Looks like somebody needs a good watering*), or you confidently proclaimed your status to the world, staring men with pruning shears right in the eye: *I'm a shrub, and I'm proud!*

Kingston also knew that he would do neither. When the woman at work poured water down his shirt, he held still for her. When the landscapers hefted him into the wheelbarrow, he crouched low to balance the load. And it was only his longstanding friendship with

Wayne that allowed him to speak up as his friend unzipped his pants and began to pee on his shoes.

They went back into the bar and Wayne planted himself next to the jukebox. A young man in a turtleneck came up with a dollar bill and paused, looking uncertain. Wayne eyed him hopefully.

'This explains why bus drivers haven't charged me a fare in years,' Kingston said, dabbing his wingtips with a cocktail napkin.

Wayne shushed Kingston and pursed his lips invitingly.

The man studied Wayne up and down, then shrugged and put his bill into the jukebox.

'It's been rough lately,' Wayne said. 'It's like they can't even see me.'

People thought Wayne was a jukebox. He had been ecstatic since the day he realised this. It hadn't paid much yet, but last week, right before closing, a bachelorette party stuffed nearly five dollars of quarters in his mouth.

'They don't even have "Love me True" on this crap jukebox,' the turtlenecked man said.

'Try this jukebox,' Kingston said, pointing at Wayne.

The turtleneck nearly fell over. 'Sorry man,' he said. 'I thought you were a bush.'

Kingston bit his tongue, took the man's bill, and shoved it into Wayne's mouth.

'Look at his hands!' the man yelled to his friends at the bar. 'He totally looks like a bush – but with hands.' Wayne was having trouble swallowing the bill, so the man kicked him.

'Where's the buttons on this thing?' he yelled.

'It's voice activated,' Kingston said. 'The latest model.'

ALLEN C. JONES 281

'Love me True,' turtleneck yelled at Wayne's face. He yelled it again as Wayne finally choked down the bill.

'Do you remember how it starts?' Wayne whispered to Kingston.

'Is this a joke?' the turtleneck yelled, kicking Wayne again.

Two of his friends came over, tall and coiffed and turtlenecked to the hilt. They proceeded to kick and punch Wayne as he mixed random Elvis songs together, hoping to approximate 'Love Me True'.

'You're making it skip,' Kingston said.

The two new turtlenecks leapt back.

'Crazy right?' the first turtleneck said. 'He's totally not a bush.'

'You can't be my jukebox if you don't know the songs,' the owner yelled from behind the bar. The bouncer grabbed Wayne and Kingston and dragged them outside.

'And stay out!' the owner yelled.

The bouncer waited for the owner to go inside.

'I'm supposed to throw you down on the ground,' he said, 'but I hurt my arm choking a guy yesterday. Do you mind throwing yourselves down? Maybe by the window where the owner can see?'

'I'm getting tired of it,' Kingston said, throwing himself down next to Wayne. 'Aren't you?'

'You've got to take some knocks if you want to make it,' Wayne said, dusting off his pants and then throwing himself down again for good measure.

'You're not a jukebox,' Kingston said. 'You are an unemployed CPA who likes karaoke.'

'I'm a jukebox, and I'm proud.'

Times were desperate when even your best friend didn't understand. But Kingston was a guy who got mistaken for a bush. Guys mistaken for a tank, or a jet plane, or even a jukebox made big moves. But a bush?

The next day, Kingston called in sick and went to the botanical gardens. He snuck behind the crystal palace and tucked himself in with the ferns. A pair of old women pointed him out and clucked. 'Needs help that one,' they said. One of them leaned over and plucked out a grey hair.

It's unbelievable the cruelty of the world, Kingston thought. Even the old women are in on it.

After three days, Kingston still couldn't break his depression. He drank gallons of water, overdosed on vitamin B-1, and left his sun lamp on night and day, but nothing helped. What he needed was to completely uproot himself. He looked down at his very human feet and pulled them up one after the other, feeling quite rootless already.

It could be worse, he thought. I could be mistaken for a weed.

On the morning of the fourth day, standing in front of the library waiting for the sun, Kingston noticed the blatant bravery of the ivy. It had scaled the arched brick entry and at the top, hung its legs right out into the air. *What a show off*, Kingston thought, knowing he would never dare make that climb.

'Excuse me,' a voice said. 'You're trampling me.'

The voice belonged to a beautifully dishevelled young woman sitting deep in the honeysuckle by the book-return.

'What are you doing in there?' Kingston asked.

'Waiting for the sun.'

'Do people mistake you for a bush too?'

'Are you mad?' she asked.

What an idiot he was. A girl finally talks to him rather than watering him, and he calls her a bush.

'It's just that people mistake me for a bush,' he said, perennially honest.

'Sit,' she said, patting the ground next to her.

Her name was Amarantha, and she had long elegant arms and a face like a flower. They sat quietly together. A bee alighted in her hair. A bird tried to pull off one of Kingston's eyebrows. It was idyllic.

For the next three days, they were inseparable. They sunned themselves all morning outside Kingston's apartment, giggled madly when the landscapers gave them rides in the wheelbarrow, and took turns dunking each other in the drinking fountain. In the evening they curled up on the sofa, entwining their limbs so thoroughly, they no longer could tell one from the other.

On day seven, Kingston introduced her to Wayne.

'How's the jukebox business?' Kingston asked, finding Wayne at the bar.

'*Wise men say,*' Wayne belted out, speaking in the pauses between singing. 'The jukebox plays on that side of that bar – *only fools rush in* – and I get this – *but I can't help* – side. I split what I make – *falling in love* – with the owner.'

'This is my new friend Amarantha,' Kingston said.

'Very funny,' Wayne said.

'What?' Kingston said.

'Actually, that's great Kingston,' Wayne said. 'It's best to just – *like a river flows* – accept it. I mean – *darling so it goes* – look at me. They're loving me tonight.'

'What a crap version of Elvis,' a guy in a blood-red turtleneck yelled from the bar.

'How can you stand it?' Kingston asked.

'Are you kidding me?' Wayne said. 'These people love it – *crying all the time.*'

'This is a sad place,' Kingston said. 'It's full of people who look a person right in the face, a real human being, and call him a bush.'

'What do you have against bushes?' Amarantha asked, bringing two pints of water from the bar.

Kingston looked around at all the beautiful people, tucked into their skin-tight clothing, not a strand of anything loose or out of place, all ducking and grimacing like unhappy soldiers under the gunfire of Wayne's atonal onslaught. A guy in a turtleneck with the sleeves cut off to display his enormous biceps threw his beer at Wayne. A petite woman with a turtleneck up to her ears and diamonds everywhere belched out, '*You ain't nothing but a hound dog*' in unison with Wayne.

Kingston looked at his old friend and smiled sadly. There was no denying that Wayne had found his destiny. The whole bar was going wild, cursing and wrestling their way to jam fives and tens into Wayne's mouth, barely able to keep their turtlenecks on.

'Let's run away together,' Amarantha said quietly.

Kingston agreed immediately, but as she grabbed his hand and they dashed for the door, he took one final look back. A woman had climbed on top of Wayne and was swinging her turtleneck overhead like a lasso. The blood-red turtleneck was punching Wayne as hard as he could, unable to believe the song never skipped. Even the owner had given in, reaching down and ceremoniously unplugging the other jukebox. And there was his friend, at the centre of it all, cheeks bulging with money.

'*You ain't no friend of mine,*' Wayne yelled happily, waving goodbye.

Amarantha told him only that they were heading west. Kingston decided to simply trust her. Plant yourself near this woman, he told himself, and the rest will take care of itself. He stocked up on B-1 for the trip and said goodbye to his family. His father tried to water him. His sister and mother held up his arms and checked for spots.

They almost didn't make it out of town. When they were packed and ready to go, some green-thumb do-gooder carried Amarantha off and planted her in a park flowerbed. It took Kingston hours to find her. Then a local marijuana grower mistook Kingston for a plant, snatched him up, and drove him fifty miles to his secret farm in the hills. It took him two days to get back, no one wanting to stop for a hitchhiking bush. And, finally, a pesticide truck doused them on their way to the bus, but even this couldn't stop them.

As the bus pulled away, they turned and took a final look at the city receding behind them.

'How can anyone grow there?' Amarantha asked.

Kingston shook his head, not sure if it was the pesticide or true joy that was making him so high. On the bus, an old woman came down the aisle, tugged lightly on both of their eyelashes, and then poured water over their heads.

Kingston expected to grow angry. Instead, he just laughed. It was all so clear to him now. Roaring away from the city, with fresh air streaming in the window and Amarantha's hand held tightly in his own, he could see the truth – this woman was simply mad.

They travelled deep into the heart of the country, staying in forgotten roadside motels, even taking turns passing as a bush so they could travel on a single ticket. Still, Kingston had his doubts. Amarantha was almost too beautiful. Her limbs were delicate as a plant's tendrils, her hair as tussled as a pile of leaves, and her eyebrows as mottled and soft as bark. Why would she pick him, a man mistaken for a bush?

After three days, Amarantha said they had arrived. Kingston looked around in disbelief. This was not what he had imagined. The bus had pulled into a desolate town full of boarded-up houses with tarp-strung roofs. A burro wandered by, his skin strung taught against the keyboard of his ribs.

Amarantha walked briskly to a rundown motel, skipping joyfully as if half the rooms were not blackened and destroyed by fire. A barren plain stretched in every direction. Not a single flower bloomed.

'Isn't it great?' Amarantha asked as they stepped into their dusty, fire-scarred room.

They scrubbed the tub clean, soaked for an hour, then climbed into bed. Amarantha slept as still as the dead, but Kingston tossed and turned and dreamt all night of losing the perfect happiness he had finally found.

In the desert, Amarantha was a woman possessed. Every day, she led Kingston out onto the mesa where the sun beat down so hot he could barely breathe, and all day they walked in the blistering heat, endlessly circling as if searching for something. Every time Kingston asked what they were doing, Amarantha would simply usher him forward, smiling as if these were the happiest days of their lives. But each evening when they returned to their rooms, Kingston saw that Amarantha was slowly dying. Her elegant arms shrivelled until they were little more than strands, and her face grew as fragile and crinkled as paper. Full of desperation, Kingston tried to make her stay home and rest, and when she wouldn't, he took to dipping her limbs into cool tubs of water as she slept.

Late in the afternoon on the third day, after hiking endless hours in the sun, Kingston couldn't take any more. The whole world might be crazy, but he would rather take her back to the city and be called a bush then let her wander around madly in the desert, her body slowly wasting away. The world might be a terrible place, but if the alternative was to come here and die, he would take no part in it.

'It's time to go home,' he said, stepping around a burro carcass and taking her in his arms.

'You're right,' she said, though she did not look at him, casting her gaze instead across the empty desert.

A hawk screamed from the bone white sky. A hot blast of wind threaded the burro's bones. Plastic bottles and bits of tarp skittered across the sand, chased by tumbleweeds.

Kingston knew he did not have the strength to stop her. He was just Kingston. He yearned for a time when being a bush was his biggest worry. He yearned to hear Wayne butchering Elvis. He even admitted that turtlenecks were not innately evil.

'Only fools rush in,' Amarantha said, curling her brittle body into a ball. The wind gusted, and as she tumbled away, Kingston could hear her beautiful laughter echoing across the mesa.

Kingston considered the things the world tells us, that we are bushes or jukeboxes or turtlenecks, that death is inevitable, that love is forever, that plant and man must sink their roots deep into the earth or perish, and then he thought of Amarantha's papery touch, her long dry legs threaded through his own, the leafy hair she'd shed around their bed like rose petals, and finally he made up his mind. Closing his eyes, imagining himself a bush so light it might fly, he tucked in his arms, leaned forward, and started to roll.

Video Capture

Clare Testoni

MyBabyMilestones: Day 42. After one month your baby should react to pain and other unpleasant stimuli.

Her scream wakes me. I jump out of bed and scoop her into my arms. Michael stirs, squints sleepily at Mia and me before rolling over with the pillow over his ears. I 'shhhh' and rock her gently. She still screams. Her face so twisted it looks painful. I tap the screen of my smart-watch – it's 3:23 a.m. I open the tracking app. I'd been sleeping for forty-nine minutes according to the pie chart. I hit the emoji of the crying baby to add it to the log. She's not due for her feed, and she's dry. So I hold her and soothe her and make more shhhing sounds like the white noise machine in the corner. She still screams. Her face is red. Her small fists are balled; her whole body strains.

Michael picks up his noise-silencing headphones. I sit in the chair in the corner and try to feed her. At first, she thrashes against my breast, batting my swollen and tender nipple that stands alert for her, but after a moment she opens wide and latches. The room is hushed. Just her little sucking sounds, the white noise machine, the faint muffled sound of Michael's audiobook through his headphones, and an electric whir I can't place. I look around for the source of the whir and realise it's the camera of the baby monitor, the one mounted on the crib. It's the camera focusing in the low light, following Mia with its glossy dark eye.

My head aches with lack of sleep. I stare at the camera in the dark and want to wriggle away from its gaze, but I can't move without upsetting Mia. Her legs twitch in little kicks of pleasure, or reflex, I'm not sure. I want to enter the little habit into my habit-journal on my watch, but as soon as I re-position my left hand slightly she wrenches away from me and bellows again. I try and re-attach her but she flails again. She writhes in my arms so that I almost drop her. I stand and pace around the room. The camera follows, swivelling on its axis, watching as I try to soothe and burp her. Michael stands with a loud sigh and picks up the doona, heading for the couch. The first week like this he stayed up with me, the second and third we took it in shifts, but now he simply needs sleep. Now, his leave is all used up and only one of us can afford to be a zombie. I scroll my phone with my free hand – the screen floods Mia's face with blue and the camera whirs again to the changing light.

KanyKane_99: BABY WONT SLEEP

Hi, my 7wk old has so far no sleeping pattern. Me (32) and my husband (35) have no idea what to do. She is sleeping for no more than an hour at a time and I'm just at the point where I can't keep not having any sleep. Please help!

MyBabyMilestones: Day 43. Your baby can now see up to 10cm in front of their face in focus. They still see in black and white.

My watch buzzes gently against my wrist. It's 1:30 p.m., Mia is due for a feed. She is lying on her back underneath her rotating black and white mobile as I drink my third cup of decaffeinated coffee. I put her to my breast and prop her up with a nursing pillow so that my hands are free to type into the Google search bar: baby not sleeping

It gives me back 2,290,000,000 results in 0.54 seconds. I read a very gently written article about how motherhood is tough and sometimes babies just cry and how it's important to seek—

New search. I start to type in 'effects of lack of sleep in babies', but I've only typed in 'eff' when the suggested searches fill:

effects of non-nurturing mothers

effects of lack of sleep in babies

effects of not sleeping

effects of sleeping too much

Why is the non-nurturing mother thing first? Am I not nurturing? I look down at Mia propped up on my breast by the pillow. My stomach sinks with guilt. I look around the empty bedroom in the soft daylight. Only the camera is watching, trained on its charge. Michael told me I could change the settings so it doesn't follow me around, but the app is very confusing.

New search: 'how do I stop my baby monitor from following me?'

There are 1,500,000,000 results in 0.75 seconds:

How To Protect Your Baby Monitor From Hackers In Three ...

Why Parents Should Stop Using Baby Monitors | POPSUGAR ...

Yes, Your Video Baby Monitor Can Be Hacked. No, You Don't ...

I hover over the 'How to Protect Your Baby ...' article, about to click, when Mia detaches and screams. I guide my nipple back into her mouth and when I look up, I can't quite face the links. Michael set it up, I'm sure it's fine. I just need to figure out how to change the setting.

GAMER_GIRL_66: MY WEBCAM IS SHOWING MY SOMEONEELSES HOUSE

When I bring up the feed from my Anpwoo YT003 on my phone (iPhone9) I'm getting a picture of a house that isn't mine. Tried to do a manual reset but it won't talk to my laptop. Has anyone else had this issue? Please help, I've tried everything!

I wake to Mia's frantic snuffles and realise I'm suffocating her with my breast. My eyes had closed of their own accord. As soon as she can breathe, she screams.

'I'm sorry, I'm sorry,' I whisper.

Tears roll down my cheeks as I let her scream at me for hurting her.

'I'm sorry, I'm sorry. Shhhhhh.'

Michael's on the couch watching television. I look at my watch and realise it's 8:42 p.m. I am covered in a thin film of breastmilk and vomit. I bring up the baby monitor feed onto my phone and put it in a waterproof pouch before stepping into the bathroom and pegging the phone onto the shower rack. I strip off my clothes and, for a moment, I catch my body in the mirror. My belly is still liquid, like a deflated balloon, my breasts are swollen and veined through my fair skin. For a moment I don't recognise myself.

Under the water, the tenderness of my breasts eases a little. The feeling of soap against my skin, of shampoo in my hair, is better than any massage, or yoga class I can remember having. I look at Mia lying in the blue light of the camera's night vision. She is quiet, still – too still? Is she breathing? *Don't be paranoid*, I think. *Ignore the pull of your hormones and instincts. Stay logical.* I remember how I used to judge my sister for her obsessive maudlin baby proofing and hovering.

'She's lost it,' I'd told Michael after meeting her for coffee when my nephew was six months old. 'Full baby brain. I'm not sure when she's coming back. We used to talk about films and books and the news. She just talked about shit, vomit, and sleep. Oh, and cot death. It was so depressing.' I had tossed my high heels in the corner and vowed never to become so boring.

I turn the shower off and step out to dry my body and wrap my hair in its moisture-wicking cap. Going to un-peg my phone from its place in the shower, I hear a loud sigh. It is not the light sigh of a baby's lungs. It is a slow exhale, deep and masculine. It rattles through the tinny audio of my phone. I walk out of the bathroom. Michael is still on the couch watching Netflix. I look down at the phone again. I hold it close to my ear and hear another rattling breath of a man. I can imagine the flare of meaty nostrils watching Mia sleep. It's a hovering breath that I know from being trapped in elevators and buses with men who stand too close. From taxi drivers who watch the backseat and not the road. It's the groan of air that some men make when I pass them on the street and their eyes linger.

I hold my panic and walk quickly into the bedroom, my towel around me. The room is empty. Mia sleeps peacefully in her bassinet.

I go loose with relief. I laugh a little at my own paranoia. I pull on an old set of button-up pyjamas and lie on the bed, hollow with tiredness. I hear the electric whir of the camera turning towards me, watching me. I hear the masculine breathing again, heavy and close. I sit up and look over at the bassinet. The camera is trained on Mia, and the room is quiet. I turn on Mia's noise machine and the sound of rain plays. I lie in the dark, listening to digital storms.

ASTRO*BOi*: AM I DOING SOMETHING WRONG?

So I set up my new webcam (running a Canon DSLR through an Elgato Cam Link) and it's working fine but I can't get the audio to work. I've set it up with USB and aux power. What am I doing wrong? I've tried everything!

MyBabyMilestones: Day 48. Your baby will smile in response to your smile.

12:30 a.m. My wrist vibrates. The room is dark and still. Michael lies beside me, sleeping. Mia is silent, the digital rain continuously falls, sporadic booms of soft thunder roll. The same thunder burst again and again. Lightning strikes over and over. I wonder if I should wake her. I want to keep the feeding schedule. She's only in the fortieth percentile for weight, the thirtieth for height. Well, she was always likely to be small like me. Her eyes are blue like mine still, but they might darken to Michael's hazel. I look over at her, at her sleeping through the mesh of her bassinet. My eyes slide closed as I watch her. They snap open again as I see the glint of the camera lens tracking me, not Mia. I freeze. I tuck in the edges of the blanket around me like I did as a child.

_Phoneix_3: AM I GOING CRAZY?

So I (f38) keep putting things down in a specific place. Like my nappy bag, or my keys and then I swear when I go to look for them they're not there. My SO (m42) thinks I have postpartum but I feel fine! Happy and normal. Is this just mommy brain? Or is there a goddamn ghost in my house? Please help! I have no idea what is going on.

MyBabyMilestones: Day 49. Your baby now follows movement with their eyes.

My watch buzzes alerting me to movement on the camera. I look down at the square screen on my wrist as I change Mia on the lounge-room floor. There is a speck of liquid shit on the white rubber band of the watch.

I unplugged the camera this morning when Michael took Mia while I had a shower and ate a proper meal. He was a little late to work, but he didn't want to hand her back. He had kissed me goodbye, smelling so clean in his suit. The kiss was full of apology.

I dress Mia again and bring up the monitor app on my phone by tapping the alert. The familiar black and white night-vision appears. I see a cot, empty, the sheets white or a very light colour, like our light yellow ones. But this is not Mia's bed. It is not our bedroom. The camera moves to track the room, rotating its head. I watch as a black shape comes into focus, the camera buzzing its lens to the correct depth. I hear the deep breathing of someone sleeping. The camera stills on a white face in the dark. A woman, her hair a dark smudge could have been anything from red to black, her face mutable in sleep.

Her eyes open and she looks straight at the camera, they are fluorescent in the dark.

I close the app quickly, my chest tight. Had that been me? I open the app again, but it tells me that my camera is not delivering a feed.

Si_ The_IT_GuY_: SEND HELP!

It takes everyone three hours to get their baby to sleep right?!! and they sleep for 30mins at a time RIGHT?!!! HAHAHAHAHAHAHA Is it too late to get an upgrade to a new model? Can I trade him in? Anyone else knows how to troubleshoot this? FML.

MyMabyBilestones: Day 49. Your baby now follows movement with their eyes.

Her screams started at 5:00 p.m., just before Michael got home, and continued through dinner and through Michael taking her for an hour so I could take a break. She calmed while I fed her, but then the screams started again. She is fed and dry and burped and held, and still, she screams.

Michael offers to walk her around the block for a few hours while I get some sleep. I nod, reluctant and grateful. There is something wrong, I feel the dread of it. I brush my teeth and look at my swollen face in the mirror. My skin is crepe-y, I look like my mother. My hair is knotted and greasy, even though I washed it yesterday ... didn't I?

I turn off the light and spit my toothpaste in darkness, not wanting to see the mirror.

twitchb1tch_: HELLO IM EXPERIENCING A LAG

My SO has tried helping but I can seem to get my 4MO LO to catch up. There seems to be an echo that pulls the image out of sync and it only seems to work when I'm breastfeeding. I have no idea what else to try. I've tried going odour free and making the room light-tight but that hasn't seemed to work. Should I just give up on an HDMI connection? It's driving me insane! Is there anything I can do to speed up or is this just something I need to be patient with? HELP!!!

MabeyMilestones: Day 49. Your camera now follows movement with their eyes.

I wake to her screaming. Where is my watch? What time is it? Michael has left for work and I realise she's been screaming for some time, that she'd been screaming in the dream I was in. My watch is on the floor, buzzing. I don't remember taking it off. My back is sore and my left arm, numb. I have slept in the same position all night. She must be so hungry.

I pick her up and take her to the feeding chair shhhing and rocking. I put her to my breast. She fusses then settles. I watch her pink lips on my mauve nipple, and I feel light, drunk. She is calm and happy after feeding. I place her in her bassinet and look at the unplugged camera above it. I want a shower and a coffee. I spin her mobile above her and plug the camera back in. Scooping up my watch from the floor, I flick off all the alarms I missed and leave it to charge as I undress and pull up the app on my phone.

I scrub my pits and get out of the shower in under one minute. I scoop up the phone as I head to the kitchen for a coffee. A note on the fridge from Michael says that he fed Mia with some freezer milk this morning. He didn't write the time. I text him for more details to put in the log. I try to open the app but it's buggy and keeps closing. Have I over-fed her now? Annoyed, I pull on a pair of knickers, a maternity bra, and a t-shirt while the kettle boils. I check the camera feed – Mia is awake, watching her mobile.

I bring my coffee and a slice of toast into the bedroom and place them on the desk in the corner. I tickle Mia's tummy and leave her there while I drink, eat, and open my laptop. I have fifty-two new messages from people and organisations I had completely forgotten existed. I skim past updates from friends and colleges. One message appears to be to me, from me, and I try and remember if I emailed myself an article or a post to read later. I open it.

It's an image. Black and white, the focus soft like a photocopy, of me in bed, sleeping. There is only one line in the email under the image:

Please help. I've tried everything.

Evisceration of the Clock

Jeimer Ng

I was there when they made the decision to rid the world of clocks. Watches, timers, sundials, hourglasses, candles. You name it, any standard method of keeping time was burned. Something about there not being enough time? I don't remember, exactly. Of course, time was still there. It never left. Never will. But it was no longer dictated through numerical increments and ticking hands on a plate. Instead, it was gauged through one's own ears. People all over the world began listening to each moment, tuning into what their situation called for until it was satisfied. There were no more deadlines. No more *due by*-s. No more *early*-s or *late*-s. Not in the conventional sense, at least. Admittedly, things did get pretty chaotic for a while. Trains crossing paths and missing each other by inches. Football games being played for days. I remember most distinctly the bedlam that ensued at airports. People arriving would land at their destination long after intended. But amidst the mayhem would be those departing who no longer left the embrace of lovers and loved ones in haste. What we were left with was the annihilation of regret, the erasure of remorse for time lost. No more *I-have-to-go*-s. No more *stay-a-little-longer*-s. No more *don't-leave*-s. What remained, is what should be.

Time well spent.

But They Sing Gloriously

R.A. O'Brien

The first baby born with nubbins arrived on 7th November at 10:03 p.m. in a small hospital in a country town in the West Australian wheat belt. Think: open land rolling away to the horizon, straw-coloured wheat-stubble, grazing, grubby-fleeced sheep, and the smell of eucalypts and dust. The town population was 1,477 + 1. Tiny. Blink and you'd miss it. The town and the hospital both. The baby, too. Tiny and very sweet. But.

The midwife and doctor both thought the new-born's bone structure looked odd, not quite right. The shoulder blades were malformed and the arm bones seemed particularly long. They sent the mother and the baby – a girl called Marjorie – to a bigger hospital. Better facilities. Medical specialists. The doctor and midwife in the country town washed their hands of it. Went home, ate, went to bed. Not together, although she wouldn't have minded, but the doctor hadn't figured that out. Tomorrow would be another day.

As happens, tomorrow faded past as well. A few days after that there was a piece in the newspaper. Then they remembered.

By the time the newspaper caught wind of the story, seven babies with nubbins on their shoulder blades had been born throughout the wheat belt. Because the big smoke was Perth, and because there was only one hospital there specialising in maternal and infant health, the babies all ended up in the same place. A funnel effect. If the nubbins had started somewhere else – in Europe or the US or South America or someplace – it might have taken much longer to piece things together. But the wheat belt is close to empty and the structure of the health system created an agglomeration of strangeness. Peculiar babies became visible quickly. The public health apparatus swung into action. The well-being of the infants was closely monitored.

The newspaper piece was written simply to fill up the pages. Summer. Shortly after Christmas. And no bushfires to report. They would surely come, but not yet. A slow news week. The paper had needed to find local interest stories. Otherwise, the story might never have seen the light of day.

Its first appearance was on page twelve. A long way in from the front and an even number. People look at the odd-numbered pages first. Sometimes they miss looking at the even-numbered ones altogether. A page twelve human-interest story. Ho-hum.

The TV stations were just as news-deprived and one of them tumbled to the idea of running the baby story. It wouldn't really be a repeat; they had the advantage of cameras. The other nine babies (now a total of ten) were sick, asleep, or crying, but Marjorie 'gooed' and smiled and didn't cry a bit. The news crew took hours of video.

Marjorie was a particularly endearing new-born. She had a fine-featured face, long, slender arms and fingers, a pretty mop of curly black hair, and wide-awake eyes. The nubbins on her shoulder blades were visible, even in the footage – no small thing given the crew was not permitted to set up lights in the hospital and the camera tended to make everything look flatter than it was. Instant poster-child.

The slow summer news continued. Cricket. Heat waves. Crowds at the beach. Sticky ice-creams. Sand so hot it burned your feet.

Got a beer in that cooler?

Put some sunscreen on.

Want to come over on Sunday for a barbie?

Didja see the story about the babies? It was on the news last night.

Yeah, pretty kid, but weird to have so many, eh?

The lack of news created opportunities. A loose coalition developed. Green-ish influencers, lobby groups (some solid, some mad as cut snakes), political parties looking for airtime, Members of Parliament, sensationalists, believers in alien abductions, concerned parents, PC academic humanists, intrigued medical researchers, anti-vaxxers, and a group calling itself the Alliance Against Coal-Fired Electricity Plants (AACFEP), all shared a concern about the babies' welfare. Strangest of all, a group of citizens worried about the discharge of bilge water into the local marine environment also took up the babies' cause. Everybody wanted exposure. The most popular hashtag in the relevant part of the cyberverse was initially *#BabyDeformities*, then *#BabyModifications*, then, finally, *#BabyMods*. Most thought the baby mods were the result of pollution. Blamed toxic farming methods, petrochemical aerosol sprays, GM foods, ground water. Blamed God (some did so, privately). Blamed science. Blamed greed.

As well as their structural oddities, at birth the babies were covered in a colourless, fine, downy hair. By three months the hair had disappeared, then the feathers started appearing. At first, only a tuft poked through the nubbins' skin, skin that seemed itchy. The babes wriggled endlessly, seemingly to scratch their backs. X-rays, MRIs, blood tests. Nothing conclusive except conclusive oddness. By week 14 there were 79 babies born with nubbins, 31 of whom were showing feathers. By week 27 the number of baby mod cases had risen to 113. Most had feathers. No new baby mod cases had come to light for five weeks. It seemed as if the avalanche of new strange kids might have slowed and the total number of occurrences peaked. That was the point at which the feathered nubbins began to stretch and open, to unfurl.

The hospital staff tried to keep knowledge of the wings under wraps, tried to give the infants and their parents some privacy. Might as well have tried to stop the planet spinning on its axis.

Medical specialists were deeply divided. Some wanted to amputate the wings immediately, arguing that doing so would give the babies the best chance of a normal life. Some argued that the functionality of the wings had yet to be established, so why assume they'd be a bad thing? Others argued that parents had a right to choose, if they wished, to have their infant's wings 'surgically adjusted'.

Meanwhile, the news leaked. Someone called them 'angels' and it stuck. The reporters had a label. The public's imagination was hooked. The supernatural was now definitely in play.

The Cathedral priests met at breakfast.

One said to the other: 'Did you see the page three photo?'

A raised eyebrow.

'I didn't think they did that sort of thing in this newspaper.'

The paper was picked up, the page turned.

'Damn. We'll have to let his nibs know.'

As they anticipated, the Archbishop was less than impressed.

'Angels. For God's sake. No one except the ignorant and superstitious believe in angels anymore. The Second Vatican Council should have done something useful and ruled them out. Well, we've lost that opportunity. Bloody nonsense.'

The Catholic Archbishop conferred with his Anglican counterpart.

'Visitations of the Virgin and appearances of saints are quite problematic enough. We don't need angels. These fantasies always give rise to fallacies amongst the faithful.'

'I agree,' said the Anglican counterpart. 'They lead the people astray from obedience to the Church.'

The Catholic Archbishop looked meaningfully across the desk. 'And they're bad press. Look at the trouble we had last time the Virgin appeared. Complaints from government. Religious tourism running out of control. Thousands of people camping out. It was a mess.'

'We certainly wouldn't be acting responsibly if we didn't protect our congregations from unscrupulous scammers, liars, and fake news,' the Anglican counterpart said, smiling.

So, they were in communion. For once. Not that it made any difference.

The babies' wings grew. An entranced public watched it all on YouTube. Especially Marjorie. She was still poster-child #1. Her father never said no to a camera. By the time the children were eighteen months of age, there were signs that their wings would eventually be able to hold them aloft. Learning to fly seemed as innate as learning to walk. Like fledgling birds, they flapped their wings endlessly. As they grew stronger, they practised tiny lift-offs. Fell short distances. Manoeuvred to gain directional control. Rehearsed landings.

Walking, flying, talking, running. Finding a ball and throwing it. Patting the family dog. Delivering big smackeroo kisses. Waving goodbye. The babies, now toddlers, were learning it all.

The press started to call the parents 'philangeli', friends of angels. Tourist companies organised pilgrimages taking the gawking credulous from home to home, driving down the streets on which the philangeli lived, all on the off chance of seeing a winged child. Some of the philangeli put out nails to puncture the tyres of the curious. Others put out collection boxes. Many moved house, changed their names.

Then someone had the bright idea of doing a genetic analysis. Check that the kids were from the right parents, hatched in the appropriate place, not from the wrong nest. Not cuckoos. And – surprise, surprise – there in the genetic code, was an anomaly. A sequence inserted that shouldn't have been there. An ornithological snip, slidden into their human code. But by what means? When they were born, the angels had been far flung, strewn over an area larger than England. There were those who said the mothers had been fucking emus, or that they had been abducted by aliens-with-plumage and implanted with rogue DNA. It remained a mystery, and about that mystery no one with a claim to relevant expertise expressed any opinion whatsoever.

By the time the children were around five years old they flew well and had started school. They were robust and healthy, they walked and talked and wanted their parents to read them bedtime stories. They liked or hated school lunch boxes, swimming and ballet lessons, drawing, arithmetic, hopscotch, video games, being alone, being at the centre of a crowd, birthday parties, burgers, dogs, cats, horses, the colour yellow, and a million other things. Apart from the wings, they were normal children. Well, the wings and one other thing: they could all sing.

Under the supervision of her parents, Marjorie continued to be the poster-child for the angels. Cute as a button and such pretty wings. She smiled willingly for the cameras. Besides, she was the forerunner of all that came. Her father thought she was the bee's knees, wings and all. Her mother wasn't so sure – she was already frightened before the Molotov cocktail shattered their bedroom window late one Friday night.

Marjorie was hurt in the ensuing blaze. One wing was burned badly, feathers seared off. What remained turned from white to black. The medicos thought they might have to amputate but decided to try saving the wing. They didn't know if she would fly again. Didn't know who they could call upon to help with her rehabilitation. In the end, they called in the people who dealt with injured raptors, got them to help with her retraining and physiotherapy. Slowly, she recovered. But she was fearful, jittery. She was no longer the same Marjorie. Her mother wasn't the same, either. Scoured by media attention and violence, she'd had enough. She wouldn't be Marjorie's mummy anymore.

The homeless man who prowled the Botanic Gardens near the opera house in Sydney changed his sign. *Repent for the Kingdom of Heaven is nigh* was discarded. The new sign read: *Some have entertained angels unawares*. In Melbourne, someone had started writing *Angels* in empty spaces on buildings, footpaths, steps, river embankments. A beautiful cursive script in glowing, golden chalk. There was talk of a new Australian movie being made – the working title was *Strangers*.

So, there we were – media, citizens, politicians, churches, and all – alone with the possibility of having to welcome something completely new amongst us. An unhappy prospect.

Canberra was busy, Parliament was sitting. 'It won't do, Minister,' Max said. He was wearing his particularly proper Minister's Adviser face.

'What do you expect me to do, Max? They're children, for God's sake. How would it look if I had them bumped off or imprisoned?'

'They are not children, they're aberrations. Things that should never have been born.'

'I've seen the photos. They look quite attractive. What's all this shite about?'

'They're birds, Minister.'

'Don't be idiotic.'

'Feathers, thus birds.'

'Feathers, thus angels. I've seen those twee Christmas cards with Raphael's cherubs on them. So have half the population. No, Max. We wouldn't be able to sell that. Birds! No parent would buy it. Besides, I'd have to have new legislation. And before you go there, it isn't going to happen. Find something else to feed the press, can't you? A dash of some new hysteria should do it.'

The Minister's Adviser drew a breath. 'There are also financial implications.'

'And what are those?'

'The scientists want special funds made available to study them. The medicos are claiming they need new Medicare-funded codes – higher rates – because they have to work harder and it takes more time to sort out ... whatever it is they sort out when one of these ...

is brought in by its parents because it's sick. The clothing industry is in an uproar.'

'Clothing? The rag trade?'

'Yes, they'll have to design new patterns for everything. It will cost them, Minister.'

'Pardon me, but don't they develop new patterns for everything each season? I thought that was the whole point?'

'And they cost schools more. Can't sit on chairs, you see. Wings get in the way. They need stools.'

'Look, Max, cut the crap. Something's got your knickers in a knot, and it's not stools or patterns.'

'There's a new paper coming out. CSIRO and some university have done the research. They sent us a copy ahead of publication. Probably thought we'd give them an elephant stamp or something.' Max paused.

'Don't keep me in suspense.'

'There are too many people involved to suppress it.'

The Minister spoke in his quietest voice. His most dangerous one. 'Why, exactly, would we want to suppress it?'

'They did some – I don't know. A genetic study plus some sort of anatomical thing. They can probably cross-breed. With us. You know, daughter marries thing-with-wings and Mum and Dad end up grandparents to an ornithological freak. It's one thing when it's someone else's kid and there's only a handful of them, then it's just weird. When they start invading your own family, though. Horrifying. Terrifying. The punters will never vote for it.'

'It'll be a while before they hit puberty. We've got time.'

'Two elections are all you can safely bet on, Minister.'

The Minister peered at his Adviser over the edge of his glass of cabernet then carefully placed it down on the table. 'I'll talk to the PM.'

The angels seem comfortable enough in the enormous aviary built for them at the zoo – government funded, of course. At first, they wept for their parents. Marjorie, especially, cried for her dad, her blackened wing trembling.

The sign on the cage reads: *Do not feed*. The unspecified nature of the occupants is a compromise. No one will approve *Do not feed the children* and mention of angels is verboten. Their meals are controlled. They don't seem to notice the contraceptives added to the food.

Someone has daubed writing on the concrete wall at the end of their cage. The paint is the same golden colour as the chalk inscriptions. Whatever was written, it's mostly illegible now.

They spend their days in the heights. They rarely speak to passers-by and ignore their keepers. They have abandoned us. But they still sing gloriously.

Endnotes

Notes for 'Ode to Uśas: This Time Let's get the Dawn Right' – *Soudhamini*

Note on title: Ś in *Sanskrit* is pronounced as 'sh'. Thus *Uśas*, in the title is pronounced as Ushas.

1. Derived from the Sanskrit √*ma*: to measure, *Māya* in Indian philosophy refers to the formative cosmological principle by which this phenomenal universe comes into being.

2. *Drupad* is the oldest form of classical Indian music, very close to Vedic recitation. It is performed even today and is best known for its elaborate *aalaap* – an Urdu word that means 'conversation' and is considered somewhat whimsically to be a conversation between the musician and their music. For it is an 'informed improvisation' of particular scales known as a *raaga*, without deviating from its prescribed notes yet exploring it freely without pre-notation or script.

3. *Riyaz* is Urdu for rigorous daily practice by musicians throughout their career.

4. *Anda* is Sanskrit for egg or egg shaped. Combined with Brahman or universal consciousness the composite word becomes *Brahman+Anda – Brahmaanda*. The Cosmos is seen in Vedic imaginary as a Cosmic Egg, with the suggestion of a womb in its elliptical form, from which all Life is born.

5.	These are the actual moves of a salutation to the four directions in *Kalaripayattu*, an Indian martial art form that Adishakti references later in the text. Just as time is defined in terms of past, present, future, space is defined in terms of the directions, both cardinal and secondary. Hence we have the reference here to south west, which is the direction Kalari practitioners face as they begin.

6.	*Dhik* is direction, *Vijay* is conquest. A term used in historical records for a King's victorious march through the territories he has conquered.

7.	Literally, salutation movement, in Malayalam, the language of *Kalaripayattu*.

8.	*Dharma* is a well-known concept in Hinduism. Literally, something to hold, *Dharma* can be understood as a principle to live by. The dharma of *Kalaripayattu* lies in the fact that it is both a martial art and a healing practice. Part of the Kalari training lies in the massage and medicine used to prepare students for the tough physical exercises, and to cure the body when bruised through the same.

9.	Indian version of Adam.

10.	A reference to *Vedic* sacrificial altars shaped like a vulcan and built to very precise measurement.

11.	*The Bhagavad Gita*, Krishna's initiation of Arjuna on the battlefield convincing him to fight, begins with the words *Dharma Kshetre Kuru Kshetre*. I change the second phrase to *Puru Kshetre*, as purush in Sanskrit refers to consciousness. *Puru Kshetre* thus refers to the field of consciousness.

12.	This is a reference to the Covid-19 virus which was the narrative context and spur for this work.

13.	Sweet Mother of God, in Rafael's native Spanish.

14. *Nattuvangam* is the rhythmic oral syllables with which 'measure' is maintained in dance. The voice is usually accompanied with cymbals.

15. The *Vaastu Purusha* or Cosmic Human is seen like the Universe to be constituted of the five elements – earth, fire, water, air and space. Though it is the male body that is traditionally referenced, I take it to refer equally to the female body.

Notes for 'Seduction: Imagining Leonard Cohen' – *Sudeshna Baksi-Lahiri*

1. Cohen, L (1988) 'I Can't Forget' [song], *I'm Your Man*, Columbia Records

www.youtube.com/watch?v=o-58u8Lyvhw (Official Audio)

2. Cohen, L (1967) 'So Long, Marianne' [song] *Songs of Leonard Cohen*, Columbia Records

www.youtube.com/watch?v=3XzAjfwQtvM (Official Audio)

3. Cohen, L (1986) 'Take This Waltz' [song], *I'm Your Man*, Columbia Records

www.youtube.com/watch?v=wfNOogGqSLA (Official Audio)

Biographies

Julia Prendergast lives and works in Melbourne, Australia, on unceded Wurundjeri land. Her novel, *The Earth Does Not Get Fat*, was published in 2018 and longlisted for the Indie Book Awards (debut fiction). Her short story collection: *Bloodrust and Other Stories*, was published in 2022. Julia is a practice-led researcher – an enthusiastic supporter of transdisciplinary research focusing creative writing and creative-cognition. Julia is Chair of the Australasian Association of Writing Programs (AAWP), the peak academic body representing the discipline of Creative Writing (Australasia); a member of the Board of Management: Australian Short Story Festival; Senior Lecturer and Discipline Coordinator (Swinburne University).

Eileen Herbert-Goodall is a creative writing instructor, editor, and sessional academic (University of the Sunshine Coast and Swinburne University of Technology). She has written fiction and non-fiction for a wide range of publications. She is the author of the 2017 novella *The Sherbrooke Brothers*. Her second novella is currently in press with Propertius Press, US. Eileen has been the Membership Liaison Officer for the Australasian Association of Writing Programs since 2019. She holds a Doctorate of Creative Arts.

Deb Wain is a poet and short story writer who is passionate about food, culture, and the Australian environment. Her work, which has appeared in *Verandah*, *Tincture*, *Verity La*, *Colloquay*, and *Meniscus*, is often inspired by the Australian communities in which she has lived. Deb lives and writes on Taungurung Country being kept company by three chooks, two dogs, many kangaroos, the occasional echidna and one excellent human. Deb is currently an office bearer on the AAWP Executive Committee.

Karen McKnight is a Melbourne-based writer/performer and social justice advocate whose stories have been published in a range of journals including *Vandal Press*, *Modern Writing* and *The Big Issue*. Her performance troupe Discourse of Handbags performed at many venues in and around Melbourne and from there she became the Literature Coordinator of The Art of Difference Festival – celebrating mixed ability within the arts. In 2016 she was awarded the Inaugural Writer in Residence at *Overland Literary Journal* and in 2019 won the Grace Marion Wilson Prize for non-fiction. She is currently Writer in Residence at Windana Drug and Alcohol Recovery.

Deniz Agraz is a bilingual writer, content creator and an ESL teacher. Having arrived in Australia from Turkey as a teenager in the late 90s, Deniz's writing regularly draws on the experiences of migrants. In 2019, her short story 'Rosewater' was shortlisted for the Deborah Cass Writing Prize. The same year, she was selected to participate in the Citizen Writes Project. Deniz finds that writing fiction is a way for her to reach reconciliation between her first and second languages and negotiate her place in Australian society. Her work has appeared in *ABC Life*, *SBS Voices*, *Meniscus* and *diaCRITICS*.

Andiopi Athanasiadou is living and working in Greece. She is the author of various books of poetry, solo (*Tetix the Wisperer*, *Al Dente*) and collective (*Defending Dreaming*), of short stories (*My Life as a Witch*) and essays on poetry and literature.

Angharad Lodwick is a writer and reviewer who has contributed to *The Guardian Australia*, *Feminartsy*, *Homer*, *Cicerone* and the 2019 Digital Writers' Festival. She was a winner in the Writers Victoria #WVFLASHFIC22 contest and in the *Going Down Swinging* Micro-microfiction Challenge 2021. She runs the book blog *Tinted Edges* and was selected for the inaugural ACT Writers New Territory program. She is the current editor of *ChinWag*, ACT Rescue and Foster's biannual rescue dog magazine. She is the creator of the zine series *AnghaRANT* and the podcast *Lost the Plot*.

Ashley Somwaru is an Indo-Caribbean woman who was born and raised in Queens, New York. As a storyteller and experimental poet, her work is immersed in her mixed tongue, religious upbringings, superstitions, and cultural traditions that have made her into the red hibiscus she is. In 2021, Somwaru published a chapbook with Ghostbird Press titled, *Urgent // Where the Mind Goes // Scattered*. Previous work has been published in *Honey Literary*, *Newtown Literary*, *Solstice*, *SWIMM*, *The Margins*, *VIDA Review*, and elsewhere.

Patrick Eades works in hospitals by day and writes by night. His work appears in *StylusLit*, *Allegory*, *Mulberry Literary* and is forthcoming in *The Westchester Review*. He lives sandwiched between the National Parks of southern Sydney and is working on his debut novel. He also writes regularly on Medium.com: @ PatrickGEades, or can be contacted through his website: https:// patrickeades.net/

Soudhamini is a filmmaker, screen educator and Fulbright research scholar from India, who has just completed a practice-based PhD in Cinematic VR at Deakin University, Melbourne. 'Ode to Uśas' her contribution in this volume was one part of her creative submission for her PhD. She comes from Chennai in the south-eastern tip of India and is a native Tamil speaker. After four years in Naarm, she considers it her second home.

Nina Winter grew up in the small mining town of South Hedland in WA and the even smaller NZ town of Whitianga. Her curiosity and innate restlessness have led to long stints in faraway places, including Tokyo, London and Doha. In 2016 she wandered for a year in the Caribbean and is writing a memoir that explores society's ideals around motherhood and what happens when your life doesn't go in the direction you thought it would. She is currently working as a technical writer in Saudi Arabia on a project to build a futuristic new city 33 times the size of New York City.

Joanna Morrison is a writer based in Perth, WA. Her short stories have appeared in various Australian journals and anthologies, including *Westerly*, *Meniscus* (Best Prose Piece Winner, April 2018), and *Joiner Bay and Other Stories* (Margaret River Press, 2017). Her debut novel, *The Ghost of Gracie Flynn*, was shortlisted for the 2020 City of Fremantle Hungerford Award and will be published by Fremantle Press in October, 2022. Joanna has a Creative Writing

PhD and a background in journalism. She lives in Perth with her husband, two sons, and miniature schnauzer, Scout.

Christina Eastman is a practising graphic designer who likes to use creative writing not only as a source of inspiration but also as an escape. She believes that creativity does not fit inside a box and can materialise itself through different practices. She loves to create within the holistic world of design, art, literature and film.

Emma Darragh lives and works in Wollongong, on Dharawal Country. Her writing has appeared in numerous Australian publications, including *Cordite*, *Westerly*, *Meniscus*, and *TEXT Journal*. Emma is soon to complete her PhD in Creative Writing at the University of Wollongong, where she is also a sessional academic. Her website is emmadarragh.com.

Dr. Sudeshna Baksi-Lahiri received her BSc in Anthropology and her MA in Sociology from Delhi University, India. She continued her education at Cornell University in the US, completing her master's *en passant* while working towards her doctorate in Cultural Anthropology. She received a Fulbright to conduct dissertation research in the Republic of Maldives for her PhD on women's power and ritual politics in a traditional Islamic society. She is a Fellow of the Dallas Institute of Humanities and Culture, where she has taught courses that question gender stereotypes in Islam, by addressing textual and contextual perspectives.

Rafael E. Fajer Camus is a Mexican-born writer, educated at NYU and Naropa University. He has travelled extensively and has lived in Mexico City, Paris, and NYC. He's been through a few rehab treatments in the US and Mexico. He's also spent time in psychiatric treatment centres. He's now aware that he's not a cyborg destined to settle humans on Mars and is working on his first book, *Notes from the Borderline*, from which this excerpt is taken. He enjoys reading the word flabbergasted. He currently resides, writes, and does stuff out of Mexico City.

E.R. Pulgar is a Venezuelan American poet, translator, journalist and educator. Their journalism has appeared in *i-D*, *Playboy*, *Rolling Stone*, and elsewhere. Their poems have appeared or are forthcoming in *Changes Review*, *Epiphany*, *PANK Magazine*, *blush*, and *A*N*U*S*. They were selected as a finalist in the 7th Rafael Cadenas Young Poets Prize. They have designed courses for Catapult, Craig Newmark Graduate School of Journalism at CUNY, and the New York Public Library. They have taught in the U.S. and Greece, and hold an MFA in poetry and translation from Columbia University, where they were a Lenfest Fellow.

Katherine Mann is a Creative Writing PhD candidate at Swinburne University. She resides in Melbourne.

Thomas Hamlyn-Harris is an illustrator and writer of comics, visual narrative and short fiction. His work has appeared in games, children's fiction, journals and anthologies including *Inkbrick*, *TEXT Journal*, *Meet Me in the Pit* and *The Incompleteness Book II*. Thomas lives in Maleny – Jinibara Country – on the Sunshine Coast and was recently awarded a Doctorate in Creative Arts from the University of the Sunshine Coast.

Linda Godfrey is a writer, poet and editor and has a Master of Professional Writing from the University of Technology, Sydney. In 2021, Linda won the AAWP's Chapter One prize and published a chapbook of prose poetry, *Count the Ways*. She has published poetry and short stories in anthologies and online. Linda was the Program Manager of the Wollongong Writers Festival 2015 to 2018. She has been a recipient of a Varuna Residency and an Australian Society of Authors mentorship. She has edited three award-winning books, including one Miles Franklin winner.

Kerry Greer is a Western Australian poet and writer. She received the Venie Holmgren Prize for Environmental Poetry in 2021. Her poetry manuscript is in development with the Publishable program, run by Queensland Writers Centre. Kerry has been shortlisted for the ABR Calibre Prize, the Stuart Hadow Short Story Prize, the Calanthe Collective Poetry Prize, the W.B. Yeats Poetry Prize, and the Bruce Dawe Poetry Prize. She is a student in the low-residency MFA program at Cedar Crest College. Her work frequently addresses the experience of widowhood and solo parenting.

Michelle Jäger is an Adelaide-based fiction writer whose work has appeared in various anthologies and journals. She won the *Elle* Australia 2018 short story competition, placed runner-up in the InkTears' 2018 short story competition, and was short-listed for the Hammond House 2019 and Aesthetica 2020 short story prizes. Her novel *Bird Bones* is due to be released by Glimmer Press in October 2022.

Dean Kerrison writes creative nonfiction and fiction, usually on the (dis)connection of outsiders in foreign environments with international relations contexts. His short form work has appeared in *TEXT Journal*, *Meniscus*, *The Bangalore Review*, *Joao Roque Literary Journal*, *The Incompleteness Book II*, *Usawa Literary Journal*, *The Lit Quarterly*, *Allegory Ridge*, among others. This year he's living in Tbilisi, Georgia and working on a travel memoir, and slowly chipping away at a novel as part of a PhD at Griffith University, Australia.

Laura Fulton is a writer, teacher and editor born in the Mississippi delta region of southern Arkansas, now a naturalised dual citizen of Australia and the USA based in Melbourne. Her commercial, critical and creative work has appeared in the US, the UAE and Australia. Her October 2020 creative practice PhD completed through RMIT explored how the adopted person may address issues of identity, origin and belonging through creative writing experimentation. Her creative work often considers themes of separation, trauma and loss, how we cope with those issues, the ways we look forward and the ways we look back.

Brooke Maddison is a writer and editor working on unceded Turrbal and Yuggera land. She is completing a Masters of Writing, Editing and Publishing at the University of Queensland and is the founder and co-editor of *Crackle* (Corella Press, 2021), the university's anthology of creative writing. Her work has been published by *Kill Your Darlings*, *Antithesis*, *Verity La* and *Spineless Wonders*, among others. In 2021 she was awarded a Next Chapter Fellowship, a University of Queensland Press mentorship, a Curtis

Brown Creative HW Fisher scholarship and a Neilma Sidney Literary Travel Fund grant. Brooke is currently working on a fiction manuscript.

Anita Thomas is a Singapore-based author and media producer/consultant. *Senserly, Amako,* the journal-memoir which she wrote and illustrated, led to a number of workshops in lit-fests and five months as artist-in-residence with the United World College of SE Asia. In the art-poetry collaboration *Camera & Quill,* thirty-one of her photographs were interpreted in poetry by Neil Daswani. Anita designed, co-owns and maintains SingaporeforKids, a website crafted around the importance of making informed choices. She has also worked in advertising, film and television, and written extensively for corporates and non-profits in the fields of advertising, design and public relations.

Deborah Huff-Horwood is an emerging, full-time writer from Canberra who weaves her life experience and imagination into short stories, novels, picture books and poetry. Her stories – for all ages – centre on themes of creativity and courage. Since committing to a writing career in 2020 she has won dozens of accolades for her work and will soon be published in twelve anthologies. Deborah was formerly an artist, primary educator, pastry chef and clothing designer. Her lakefront home holds collections of art papers, children's literature, chocolate moulds, and lustrous silks and is the perfect eyrie for her life of silent writing.

Sarah Giles (she/her) is a writer and PhD candidate at Swinburne University researching the possibilities of the contemporary short story cycle exploring women's experiences of isolation, trauma, and mental illness. Her writing has been published in *The Incompleteness Book*, *TEXT Journal*, *The Victorian Writer*, *Science/Art Network* (ScAN) & *Australasian Association of Writing Programs* (AAWP), *Melbourne Noir Cards*, *ILLUMINATE*, *Lip Magazine*, *SMUT*, and *Underground Writers*. Sarah lives, works, and studies in Naarm (Melbourne) on the stolen lands of the Kulin Nation. Sovereignty was never ceded. This is, and always was, Aboriginal land. http://sarahgiles.work/

Emily Gray lives in Austinmer on the South Coast of New South Wales, on Dharawal land. Her short stories have appeared in the *Legacies* journal of the South Coast Writers Centre, and been longlisted for the Heroines/Joyce Parkes Writing Prize for 2022. Emily's poem, 'Blue Ship,' was longlisted for the 2022 South Coast Writers Centre Poetry Prize. Emily studied creative writing in New York, and was recently selected for an Emerging Writers Mentorship with Hayley Scrivenor, a creative writing residency at Bundanon, and for the Merrigong Playwrights' Programme. Emily is currently working on a novel.

Kristen Dagg is a television writer, producer and editor who writes regularly about women's issues for *Kidspot*, *Mamamia*, *Babyology* and other online publications. She has been writing her whole life and is currently working on her second novel. She received an award for a short story in a Voices of Women competition. She lives in Newtown, Sydney, with her deliciously complicated pre-teeny kids, a big rescue mutt and a rescue boyfriend.

Jane Cornes Maclean is a multi-award-winning author and songwriter. She has edited numerous non-fiction titles and has contributed feature articles to a wide variety of magazines and newspapers. Jane's first book *Lazy Fare* won a special category award at the Gourmand International book awards. In 2020, Jane was named national winner of the AAWP short story competition for her story 'Cockroach'. Today her greatest joy is helping others explore their creativity, and she teaches at creative writing and songwriting retreats throughout Australia and overseas. Jane lives in Queensland with her husband Neil. She is a survivor of breast cancer.

Ned Hirst is a lawyer and writer based in Sydney. His work has appeared in *Meanjin, Overland, ArtsHub* and elsewhere.

Danii Jasmine is a 25-year-old writer based in Sydney, Australia. She recently completed her first poetry collection and is working to publish and promote it while finishing a Bachelor of Arts degree, majoring in Creative Writing at Macquarie University. Her writing borrows from the unconscious as much as it is allowed to. Some have described it to her as 'Dense with image, which makes it feel alive, like fresh soil infused with an occult glow. Dirty and breathing.' When she releases poetry or prose it no longer just belongs to her, but the reader – this writing is theirs.

Allen C. Jones is an award-winning California writer; he has an MFA in poetry and a PhD in English, and he presently serves as Associate Professor of Literature at the University of Stavanger in Norway. His scholarly research investigates the literary and educational potential of paper, digital, and augmented reality (AR) reading and writing games, and his creative work includes a novel, *Her Death Was Also Water*, forthcoming from MidnightSun Publishing, and an experimental book of poems, *Son of a Cult*, forthcoming from Finishing Line Press. Find more of his writing and research at allencjones.com.

Clare Testoni is a playwright, fiction writer, and puppeteer. Clare won the AAWP/ASSF Emerging Writers' Short Story Prize in 2021 and has been published in *Westerly*, *UNSWeetened*, and in the anthology *South of The Sun: Australian Fairy Tales for the 21st Century*. Originally from Sydney, she currently lives in Walyaup/Fremantle and is a PhD candidate in creative writing at The University of Western Australia.

Jeimer Ng is an occupational therapist and emerging writer from Western Australia with a fervent love for flash fiction. He has deeply valued, more than anything, the utility of the flash medium to express that which he could not otherwise voice (and there happens to be a lot of it). It is within his chase of catharsis that the dance between the epic and the intimate of everyday life becomes most palpable to him, and he hopes to share this with people willing to lean in with an open heart.

R. A. O'Brien is a social scientist who has studied fine art, run a chicken shop, and worked in a bank. More recently, she has been employed in universities and in government. She has written and published a serious scientific paper with a Martian as well as articles and reports with more conventional co-authors, but stories are the thing that drive her. She writes speculative fiction, often influenced by her PhD on unconscious learning and by her experience in the labyrinthine ways of government. Her short stories are usually about who or what we chose to value or to love.